Under the Highlander's Spell

Other **Avon Romances**

A Belated Bride *by Karen Hawkins*
Lessons from a Courtesan *by Jenna Petersen*
Let the Night Begin *by Kathryn Smith*
Passion and Pleasure in London *by Melody Thomas*
Secrets of the Knight *by Julia Latham*
Surrender to Me *by Sophie Jordan*
Too Dangerous to Desire *by Alexandra Benedict*

Coming Soon

The Bride Price *by Anne Mallory*
Her Secret Lover *by Sara Bennett*

And Don't Miss These
ROMANTIC TREASURES

Bold Destiny *by Jane Feather*
The Devil Wears Tartan *by Karen Ranney*
The Mistress Diaries *by Julianne MacLean*

DONNA FLETCHER

UNDER THE HIGHLANDER'S SPELL

AVON

An Imprint of HarperCollins*Publishers*

AVON BOOKS
An Imprint of HarperCollins*Publishers*
10 East 53rd Street
New York, New York 10022-5299

First Avon Books paperback printing: October 2008

UNDER THE HIGHLANDER'S SPELL

Chapter 1

"Burn, witch, burn!"

The crazed chant rang throughout the village while Zia watched two men continue to pile kindling around her feet. Struggling was senseless. The coarse rope scraped her bare arms and dug into her stomach.

She had done nothing to deserve such unfair judgment. She had simply responded to the village of Lorne's need for a healer. Instead of being grateful for her help, the villagers had begun to gossip about her extraordinary powers, especially after she brought a babe back from the brink of death. Wagging tongues immediately claimed her—a witch.

Zia had tried to reason with the people, but it seemed to make it worse. They did not understand her explanations of how specific mixtures of herbs and poultices could aid in helping the ill heal. They argued her concoctions were works of the devil, and her beauty was even called to task. Why else would every man in the village be unable to keep their eyes off her? And the mark of the devil was on her for sure in the unnatural color of her long, dark red hair sparked with fiery blond streaks.

She had realized that her only choice was to run and leave the ignorant to their fate. Unfortunately, she had reached that decision too late and several men had burst into the small cottage, the village had first so eagerly provided for her. Two men grabbed hold of her and while another man burned her few possessions and healing items in the hearth, the others shoved her face down on the worn wooden table and a woman took a knife to her hair, chopping it short.

She had then been dragged, by no means passively, and tied to a stake in the middle of the village for the jeering crowd to torment. And in mere moments the torch a stout man with a grim expression gripped tightly in his beefy hand, would set the pile of kindling aflame and the villagers would cheer as they watched her burn.

Her fate appeared sealed. She could think of nothing to save her. Words were useless; they would fall on deaf ears and frightened minds. The only thing left to her was prayer, but before she could recite the familiar and hopeful words, her grandmother's ageless face popped into her head.

Zia couldn't help but smile. She loved her grandmother dearly. It was she who had taught Zia all about healing. Her grandmother had even chosen her name. Zia meant staff of life and her grandmother claimed she had been born to preserve life. Zia had worked diligently at learning all about the healing arts and had been willing to travel to wherever her skills had been needed. She also learned that not all people thought highly of healers.

Zia understood the risks, especially being an exceptional healer, though she believed her skills natural. As her grandmother had predicted, she had been born to preserve life like so many in the long line of healers before her.

Unfortunately, her life would be a short one and she so wished for more time to help people and to gain more healing knowledge.

Zia.

She glanced around, certain she had heard a familiar voice call her name. She recognized no friendly face in the grumbling crowd.

He comes to save you. He is good for you.

Zia smiled hearing in her head her grandmother's voice. Her grandmother had always been there for her even when they weren't together. It was a strange connection they shared but one she never questioned or doubted. Her grandmother subscribed to the Old Ways, the old beliefs and she had passed them on to Zia, and she was grateful she had.

Zia searched anxiously past the jeering faces in the distance for her rescuer, but disappointingly saw no one. She would wait. Even as the man holding the torch walked toward her ready to light the kindling, she kept faith in her grandmother's words.

Suddenly, thunder erupted and she glanced overhead

at the canopy of dark clouds that had moved in ever so swiftly, and her smile grew as fat raindrops assaulted her face.

Accusatory shouts sparked the air as many cried out that she commanded the weather to do her bidding.

Was there no end to their ignorance?

Just as she prepared to whisper a prayer of gratitude for her abrupt reprieve, she spied riders on the outskirts of the village.

Four men approached, the leader easily distinguishable. He sat his stallion tall and proud, a good-sized dog following at the horse's heels. A few in the crowd followed her stare and hurriedly alerted all to the arrival of strangers. A rash of mumbling gave way to hushed silence as the riders entered the village, and the crowd parted slowly, clearing a significant path for the imposing leader and his cohorts.

Apprehension crackled in the air along with the thunder as Zia met the leader's dark brown eyes and felt a jolt to her senses. Surely, the deep color was born from the depths of the earth where the soil was the most fertile, where roots dug deep to reach and from which all life sprung.

He broke the contact, glancing over the crowd, and announced in a clear, confident voice, "I am Artair Sinclare of Caithness, and I have come to speak with Zia the healer."

Gasps and murmuring circled the crowd before the village leader, Harold, stepped forward. "Zia the healer is a witch and has been sentenced to burn at the stake."

"Then I have come in due time. I will speak to her first," Artair commanded.

Zia wasn't surprised by his authoritative nature. One would have to be blind not to see that he was a great warrior. Not only did he sit astride his horse with pride, but he held himself in the same manner, his broad shoulders drawn back, his firm chest expanded, his long lean fingers heavy on the hilt of his sword.

"I can't permit it," Harold insisted, shaking his head.

"Can't or won't?" Artair asked bluntly.

Harold began to tremble. "I must think of our safety."

"Your safety rests on me speaking to the healer," Artair warned.

Zia felt hopeful since he hadn't referred to her as a witch, but rather, acknowledged her as a healer. Could this man really be her savior?

"Have done with it then," Harold begrudgingly said. "But keep your distance, she will entrap you."

The caution didn't dissuade the warrior. He moved his stallion nearer to her funeral pyre, and she got a closer look at his staggering good looks. His features were a work of pure talented artistry; the heavens couldn't have made him any more stunning. He stared directly at her, his dark eyes once more locking with hers and sending her senses soaring. You would think that the kindling had been set aflame, her body heated so rapidly.

"I search for my brother Ronan Sinclare. It has been said that you have tended him?"

"I have," she admitted, recalling the man and facial similarities between the two.

"How is he?"

"I left him healing nicely from serious injuries when word was received that the village Lorne was in desperate need of a healer."

"Where is Ronan?" Artair asked, his horsing growing impatient while he looked to remain calm and confident.

"Where he is has no name and no direction."

"You speak in riddles," Artair accused.

"She is a witch. She tries to trick you," Harold warned, jabbing his finger in her direction.

"I can take you there," she said.

"You will burn, witch," Harold proclaimed, his finger trembling in anger.

The crowd agreed and chanted for her demise.

Artair rose suddenly in his saddle and turned to glare at the people. His voice rose over theirs. "I will speak with this woman."

Voices quieted, though whispers rushed around the crowd.

Artair turned back around to face her, ignoring the quiet protest. "Tell me how to find my brother."

"I cannot. I can only show you the way."

"She enchants you and makes you do her bidding," Harold disputed adamantly.

Artair shot him a scalding glare, and the man retreated, bowing his head and taking several steps back.

"Tell me where my brother is," he demanded, turning to Zia.

"I cannot. I can only take you to him," she said and couldn't help but admire the way he remained calm and in control as if her words did not disturb him, but rather made him consider his options.

"Further discussion will not change your mind, will it?" he asked.

"It cannot, for I speak the truth."

He appeared to accept her words as fact, for he turned to Harold. "Release her to me."

"I will not," he said indignantly. "She is a witch and she shall burn for her sins."

"I require her assistance," Artair said firmly.

"This village requires that she pay for her evil ways."

"What is it that she has done to this village?" Artair asked.

"She has worked her evil magic on us."

"Your people suffer?"

Harold shook his head. "We continue to heal."

"Then what are her sins?"

Harold shoved his finger at her face. "She has used her evil ways to cure us. What now will happen to us?"

"Is that not up to you?" Artair asked.

Harold sputtered and shook his head. "She will burn, I tell you. She will burn."

Zia watched as Artair studied the man and once again she thought that he reasonably weighed alternatives. He was not at all ruffled by the exchange with the agitated man, rather he seemed in control and sure of having his way, which certainly would benefit her.

He summoned the man to him with a brisk snap of his hand and Harold did not deny the warrior, he scurried over to him. Zia was close enough to hear their exchange.

"How much?" Artair asked.

Harold appeared confused.

"How much for her release?"

Harold shook his head and his voice turned bold. "She will harm us if released."

"I will make certain that she doesn't," Artair assured him. "And I will pay you handsomely to take her off your hands."

The man seemed to consider his offer, and Zia understood why. Artair Sinclare made it sound as if he had the power to do as he claimed, though she had no doubt the promise of generous coins made Harold think twice.

"Burn the witch!" Someone yelled, and others joined in.

Harold, hearing his people call for the witch's life and probably fearing disappointing them, continued to argue with Artair. The debate seemed to go nowhere, though Artair seemed determined and that led Zia to believe that the handsome warrior would have his way—and she would be freed.

She just wished that the rain had continued. It would have prevented the torch bearer from preparing another torch and creeping closer to her, ready and willing to please the crowd. But the rain had ceased when the four men entered the village.

Artair seemed to tire of the useless exchange and reached into the fold where his plaid crossed his chest and met his waist and extracted a small pouch. He dropped it to the man.

Harold greedily seized it, tugged it open and dug inside. He stepped closer to Artair. "You'll take her far and make sure she doesn't return here and about?"

"I'll see that she has no more dealings with your village."

"Take her, then, and be done with it," Harold said with a dismissive wave.

Artair didn't waste a moment. He gave a nod to his men and they in turn drew their swords. The crowd instantly halted their shouts and fear held them silent.

Artair drew his own sword and with accurate aim he sliced the ropes that held Zia without marring her flesh. He then replaced his sword at his side and reached out his hand to her.

Zia seized hold, and when he clamped his hand around her arm, she watched the muscles grow taut along his bare forearm and bulge with strength as he easily swung her up to sit in front of him in the saddle. His arm went around her waist and he yanked her close, adjusting her against him, while her legs rested over one side and came in contact with his bare one.

Her skirt had ridden up just enough for her flesh to feel his, and he was warm and muscled, and once again she was made aware of his strength.

She met his dark eyes as he guided his horse away from the funeral pyre, and they were even more enticing up close.

"Keep away from her eyes, she'll bewitch you," Harold warned as they passed him.

Zia wasn't surprised when Artair paid the man no heed. He obviously was making it clear to all, and to Zia, that he didn't fear her. Could he also be letting her know that he didn't believe in witches or magic?

At the moment, it didn't matter to her. Her only concern was that she was free.

Zia smiled at her rescuer. "Thank you," she said, and rested her head on his shoulder. After all, it had been a very difficult morning.

Chapter 2

Artair stared at the supposed witch wrapped in his arms. He was a practical man and didn't believe in witches, though he believed in the ability of a beautiful woman to bewitch. And Zia was undoubtedly a beautiful woman.

Her dark red hair had obviously suffered a shearing, and blond spikes vied with dark curls for attention around her slim face, enlarging her beguiling green eyes. He recalled how she had held his gaze after he planted her in front of him on his horse, and how her eyes not only radiated a fierce intelligence but sparked with an undeniable passion.

She was taller than most women, maybe four inches shorter than his six feet, and though slim, she was curved and rounded in all the right places.

"Keep on the road that brought you to the village. It is a place with no name. I will tell you where to turn," Zia said pleasantly.

She certainly was relaxed for a woman who had just escaped death, and now seemed not at all troubled resting against a complete stranger. She was a woman who obviously did not frighten easily, or perhaps she felt quite comfortable with her abilities to protect herself—though her skills hadn't helped her in the village.

Curiosity nagged at him and he asked, "What happened back there?"

She sighed and ran her fingers through her hair. "I got sheared for healing them."

"It doesn't look all that bad," Artair said, meaning it. He wasn't accustomed to seeing a woman with short hair but had to admit it did Zia justice. If possible, it made her appear more beautiful than the women he was used to.

She laughed and rushed her fingers through her hair once again. "And here I thought you were a truthful man, Artair."

His innards jolted hearing his name spill with light-hearted laughter from her rosy lips, though was it that even jokingly she doubted his integrity?

"I am a truthful man," he said. "Your short hair seems to enhance your beauty."

Her green eyes sparkled and her smile deepened and turned lopsided, and he thought it the most enchanting smile he had ever seen.

Enchanting.

Was she enchanting him? *Only if he allowed her to.*

"What a charming compliment," she said. "Thank you."

"You are most welcome, but tell me . . . You are

obviously an intelligent woman. How did you ever get yourself in such dire straits? You must have realized the situation in the village had turned dangerous for you. Why didn't you leave before it got out of hand?"

"An ill babe," she said, her smile fading. "I couldn't leave the darling lad. He had yet to reach his first full year. He had a right to a longer life, and I had the ability to see that he got it. He required constant care until I was certain the worst had past and he would survive. By then . . . "

"It was too late."

She nodded. "In saving him, I condemned myself. No one had expected the lad to live, though the mother hoped and the lad fought bravely for his life."

"I admire your courage. There are not many who will give their life for another."

"I think I like you and your compliments," she teased. "But alas, I cannot accept compliments for doing my duty. I am a healer; it is my obligation to heal."

"Even at your own peril?"

"I take a risk whenever I tend the ailing. I never know if I will fall to an illness that plagues a village. I can only trust in my knowledge and have faith that all will turn out well."

"Did you have faith while tied to the stake?"

"It was *all* I had."

"Have you ever been accused of being a witch before?" he asked.

"No. I have been fortunate, though aware of the risks."

"Yet it doesn't stop you."

"You are a warrior?" she asked.

"Yes," he answered proudly.

"You know the risks when you enter a battle. Yet you enter it knowing you could die."

"I am defending my land," he argued.

"I am defending life," she said with equal pride.

"But you are only a wo—"

"Do not say what I think you mean to say, for it will surely insult me."

He noticed her eyes twinkle with mirth and her lips fight a teasing smile, but her words had been edged with a boldness that cautioned him. She had meant what she said.

She sat up suddenly and pointed a few feet ahead. "There's a narrow path to the left."

They turned where she directed. It could hardly be called a path. Tree branches threatened to knock Artair and his men off their horses and forced them to hunch down over their saddles. He did, however, find being hunched over Zia . . . pleasant. Her hair smelled sweet, like a freshly plucked bouquet of flowers, the spiky tendrils tickled his cheek, and damned if her plump lips weren't ripe for kissing.

He was glad to see that the path cleared just ahead. If he remained hovering over her much longer he damn well was going to kiss her.

With that thought heavy on his mind, Artair lifted his head too soon and a tree branch smacked him in the forehead.

He grunted and squeezed his eyes shut against the rush of pain.

He jolted when he felt her fingers explore his forehead and slowly opened his eyes. She was focused on seeing to his care, but to him her fingertips felt cool and her touch more like a caress.

"Nothing serious. It leaves a welt that will disappear soon enough," she advised.

He had hoped her fingers would linger longer, but with her examination finished, her touch vanished and disappointment rushed over him.

"There is another turn a few feet ahead and it would be best if your men walked the horses."

He followed her lead and ordered his men to dismount. Zia slipped out of his arms and off his horse before he could help her and walked a few feet away from him. It wasn't a far distance, but oddly enough, he felt as if she had slipped from his grasp.

He watched her stretch her shoulders back, swing her arms out and roll her head from side to side. Then she smiled wide. Her beauty stunned him and for a moment, a sheer moment, he wondered if she was a witch for she certainly seemed to be bewitching him.

Her clothes—dark blue skirt and pale yellow blouse—while common, fit her body like the silks and velvet garments tailored for royals, and she carried herself with the same distinction.

Nessie, his dog, went over and immediately made friends with her, but then Nessie did whatever she wanted to do.

"She is a beauty, so friendly and obedient," Zia said.

Artair laughed. "Nessie is far from obedient. She has a mind of her own."

Zia kissed the mutt on the head. "Smart lass."

"Is this no name, no direction place close?" Artair asked returning to the matter at hand.

"We will reach it by noon tomorrow."

She walked ahead leading them, Nessie following her. Artair's only recourse was to do as Nessie did, follow Zia. His men trailed behind grumbling. While he did not believe in the power of witches he knew some of his men did and at the moment he was sure that they thought following her unwise.

After a few more twists and turns he wondered if he didn't agree with them, for suddenly he felt in unfamiliar territory and worse, confined and confused, by the dense growth of trees and foliage.

"What is this place?" he demanded.

Zia glanced over her shoulder with a smile. "My home."

She hurried ahead and when she drifted from sight he grew concerned that perhaps he had been foolish not to have been more cautious with her, but then she popped up in front of him, her smile glowing like a bright full sun.

"This way," she said pointing. "I am starving. There is a stream, and I"—she tapped her chest proudly—"am very good at catching fish."

"Did you hear that, James?" Artair called to one of his men. "She is very good at catching fish."

"Not as good as I," James shouted back.

"A challenge. I love it," Zia said with a laugh, and hurried ahead of them, Nessie on her heels.

"No fair," James yelled and the short, stout man quickly handed his reins to the warrior behind him and took chase.

Not long after, Zia caught the first fish. James frustrated, threw down the pole he had quickly fashioned from a branch. Artair assumed Zia would take delight in her success, but instead she shared with James her secret to catching fish so quickly. With leaves dangling from his hook James caught a fish and before Artair knew it they were all sitting around a fire waiting eagerly for four fish to finish cooking.

The smell was phenomenal, Zia having added to the cleaned fish a mixture of crushed leaves she had gathered from the surrounding woods. His men had eyed her skeptically but when the scent had turned mouthwatering their grumbling halted.

After tasting the fish the men attacked it, licking every morsel off their fingers and grumbling because she insisted that each give a share to the dog.

"A great cook besides a great healer," Artair said.

The others nodded, grinned, and patted their stomachs.

Zia bowed her head in appreciation. "Food can sometimes be more healing than potions."

A lively conversation ensued, and Artair was amazed at the way his men so easily befriended her. But then, he was beginning to realize that Zia embraced life with such zest, it was hard not to like her. He could also understand how her passionate nature might intimidate some and possibly cause jealously in others.

Within the last few hours he had gotten a good insight into her and was eager to learn more. She had surprised him from the beginning. He had expected a shivering, frightened woman after being so close to being burnt at the stake, but once free she seemed unbothered by her brush with death.

Courageous or foolhardy?

He still wasn't certain.

On the road once again, they alternated between walking and riding, the path narrowing, winding, then yielding to easy terrain. The sun had surfaced as soon as they left the village, and it remained strong all day. Summer might be waning, but today she was at her peak.

Artair realized that there was no keeping Zia beside him, or Nessie for that matter. She would talk with him awhile, and then be off foraging in the surrounding woods, returning with a flush of excitement, waving bunches of foliage as if she had discovered gold.

But when she returned carrying a twig basket she had obviously fashioned to carry an abundance of berries, the men grabbed handfuls with appreciative grins. Nessie lingered nearby, and from the way the dog licked her lips, it appeared she had already had her share.

"Leave some for me," Artair warned, laughing.

"We got here first," James argued good-naturedly.

Zia hurried alongside him afterward, filling the empty basket with her bunches of leaves, and he was glad for her company. Though she was in truth a stranger, he felt comfortable with her, as though they had been longtime friends.

Bewitched.

Women could certainly bewitch, and he supposed Zia did bewitch with her contagious enthusiasm. But being a healer, she balanced it with a reverence for life. She certainly appeared a complex woman, and that enticed him.

After several hours he ordered James and Patrick to hunt a couple of fat hares for supper.

Surprisingly, the two men looked to Zia, and it was James who asked. "Will you cook for us?"

Zia smiled with glee. "Wild onions and I think . . . " She tapped her chin in thought. "I know . . . " And off she ran, the dog running after her.

"Be careful your arrows don't find her," Artair warned his men.

"Worry not, I'll hear their approach," Zia called out.

The men stared wide-eyed after her, and Artair just stared, his mouth slightly agape, too late to respond to her for she had already disappeared into the woods.

How she had heard words meant only for his men he didn't know.

"You know witches have powers we don't," James whispered to him.

"You think Zia a witch?" Artair asked bluntly.

James scratched his bushy hair. "She is a strange one."

"So that makes her a witch?"

"She is a beauty," James said even lower, as if afraid she'd overhear him.

"That makes her a witch too?"

"I'm just saying maybe we should beware."

"You asked her to cook the hare, giving her ample opportunity to poison us."

James had to think a moment, and then grinned as if he'd settled his own doubt. "She smiles too much to be a witch. Witches don't smile. They're mean buggers."

"I'm glad we've settled that," Artair said, though he wondered how often others questioned the same about Zia. The thought plagued him the whole hour before a campsite was decided on for the night.

Zia had suggested the place, which was near a stream, so the horses could drink their fill. She had returned to her foraging, promising to meet them at the location. Artair truly should not have allowed her to wander off on her own. There was always the chance she wouldn't return, and with no knowledge of the area, he and his men could very well be lost for days.

However, he believed Zia true to her word that she was a healer who did her duty. She would want to return to see how Ronan was healing. She had re-marked about how he had been healing nicely when she left, so she had to be curious as to how he'd been during her absence.

Artair planned on questioning her about Ronan tonight, after they ate and one of the men took watch while the others slept. He would find out as much about Ronan as he could for he wanted to be prepared to help his youngest brother however possible. He'd been missing over a year now, and everyone missed him terribly and wanted nothing more than his safe return home.

His thoughts were interrupted when the two warriors returned boasting of their hunt and showing off two plump hares each had caught. Zia followed them, her basket overflowing with a variety of greens and several wild onions. That her foraging proved beneficial was obvious in her brightly flushed cheeks and sparkling green eyes.

She was a tempty morsel, but Artair's hunger was for information and food and he intended to assuage both as soon as possible.

The meal was amazingly delicious, and the men ate with vigor, not one of them mentioning anything about witches. With everyone relaxed, conversation was lively, and when all the meat had been cleaned from the bones, James stood and volunteered for the first watch.

"That's not necessary," Zia informed him.

"And why is that?" Artair asked.

"These woods are safe."

"No woods are safe," Artair said.

"These woods are. Trust me."

James glanced around the landscape skeptically. "Are there wee folk about?"

"James!" Artair warned sternly.

"Don't tell me you don't believe," James argued. "You heard yourself how the wee folk stole all of Bogg's coins and left him near the river to almost drown."

"Bogg drank himself drunk and had to concoct a good tale to appease his wife, or she'd have drowned him herself."

The others laughed.

"He knew no one would dare speak against the wee folk," Artair finished. "Bogg used his head, once it cleared, and told a tale that keeps growing taller with each telling."

The other men nodded in agreement.

James looked to Zia for clarification. "If not the wee folk, then how are these woods safe?"

"Sentinels."

Artair sprang to his feet, he and his men drawing their swords as Nessie sprinted to his side.

Chapter 3

"**Y**our weapons are not necessary," Zia said. "Besides, they are useless. Our sentinels are excellent archers. If they intended to kill you, you would have been dead when you first stepped on our land."

Artair ordered his men to put away their swords. "They have been watching us all day?" he asked.

Zia could see uncertainty in his eyes. He was probably debating his next move, though ordering his men to sheath their weapons was a wise choice. She didn't wish him to suffer needlessly. After all, he had saved her life.

"There is nothing for you to fear. They will not harm you. They are there to protect our land."

"Our land?" Artair questioned.

"The village Black. It belongs to all of us who live there, though it is named after my family, who founded it. Believe me, Artair, we mean you and your men no harm. The village is probably grateful you rescued me."

"How would they know? I have only rescued you today."

He was quick-witted, though cautious and he seemed to apply sound reason to his decisions. He had realized fast enough that the only way he would be able to have what he wanted from her was to free her and he had paid handsomely for the decision. And he hadn't hesitated in paying the coins, which made her realize how important his brother Ronan was to him.

It seemed every step he took was toward finding his brother, and she couldn't blame him. If she had a missing sibling, she would do the same. Unfortunately, she was alone, without father or mother, but she was ever so grateful to have her grandmother.

"They keep track of my whereabouts," she answered, not ready to admit to the odd connection between her and her grandmother.

"You give me your word that we are safe?" he asked.

Strange, but comforting, that he would accept her word. It meant he trusted her, and that pleased her.

"You have my word that no one will hurt you or your men. The sentinels protect from danger. You and your men are no danger to us. You can rest easy tonight."

Artair signaled his men that there was no threat, and the other three men spread their blankets and sought a good night's sleep.

He however did not, and Zia knew he intended to speak with her. She was ready. Actually, she looked forward to the discussion. Artair intrigued her. He had remained calm and in control throughout the whole ordeal in the village as if none of it had disturbed him. Even now he seemed in control and unperturbed, and she couldn't understand why that troubled her.

His men were soon snoring around the campfire, and she and Artair were left to themselves, Nessie cuddling beside her. It didn't take long for him to begin questioning her about Ronan.

"My brother was brought here to your village?"

She had questions of her own as she responded with a nod. "Ronan made mention of three brothers."

"Cavan, the oldest; then there's me; Lachlan follows; with Ronan the youngest."

"Ronan worried about Cavan."

"Cavan and Ronan were captured by barbarians during a battle. They were separated, and Cavan finally returned home after a year of captivity. He worries daily over Ronan's fate," Artair said. "He also worries about his new wife, Honora, who is to give birth in a couple of months."

"And Lachlan? Is he wed?"

That brought a smile to Artair's face. "Lachlan wed? Not likely. He likes women too much, as they do him."

"Ronan missed you all, especially his father and mother."

Artair's joy vanished as quickly as a snuffed out candle, and Zia realized the news wasn't good.

"Our father was murdered a few months ago, and while the culprit was caught and punished, my heart breaks to have to tell Ronan."

"I am sorry for your loss. It must be difficult for your mother."

"She claims she is fine, but we all see how much she misses our father. They were together many years and never tired of each other. I never heard either of them speak ill of the other. They respected and loved each other from the day they met."

"They made a good match."

"A perfect match, my father claimed, and urged all his sons to do the same."

"You look for a perfect woman?" she asked, curious.

His smile returned. "There is no such thing."

"Isn't there?"

"No man or woman is perfect."

Zia sighed dramatically. "When you're in love, everything is perfect."

"You know this from experience?"

"No, only from what I've been told, though I'm looking forward to experiencing it firsthand. And what of you?" she asked. "Have you known love?"

"No, duty comes before love."

Zia's eyes popped wide. "You would marry out of duty?"

"I almost did," he said. "Cavan's wife Honora was to be my bride. We even exchanged vows."

She gasped. "What happened?"

"Cavan returned on my wedding day, but due to the marriage papers stating that Honora was to wed the next chief of the clan Sinclare, she was actually wed to Cavan and not me."

"You had no feelings for her at all?"

"I barely knew her. What mattered was that I was doing my duty as the next clan chieftain."

"But you said your father encouraged you to find love."

Artair nodded. "Yes he did, and I chose a woman who I felt would make a good wife, and in time I believed we would grow to care for each other."

"Caring for a wife is far different from loving her."

"Caring is an essential part of love," he argued.

"I care for many. I wish to love—passionately love—the man I wed."

"Passion eventually dies; caring lasts forever."

She smiled. "Passion only dies if you let it, and it is not only the passion of intimacy I refer to, it is pure passion for life." She stretched her hands up to the night sky. "Life is full of passion. You only need embrace it."

Artair stared at her, his eyes narrowing.

"You think me crazy," she laughed. "But I will take being crazy over your mundane sense of duty."

"You do *your duty* when it comes to your healing."

With a huge smile, she hugged herself tightly. "With joy and gratitude and tons of enthusiasm."

Artair smiled, her zest contagious.

"What of your brother Cavan?"

"What of him?"

"He found himself wed to a complete stranger. Didn't he object?"

"At first, adamantly."

"But he realized his duty and did it?" she asked.

Artair nodded. "It actually turned out well for him and Honora. They fell in love."

"Love found them, which is usually the way."

He chuckled. "You believe love finds us, we don't find love?"

"I do," she said bluntly. "I believe love is much wiser than we are."

He rubbed his chin. "You are a strange one, though interesting."

"Another compliment. You do touch my heart, Artair," she said with repeated taps to her chest.

"You're an easy woman to compliment, Zia."

She sighed. "How lovely my name sounds coming from your lips. It's as though you felt my name and somehow touched me with it."

Artair coughed lightly and shifted his legs where he sat on the ground.

Had she made him uncomfortable? And why did it matter to her? She did find him appealing. He was a handsome one, but she actually found his company more enjoyable. After she got past his sense of duty, she spied a different man—one she wouldn't mind getting to know better.

It was best to end the conversation now, so she gave an exaggerated yawn. "Time to sleep. The sun will rise soon enough." She hunkered down on the blanket Artair had provided for her. "Pleasant dreams."

"The same to you," Artair answered.

Artair watched Zia's chest rise and fall in a slow, steady rhythm as she slept. The firelight danced over her hair, making the golden strands appear as flickering flames.

He had enjoyed their lively conversation, and only now realized that he had learned nothing about Ronan from her, but she had learned much about him. He hadn't realized at the time that she was asking most of the questions, and that he generously supplied the answers. She certainly knew how to get what she wanted from a man, and she did it so effortlessly.

He could understand why any man would declare her a witch. Without candor or malice, she made men feel inferior to her. Hurt a man's pride and he would go to any lengths to seek retribution.

Zia, however, was who she was. There was no pretense to her, and that made the knowledge of a man's own stupidity too much to bear.

He laughed at himself, and he hadn't done that in a long time. He hadn't been able to. With Cavan and Ronan's capture came more duty for him, and he embraced it for he knew he had to. There were times when he hadn't wanted it. So many times, he had wished for his brothers' safe return, but time passed and his duties increased.

He had never told anyone that he was relieved when

Cavan returned. Many wouldn't have believed him. After all, with Cavan gone he would be the next chieftain of Clan Sinclare. But he hadn't wanted that distinction. It belonged to his brother Cavan, who had been raised since childhood knowing it would be his. Artair felt the same. Cavan was born to be chieftain, and he would serve Cavan, as would his brothers. It was the way of things, and Artair had no difficulty accepting his station in life.

He was actually pleased with it. His desire was to meet a good woman, settle down with her and raise a brood of children. He would always serve his clan and family well. That was the way of it and that was his intention.

Passionately love.

Zia's words rang in his mind.

Even though his father advised him to find love, Artair was more practical and knew that finding a good woman who would share his plans for the future would serve him much better than finding love.

Love could be unsettling, uncertain and unpredictable. He favored the opposite. A settled relationship, whose predictability he could rely on. And yet her words nagged at him.

Passion eventually sizzled, while commonality remained dependable.

Passion only dies if you let it.

More of her words to haunt him. And his father and mother were proof of Zia's statement. They loved passionately, each other, family, clan, and life. They were always there for one another. His father had respected his mother and often sought her counsel when matters proved difficult. They would huddle away in their bedchamber, and if he and his brothers happened to sneak by, they would hear them talking, laughing, and . . .

Artair grinned. It wasn't until later, when they were old enough to be aware of what their parents were up to in their bedchamber, that they stopped sneaking by. The thought that his parents continued to love each other so passionately had pleased him. It was good to know their love was strong and firm, for it told him that they loved their sons just as much.

He finally settled down on his blanket to sleep, his thoughts still heavy on his mind. He shouldn't be thinking of Zia, passion, or love. His only thought should be his brother Ronan. Tomorrow, God willing, they would finally reunite.

He prayed that nothing would prevent their reunion, but couldn't help but worry. It had been over a year of searching and following gossip and messages that proved false. With so many paths that led nowhere, he worried this would turn out the same and once again he would be left wondering the whereabouts of his brother.

Cavan had ached to join him on this mission, but Honora hadn't been feeling well, and even though she urged him to go, he felt he could not abandon her. Artair understood. If anything had happened to Honora and the babe while Cavan was gone, he would have never been able to forgive himself.

Cavan still continued to blame himself for Ronan's capture, though he had actually come to his brother's defense in the battle that saw them taken as prisoners. But that didn't matter to Cavan. He was obsessed with finding Ronan, and Artair knew there would be no rest for any of the clan until they did.

Whether they found Ronan alive or dead, Cavan wanted him brought home. It was Sinclare land he belonged on, and it would be Sinclare land where he would rest.

Artair fervently hoped that tomorrow would end their tireless search, that he would return with Ronan, alive, and they all could finally lay the past to rest and embrace the future.

He yawned, sleep poking at him, though he fought it. He had to make certain he had thought of everything, covered every possibility, prepared for the unexpected. He could not—would not—fail either brother, Cavan or Ronan. Both had suffered enough, and it was time for family to be reunited once and for all.

In the meantime he would learn more about Zia. She appeared a good woman, and he was looking for a good woman to make his wife. She seemed a viable candidate, and she was a healer, another good quality and definitely an asset to the clan.

Artair shook his head.

It was a thought, no more than a thought.

Chapter 4

"**W**hat was that you said?" Artair asked. He stood beside his horse at the mouth of two mountains that looked almost as if they touched, though on closer inspection a trail that separated the two could be spied past the dense foliage.

"Your men will have to wait here," Zia repeated.

"Why?"

"They have no business in our village. Only those who have a reason for being there are allowed entrance."

Artair offered a sensible reason. "They are with me."

"But *only you* have business there."

He knew it wouldn't sit well with his men for him to continue on without them, and he felt the same. They watched each others' backs; in a sense, they were one.

"We are family, of the same clan. It is all our business," Artair said, confident he had settled the dilemma. His men nodded and smiled, showing the same confidence.

Zia smiled graciously and shook her head. "Your men stay here and you go on with me, or I go on alone and you all take your leave."

"Who's going to stop us from following?" James asked boldly.

"The sentinels that surround you," Zia answered calmly, and began walking toward the mouth of the two mountains.

Artair remained as he was, but his men placed heavy hands on the hilts of their swords and their eyes went immediately to the trees. Zia didn't break her stride, and Artair realized the choice was no longer his. He had to follow her and his traitorous dog.

"Make camp here—"

"You can't mean—"

Artair cut off James's protest. "If this is the only way to see if my brother is in the village, then so be it. Make camp and remain alert. I will remain in touch. If you do not hear from me each day then know that something is amiss. John, you return to Caithness and advise Cavan of our whereabouts and circumstances, tell him to take no action until he hears from me."

John scratched his head. "I'm not sure if I can find my way back."

Zia, though a good distance away, stopped and turned. "I will have one of our men take you."

"You have exceptional hearing," Artair said.

Her lovely face brightened and soft laughter spilled from her rosy lips. "Most people hear only what they want to hear, while I want to hear everything. Do you wish John to leave now?"

"I want him set to leave as soon as I have news of Ronan," Artair said.

She nodded, searched the treetops and gave a wave. Suddenly, a young lanky man with bow and arrow dropped to the ground. "Terrance, please wait here with these men and as soon as word is received, escort John to the main road."

"How will I find my way back?" John asked.

"Someone will see you when you return along the main road and direct you here," Zia said.

Artair admired the way she seemed to have a solution to most situations. He prided himself on having the same ability and thought that perhaps she was more practical than she appeared.

With everything settled, he followed Zia through the pass, his horse following behind him. It was a narrow passage, the entrance easily missed by the visible eye. A few feet ahead the mountain pass ended and they were greeted by a dense forest of trees, or at least he thought it was.

A short distance into the forest a path led them directly to the village. He spied it just up ahead and he felt a sense of exhilaration mixed with fear. Shortly, the long, exhausting search for his brother could be over. He didn't want to count on it, though. Too many times he had been disappointed following leads and information that proved false.

He knew he had taken a chance freeing Zia, for she

could have lied to gain her freedom, but it was a chance he was willing to take, had to take. Even if it proved false, he needed to know if his brother was there or had ever been there.

The village Black welcomed them with open arms. Smiles shined on everyone's faces, fields and gardens bloomed abundantly and everyone seemed generous with health.

There was no keep; rather, cottages dotted the landscape, though there looked to be a large communal lodge at the far end of the village. He followed Zia to a good-sized cottage that appeared partially tucked in the edge of the woods.

"Is this where my brother is?" he asked.

"This is where I left him," Zia said, and smiled. "It's my grandmother's home."

Her smile offered encouragement. Here, he knew, his brother would have found solace. It was a place of peace and healing. He could feel it, strange as it seemed, knew it deep inside.

The door swung open and a tall, slim woman with long, pure white hair that hung in a braid over her chest and fell to her waist greeted them with a huge smile and arms spread wide.

Zia rushed into them. "Grandmother," she cried, hugging the woman tightly.

Artair observed them. Zia's grandmother appeared ageless. Few lines and wrinkles graced her lovely face, but not enough to determine age. It was as if each glance offered a different observation and by the time glances were done one could only assume the woman defied aging.

"Welcome to village Black, Artair," she said with an offered hand.

Had Zia informed her of his name? He didn't recall hearing her say it, but then, enthralled with the woman's presence, perhaps he hadn't heard.

He reached out and accepted her welcome. "Thank you for having me to your village."

"Bethane," she said, her smile growing. "My name is Bethane, and you are most welcome here. Come. You most be parched and hungry from your travels."

"Stay, Nessie," Artair ordered, but the dog ignored him and followed Bethane into the cottage. "Nessie!"

Bethane turned. "She's welcome in my home."

Artair entered the cottage behind his dog and Zia, thinking Nessie definitely needed a firmer hand. He was amazed at the size, the room being large with beautifully crafted furnishings and pottery that were certainly crafted with a skilled hand.

He gave Nessie a reproachful glare, but the dog just parked herself beside Bethane and ignored him.

"Please sit," Bethane said, extending her hand to a chair at the table in front of the hearth.

Artair remained standing, wanting to see his brother. "Zia says my brother Ronan is here?"

"He has left the village," Bethane answered gently, and once again offered him a seat. This time he did.

Zia was busy filling a pitcher with a brew from the

caldron that hung over the flames when her grand-mother said, with concern, "He was too ill to travel."

Artair looked to Bethane along with Zia. "Why did he leave?'

"I do not know. He was gone when I woke one morning."

Artair felt the familiar punch of disappointment to his gut. He had hoped beyond reason that this time would be different, but in truth he wasn't surprised that it hadn't. It seemed too easy that he should enter a village and simply find his brother there.

"I am sorry," Zia said.

Her apology was sincere. It was obvious she had expected to find Ronan there, which brought him some relief. She hadn't lied to him.

"When I left, he needed more time to recover," Zia added.

Artair could see worry written on her face as she occasionally gnawed at her plump lower lip. She obviously had reservations over Ronan's departure.

"I agree, but something continued to trouble him. I can only assume that was the reason for his departure," Bethane said with her eyes on Artair.

"He must have been well enough to leave, if he walked out on his own accord," Artair said and knew his brother well enough to know it was the truth.

"He was healing nicely," Bethane said. "He was eating well, resting and growing stronger each day. He had improved greatly from when he first arrived."

Zia sighed. "I feel better knowing that."

Bethane placed a comforting hand on Artair's arm. "I only wish I knew where he went. I can imagine how disappointing this is for you."

"I had hoped," Artair said, and was suddenly struck by the resemblance between Bethane and Zia, elegant lines and angles with softness in every tender curve of their faces. It was as if the same craftsman carved them from the same stone, and Artair realized he was seeing for himself how beautifully Zia would age.

Zia placed filled mugs and sweet bread with bramble jelly on the table. "I would have made him stay here until he was well enough to leave."

Bethane chuckled. "And for you, he probably would have stayed."

Artair bristled. "He found you appealing?"

Zia looked affronted. "I was his healer."

Bethane smiled. "Most men find my granddaughter appealing. I believe it's her passion for life that attracts them, though her exuberance could eventually wear a man down. It will take a special man to love her."

"It is who I am," Zia said without apology, and plopped in a chair opposite her grandmother, leaving Artair at the head of the table.

Who was she? Artair could not say he truly knew her, though one day had given him a good indication of her nature, and left him wishing to learn more about her. How, though? How did he learn more? His brother wasn't here. He had no reason to stay, yet didn't want to leave. Besides, there could possibly be others in the village who might have seen something that would help him track Ronan.

"Would you mind if I remained here for a few days and talked to the villagers? You never know what they may have seen or heard."

Bethane placed a slice of bread on his plate and a heaping of bramble jelly. "We would be honored to have your company, Artair. Remain as long as you like."

He caught the way Zia scrunched her brow. She obviously wondered over her grandmother's invitation. Was there more to it? The only way he could find out was if he remained and snooped around.

"Zia, you have an extra room in your cottage. Artair could stay with you," Bethane suggested.

Artair raised a brow. "Would that be proper?"

"Do you intend any improprieties with my granddaughter?"

"Absolutely not," he said adamantly.

"Then what's the point of him staying with me?" Zia asked, disappointed.

Artair stared at her, confounded.

Zia burst out laughing, as did Bethane.

"Your word is good enough here," Bethane said between laughter.

"You are welcome at my cottage," Zia said, her face bright and her words honest.

"You trust me, a stranger?" he asked with a thump to his chest.

"I don't consider you a stranger," Zia said.

He was surprised, and spoke his thoughts. "We've known each other barely a day, and how can I trust you when I rescued you from being burned at the stake for being a witch?"

Bethane gasped. "You were tied to a stake?"

"Only for a short time, Grandmother," Zia said, and sent Artair a scalding look.

Artair felt a stab of guilt. He hadn't meant to upset or worry Bethane, but he intended to view the situation reasonably and sensibility would show that he had taken a huge risk in taking a chance with her.

"With your intentions to remain for a while, we should be able to get to know each other better," Zia challenged. "Then you can determine for yourself if I am a witch."

"A reasonable offer," Bethane declared. "Now with that settled let me tell you about your brother."

Artair gave her his immediate attention wanting to hear all she had to say, but his mind lingered on Zia, the way she quirked the corner of her mouth, the way her eyes danced with joy, the soothing tinkle of her laughter and her generous smile when she found something amusing or pleasing, which was often.

"He fought against his pain, all his pain," Bethane said. "I would hear him whispering to himself to stay strong, fight, not give up. And he would laugh when he spoke of his brothers, telling me stories of when he was young and how Cavan—I believe he told me that Cavan was his oldest brother?"

Artair nodded, the knot in his throat preventing him from responding.

Bethane continued. "He claimed Cavan always protected him from his other brothers or his own stupidity, or as I advised his youthful innocence."

"Cavan did that," Artair said with fond memory. "He always protected Ronan, always kept him safe from harm."

"I believe Ronan felt obliged to return the favor," Zia added. "He wanted so badly to heal. He was determined to regain his strength and . . . "

When she didn't finish, Artair asked, "And?"

Zia's smile faded and she seemed reluctant to continue, but she did. "He wanted to rescue Cavan and seek revenge against those who had caused him and his brother such pain, such grief. He was as determined to seek revenge as he was determined to heal."

Bethane nodded. "That surely was the way of it."

Artair raised a proud chin. "Then he truly is a Sinclare."

"Revenge serves no purpose," Bethane warned.

"I beg to differ," Artair said strongly.

"As a warrior, I would expect no different," Bethane said.

Artair didn't care for the way she spoke to him as if he were a child needing guidance. "Warriors are necessary."

"I won't argue that," Bethane said. "I respect warriors and the need for them, but revenge?" She shook her head. "That can only bring more sorrow and regret than is necessary." She stood, tall and regal, like a queen who had finished speaking to her subjects. "Zia, show Artair to your cottage, and Artair, feel free to speak to anyone in the village. We will all help you as much as possible. I must take my leave now. Bless you, my son."

Artair stood as she walked out of the cottage with poise and dignity. She was a gracious woman, and Artair believed an intelligent one. He looked forward to future discussions. It took him a moment to realize that Nessie had followed her, and he called out for the dog.

"My grandmother is wise. You should listen to her," Zia said, then grinned. "You've lost Nessie to her."

"We'll see about the dog, the advice I might take."

As they walked out of the cottage his eyes settled over Zia and the seductive sway of her hips. He realized as he watched her that it wasn't intentional or meant to entice. She simply possessed a unique rhythm, one that fit her body comfortably, the provocative sway as catchy as a repetitive tune.

Chapter 5

"**K**eep your eyes on the path," Zia warned, and heard Artair stumble behind her. She turned as he easily righted himself. "There are some twist and turns in our village. I don't want you getting lost."

He nodded, and she heard him keep pace as they continued on.

She felt terrible about his brother having left before he arrived. She hadn't expected him to be gone, and she didn't believe he had been well enough to leave. What then had happened? She supposed revenge could fuel the body, but like her grandmother, she would not have advised it. Revenge never allowed for full healing.

She was glad Artair decided to remain for a while longer. She had hoped he would. It would not only do him good to be here, to cease his hunt for his brother, if only briefly, but give her time to get to know him better. She found him appealing in so many different ways, and she wanted to know why. He was handsome and intelligent, but that wasn't the whole of him and she wanted to know the whole of him.

Zia stopped before a quaint cottage, neither small nor large and with a front flower and herb garden that bloomed profusely. "My home," she said proudly, stepping aside for him to precede her down a pebbled path to the weathered, arched front door.

He hesitated, and she was pleased to see him break into a broad smile after taking his time to view the place.

"It's lovely and it fits you perfectly."

"Another compliment," she sighed. "I will certainly miss them when you leave us."

His smile faltered briefly though he reclaimed it as easily as he had his stumbled steps. She wondered over his strange reaction and her own sudden apprehension over his inevitable departure, for she didn't want to think of when he would leave. She enjoyed his company and certainly his compliments pleased her, but how odd? She knew him only a day, though it felt much longer.

Once inside, Zia showed him where he would stay. "It's a small room but adequate for your needs, a soft bed with fresh linens and a chest if you wish to store any of your things."

Artair looked it over, his glance going from the small room to her bed and the slim curtain that separated the two rooms.

She smiled and settled his unspoken query. "The room is used for someone who needs constant care."

"Will you care for me?"

His question didn't surprise her as much as the seriousness of his tone. He sounded as if he actually meant it rather than that he simply teased her.

She thought to tell him that if ever he needed caring, she would tend him, but instead she simply answered, "Yes."

"I am pleased to know that," he said.

His gentle smile sent quivers through her, while making him appear all the more handsome. It was hard not to stare at him, drink in his beauty and melt in his dark eyes. She wondered if Artair knew how he affected women. She had seen it for herself from when he first rode into the village and saved her.

Even amidst the chaos, there wasn't a woman who could keep her eyes off him. Even here in her own village she had seen the way the women's eyes followed him, though she knew the women here simply appreciated his handsome features, since most were in happy unions.

So far from what she knew of him he didn't seem enthralled with himself, but rather a warrior of fine standing and a man determined to find his brother.

"You will want to give John a message to take to your brother," she said. "Then if you like, I will show you around the village."

He nodded. "Thank you, but I am not keeping you from your duties, am I?"

"Not at the moment."

"Then I would be pleased to have you show me around."

Zia took a few moments for herself while Artair

went to deliver his message to John and see him safely on his way. She quickly freshened herself in the stream behind her cottage and slipped into clean clothes, a lovely buttery colored skirt and pale yellow blouse, sandals, the strips adorned with smooth pebbles, graced her feet. And she could do nothing with her short hair but run her fingers through it and let it have its way.

She finished with a quick dab of rose water around her neck, in the crevices of her arms and around her wrist. She sighed once done, feeling her old self.

A gentle knock had her swinging the door open and once again she found herself catching her breath at the sight of Artair. But she didn't admonish herself, she told herself to enjoy every palpitation and flutter. It was the way of things, the way of life, and she loved every minute of living it.

"You are beautiful," he said.

His remark was said so simply and yet so profoundly, her joy soared. Stepping out of the cottage, she wrapped her arm around his, moved in close beside him and said, "I will never tire of your compliments."

They walked off, Zia taking delight in showing him the village while inwardly more focused on the sensation of his muscled arm and the feel of his taut thigh when she accidentally brushed against him. He exuded strength, she could feel it, and it tingled her flesh.

They lingered by a weathered fence, beyond which grew an abundance of crops.

"Your village thrives considerably," he said. "And in everything I have seen."

"We all work together to see that it does."

"Then you all work very hard, yet none of you seem to struggle. I am impressed," he said. "It seems that you and your grandmother keep everyone and everything healthy."

"We all do our share," she insisted, not willing to take the credit when it belonged to all in the village.

A bell rang out.

"I am needed. Feel free to wander about," she said, and with urgency took off.

Artair had seen enough to know the village Black possessed a powerful pride in their land and themselves. A common goal always united people, and these people obviously shared a common goal.

However, he was curious how the village Black came into existence. It wasn't a place you would stumble upon. Unless you knew precisely where it was, one would never find it, which could explain why the people lived in peace. No one knew it was there, and with sentinels posted and the undetectable entrance, discovery, much less attack, was unlikely.

He meandered through the village and was frequently offered a hot brew or something to eat or simply a moment of conversation. All knew who he was and all offered their hope that he would be reunited with his brother soon. And all spoke of Ronan as if they knew him personally.

"Fine lad."

"A strong one."

"Determined."

"Good to talk with."

"Brave."

He stopped after a while and settled under a large tree, resting against its thick, aged trunk, to think about his brother. They spoke of Ronan far differently than he had expected. He didn't doubt his brother's strength, but Ronan was the youngest, the one he himself and his brothers always looked out for, the one who always listened to their every command. To the villagers, however, he was a strong, independent man, and one with whom it was easy to talk.

This was a new Ronan to him, or perhaps he had just never noticed those aspects of his brother.

His attention caught by a flurry of activity around Bethane's cottage, he decided to see what was going on and if he could be of assistance. After all, the villagers had been gracious to him right from the start, and it was only right that he return their kindness.

A young woman hurried past him, and he quickly asked, "What's wrong?"

"An injured warrior has been brought in," she said, and hurried off.

Artair didn't think the village had warriors—sentinels, yes, but no full-fledged warriors. So where had this one come from? Curiosity and his warrior instincts had him headed straight for Bethane's place.

He noticed people coming and going from around the side of the cottage, so that's where he went. It appeared as if a small cottage had been attached to Bethane's, and he assumed it was for the purpose of tending the ill.

He entered and was startled by what he saw, though he didn't show it. On a long, narrow table, draped with a white linen sheet soaked with blood, lay a barely recognizable man.

Zia and Bethane worked frantically on him, their arms and the linen aprons they wore to protect their clothes covered in blood.

The man didn't move, didn't make a sound, and Artair knew it was better that way, for if he was conscious, he'd be screaming in pain. He turned around to leave the healers to their work when he caught sight of the man's garments heaped in a bundle on the floor. Common sense had him rushing to the table.

"This man is a barbarian."

"This man is injured," Zia said firmly.

"He's a *barbarian*," Artair emphasized, thinking they hadn't heard him clearly.

"It matters not who he is," Bethane said. "He is a man in need of healing, and we are healers."

"His kind does not honor life; they take it without thought or caring."

"Perhaps, but we are not barbarians and we do not live by their creed," Bethane said calmly. "Now please, we need no more distraction. We can speak of this later if you wish."

She was dismissing him, though not his protest, and

for a moment he simply stood there astounded, then he quickly turned and walked away.

Barbarians had been his enemy for as long as he could remember. They descended on villages like vultures, leaving nothing alive in their wake. The only way to combat them was to do away with them, and here he was waiting while Zia was trying to save a barbarian's life. How did he make sense of it? Could he? Did he want to? What choice did he have? He sat amidst a healing village. He had to try and understand.

He remained where he was, Nessie having joined him, until shadows slipped across him and he realized several hours had passed and it had grown quiet around Bethane's cottage. He was about to get up to see how the barbarian was doing when Zia walked out.

She was minus her apron and stood rolling her head and then squared her shoulders as if stretching out her aches. She spotted him, waved and walked to join him beneath the tree.

"How is he?" Artair asked, anxious to know.

"He's alive, but it's questionable that he will live through the night."

He wanted to ask why she had even bothered to try and save the barbarian, but he knew she had fought a valiant fight, and thus he couldn't simply dismiss it as senseless. He had to respect her position as a healer, for she had fought as valiantly to save his brother. That was the realization his solitary time had brought him. Zia was a healer and would heal whoever needed it. It was her way.

He knew she was weary, but there were questions he needed to ask. Questions he had failed to ask at the start. "Precisely, how bad was my brother when he was brought here? And how did he find his way here?"

She surprised him when she asked, "Would you find me too bold if I rested my head on your shoulder? I am quite weary, and if you recall, I have already pillowed my head on your chest."

He did recall how after he had rescued her, while on his horse, she had rested her head to his chest but he had thought nothing of it, merely her need to feel protected after a frightening ordeal.

This, however, was different, and he liked the thought that she would seek his shoulder to rest upon.

"It would be my pleasure," he said.

She smiled, rested against his side and dropped her head to his shoulder with a sigh. "Your brother suffered a severe wound to his shoulder, his leg, and he had several damaged ribs. His face had been badly beaten. A friend of our village brought him here."

"A friend?"

"A friend to us is anyone who knows and respects this as a place of healing."

"How would one know that?" he asked.

"They are informed."

"How so?"

She yawned and moved her head from his shoulder to his chest. "By people who trust."

He slipped his arm around her, liking the feel of her body against his. "You avoid a direct answer."

"Not true."

"Don't trust me?" he asked, giving her arm a rub and catching the soft hint of roses drifting off her.

"Actually, I do. Though I don't know you long, you have demonstrated your trustworthiness. You didn't anger when you learned of the sentinels. You didn't fret when I wouldn't let your men into the village. And you left the cottage when my grandmother dismissed you, though you did not want to."

"You realized that?"

She nodded. "I can understand why you feel the way you do about barbarians, and I can't say I blame you. I have tended many who suffered at their hands, but as a healer, I do not choose whom I heal; I only know I must heal those who need it."

"I realized that myself after giving it thought."

"A quality of yours I admire. You look and find reason in situations, instead of acting foolishly first and thinking it over later."

"While you rush in," he said, and gave her a playful poke in the arm.

"With reason," she defended.

"Or is it foolishness?"

"Or life saving," she argued.

"Or life threatening." He didn't like that thought; the idea that her need to heal could continue to place her in danger. He could save her only so many times, and then, one time . . .

He could be too late.

The idea ate at his gut. After all, he was a warrior, and a warrior protected the weak.

He almost laughed. He could never envision Zia as weak. She was too full of life, too passionate about all she did.

She yawned again. "I can take care of myself."

"Can you, now?"

Another yawn followed and she burrowed deeper against his chest. "I most certainly can."

Artair didn't respond. He remained silent and waited, and sure enough, in a few minutes she was snoring lightly.

Bethane approached him and he cautioned silence with a finger to his lips then whispered, "She's exhausted."

Bethane kept her tone soft. "She fought hard for him."

"He is?"

"Still holding on. The night will tell. You will see her tucked in?"

"I will. You need not worry, she is safe with me," Artair said.

"I know," Bethane said with a smile, then walked away, Nessie following her.

Chapter 6

Zia woke with a stretch then bolted up in bed. She was wearing her skirt and blouse from yesterday and it took her a moment to realize why. When she did, she smiled. She recalled being with Artair under the tree. He had to be the one who carried her to bed and tucked her in, clothes and all. How gallant of him.

She looked over at the thin drape that separated them and saw that it was pulled back, the sparse room empty. She hurried out of bed and quickly changed garments, choosing a violet skirt with a white blouse, sprigs of heather skillfully embroidered around the low neckline. After slipping her sandals on, she entered the main room, to find that empty as well. She made haste to the stream behind the cottage, scrubbed her face and hands with the cool water and saw to taming a few wild strands of short hair by dampening them.

Finished and feeling famished, she headed to her grandmother's cottage, where she usually took breakfast. Besides, there was an ill warrior to tend, and since her grandmother hadn't disturbed her during the night, that could mean only two things. The warrior had succumbed to his wounds or survived the night without incident.

She hoped Artair was with Bethane. She was looking forward to seeing him, recalling with pleasure the feel of his hard chest, though it had pillowed her head comfortably enough. But it was the elemental scent of him that had enticed her most; earth, wind, and fire. He was scented with all three, and oh how she loved it.

Zia entered the cottage with a flourish and a smile.

"You missed Artair," Bethane said.

Neither her flourish or smile faltered. It was not her way. Life was too precious to waste on disappointment and too short not to enjoy.

"I'll find him, though Nessie prefers your company," Zia said, and plopped down at the table to join her grandmother in her morning oatmeal porridge drizzled with honey.

Bethane patted the dog's head. "She's grown attached to me."

"I'd say so. She follows you all over and listens to you much better than she does Artair."

"She has a mind of her own and I understand that," Bethane said, and received a lick from the dog.

"How is the warrior?"

"Surprisingly, he continues to sleep and heal."

"Good," Zia said with a firm nod. "I hoped and prayed for his recovery."

"Artair heals as well, though in a different way, and will seek more questions," Bethane said.

Zia scooped up a spoonful of porridge. "He already has. He asked who brought his brother here."

"And?"

"I spoke the truth. I told him a friend."

Bethane nodded. "That is the truth, but we both know there is more to it, and when he discovers—"

"I will tell him when the time is right," Zia said. "Do you know where he is?"

"He has gone to speak with his men. What do you think of Artair?"

Zia rested her elbow on the edge of the table and her chin in the palm of her hand. She tapped her cheek with her fingers while thinking over her grandmother's question. She knew Bethane would not rush an answer out of her. She would want her to think it through and reach a sensible conclusion.

She sputtered at the silly thought of thinking it through and being sensible and laughed out loud, "He's gorgeous!"

Bethane nodded. "I thought as much. Have you looked inside him yet?"

"There's goodness there." She scratched her head. "But he has an overly sensible nature and a strong responsibility to duty."

"Good qualities," her grandmother assured.

Zia shrugged. "He knows nothing of passion."

"You could teach him."

Zia's grin grew large. "I plan to."

After finishing breakfast with her grandmother, Zia went straight to the see how the barbarian was doing. Bethane would be busy making the rounds of the village, visiting with the women whose birthing time was near.

The women of the village took time to sit with the ill and those recovering so that Bethane and Zia would be free to tend others. Zia had long ago found that being a healer had benefits and one of those was the many friendships she formed with women and the ease with which they spoke. It was also how she had learned so much about men, women and sex. Women openly discussed intimacy, some fearing there was something wrong with them because they enjoyed it so much while others complained that they couldn't stand it. The many chats had helped her to help other women and to better understand her own desires.

Tara, a robust woman with a gentle smile, who often spoke candidly with her, was busy working on a piece of embroidery while the barbarian slept.

"Has he stirred?" Zia asked, placing a tender hand to his head. There was no trace of fever, which boded well for him.

"He's rested soundly," Tara said, gathering her things.

"You gave him the broth?"

"On schedule. You will look after him now?" Tara asked.

Zia nodded. "I will keep an eye on him while I tend to any who seek healing today."

It was busier than usual, a few scrapes, an abrasion that required stitches, a stomach ailment that actually had Zia concerned, and Artair showing up worried over one of his men.

"It's James. He's complained of these ailments before but no healer has been successful in helping him."

"Bring him here," Zia said, not doubting his word, not thinking that he just wished one of his men in the village. He would not do that. Concern showed on his face, and he'd sought her permission first.

The stout man was in agony when Artair hurried him into the healing cottage. Zia saw to him immediately, concerned for the man she had enjoyed fishing with.

She questioned him and learned that his stomach problem occurred on a regular basis. She mixed a combination of herbs and had him drink the potion. It was sweet tasting so he made no objection.

In minutes his stomach soothed and he smiled. "It feels better," James said rubbing his healed stomach in amazement.

At that moment a painful roar filled the air and Zia dropped the cup in her hand and rushed to the other room, Artair and James following.

Zia fought to keep the barbarian still, trying to soothe him with calming words, but he raged in fear and pain.

To her surprise, Artair came to the rescue. He clamped heavy hands down on the man's shoulders and ordered James to hold his legs still.

"It's all right. You're safe. No one will hurt you. Be still and you will grow strong," Artair ordered.

The barbarian responded to the commanding tone and settled down.

"Are you in pain?" Zia asked, leaning over the man.

He nodded vigorously.

She quickly ladled broth into a cup from a warming caldron and held it to his lips. "This will ease your pain."

He eagerly sipped at the brew until there was nothing left, then grabbed her arm. Zia had to stop Artair from ripping the injured man's arm off her.

"I—I—"

"You will recover if you rest and trust that we will help you," Zia assured him, placed a cool cloth to his brow in hopes it would keep fever away, and gently caressed his shoulder.

He settled, but only after taking hold of her hand. "You won't leave me?"

"I am here, as are others."

He shook his head. "You. You must stay with me."

"I will," she assured him, and felt Artair bristle beside her.

Then the barbarian drifted off to sleep, and she, Artair, and James left him to rest comfortably.

James excused himself, feeling fit and ready to return to Patrick the lone Sinclare warrior who waited outside the entrance of the village.

Zia stopped him. "Bring Patrick here. I wish to keep

an eye on your stomach ailment and there is no sense for him to remain alone."

James nodded appreciatively and took his leave.

Artair took hold of her arm and moved in close. "Were Ronan's injures as bad as the barbarian's?"

"No, but bad enough," she answered.

Artair ran his hands through his hair. "He shouldn't have left here. His injuries needed time to heal. He's left himself vulnerable."

Zia took strong hold of his hand. "I would have preferred he remain here, but you must understand that when Ronan chose to leave here, he probably unwittingly took what was necessary to help him *survive*."

Artair arched a confused brow. "Explain."

"Potions necessary to his healing were added to the various foods he was given so that his healing would not be interrupted. Every bite of food he took fortified him. I doubt he left without taking some sustenance with him. He probably grabbed the first available food which meant he took the food kept in his room, which contained healing herbs. He continues to receive what he needs to heal."

Artair shook his head and stepped away from her. "Your ways are strange to me."

"To most," Zia corrected.

"How do you do it?"

"We care for each other and those in need. It makes a difference."

Artair stared at her unable or unwilling to respond until finally he reached out to her.

She took his outstretched hand and once again held it firm.

"Tell me my brother is strong enough to survive his wounds."

Zia nodded repeatedly. "Ronan is more than strong enough to survive and more than determined to survive. You will find your brother."

"It is my most devout wish to see him again. To grab him and hug strength into him and know—" He shook his head slowly. "—know that he is finally safe."

"Zia!"

At the tearful cry, both she and Artair turned to see a chubby young lad, barely four years old, struggling to hold a plump pup in his arms. "Brute needs help."

Zia went to his aid. "What's wrong with him, Thomas?"

A fat tear dropped on his pudgy cheek. "His paw."

Zia gently wiped it away. "You were smart bringing him to me right away." She eased the pup out of his arms and talked reassuringly to the animal as she entered the other part of the cottage and placed the dog on a small table. "Let's see what's wrong with you, Brute."

Thomas hurried to the table and patted his pup on the head. "Zia will fix you, Brute."

She hoped that she could, and after a quick exam, smiled with relief. "Brute has a big splinter in his paw."

"He does?" Thomas cried out and shook his finger at the dog. "I told you not to play in the wood pile." He looked back at Zia. "Is it going to hurt? I don't want Brute to hurt."

Artair hunkered down beside the lad. "Zia has a tender touch. I bet it doesn't hurt Brute at all."

Thomas smiled wide, his full cheeks flushed. "Hear that, Brute? It won't hurt."

Zia had the dog repaired in no time and without as much as a whimper. Actually, she received numerous licks for her good deed. She sent child and pup off with honey biscuits and a promise from Thomas that he would return with Brute in a couple of days so she could make certain his wound was healing properly.

Thomas thanked her with a big hug before he and the pup bounced off, sharing the biscuits.

An old man hunched over from age shuffled into the cottage after Thomas left, and stopped when he spotted Artair. "Sorry, I thought when I saw Thomas leave that you were done. I will wait outside."

Zia went immediately to his side, her arm going around his frail shoulder. "No, Charles, I can see you now. This is Artair. He is Ronan's brother."

"Good lad, Ronan," Charles said as Zia guided him to a chair.

"You knew my brother?" Artair asked eagerly.

"I visited him from time to time. Smart and curious."

"About what?" Artair asked.

"Just about anything, though he showed a lot of interest in bows."

"Charles is Peter the bow maker's father," Zia said.

"You passed your skill on to your son," Artair said.

Charles nodded. "And he's made a better bow maker than me."

"And Ronan was interested in bow making?" Artair asked.

"We spoke more about aim and accuracy. And how a skillful archer can hit his target even at distances thought impossible."

The old man was hit with a coughing fit, and Zia shooed Artair outside, though not before Artair told the man they'd speak again.

Zia wasn't surprised when almost an hour later Charles left the cottage and she saw Artair join the old man and follow alongside him talking. But then that was what he was there for, to find out all he could about his brother's stay here. And many would have stories to share with him, for many had visited with Ronan.

However, she didn't know if any would be helpful to Artair, at least not helpful in the sense of what he searched for. Their stories wouldn't tell Artair where his brother went, but they would help him to better understand his brother and what he had gone through, and she wondered if he would realize that.

Several hours later Zia finished her duties and decided to dig up some woodland herbs to flavor that night's fish. Bethane returned and suggested that she find Artair and ask him to help her.

"Matchmaking, Grandmother?" she asked teasingly.

Bethane grinned and placed a hand to her chest. "Me? Never!"

"You like him, don't you?" Zia asked more seriously.

"From what I see of him, yes."

"You see more than most."

"I look deeper than most," Bethane said. "But there is much on the surface of Artair that shows me he is a good man. Dig deeper and you will find even more sterling qualities."

"Are you suggesting I dig deeper?"

She gave a wink. "Isn't that what you're about to do?"

Chapter 7

Artair walked through the village a bit surprised that so many had spoken with his brother. It was as if the whole village knew Ronan and had been concerned for him. Most commented on how worried he'd been over his brother Cavan, and how he missed his family. But he heard nothing that warranted Ronan's sudden departure from the village.

The only sensible answer was that he had been anxious to return home. He thought of sending a message to Cavan, alerting him to the possibility, but decided against it. His family had been disappointed too many times by false leads. And at the moment he had the strange feeling that his brother was running, but from whom and to where? He would investigate more before he shared any opinions with his brothers.

Artair stopped, sensing Zia's approach, then caught the familiar scent of her before hearing her footfalls. He shut his eyes and envisioned her. She'd be smiling; she always smiled. Even when she was tied to the stake bartering with him for her freedom, he had thought he detected a hint of a smile. And then there were her sparkling green eyes. Always alight with passion. Damn, but he found her appealing, and the more he got to know her, the more appealing she became.

If he felt so intense about her in such a short time, he could only imagine how he'd feel about her given time. And he had decided he wanted extra time to spend with her. How he'd manage that, he wasn't certain, but he would.

He turned slowly and burst into a smile, his vision having taken solid form.

"I found you," Zia said exuberantly.

"I didn't know I was hiding."

She laughed, stopped in front of him and rested her hand against his chest. "You can't hide from me; I will always find you."

He placed his hand over hers, the feel of her warm, soft flesh, tingling his own. "Why would I want to hide from you?"

She scrunched her face in thought and he almost laughed. She looked even more adorable to him. No matter what expression she wore, she remained a beautiful woman.

She answered in a seductive whisper. "I will let you find that out on your own."

He lowered his head and returned the whisper. "Do you warn me that you're too much to handle?"

She pressed her hand more firmly against his chest. "It's a possibility."

"I can handle anything."

"You don't have much luck handling Nessie."

She stepped away from him laughing, and he muttered beneath his breath as he followed her. There would be time for him to show her just how capable he was of handling anything.

"Would you like to gather plants with me?" she asked, reaching out to take his hand.

"Do I have a choice?" he asked laughingly as she tugged him along.

"Not really."

He followed along willingly, eager to spend time with her, even if he had to collect plants to do it.

Artair wasn't surprised when Zia snatched a basket from the side of a cottage. He was learning that the village Black shared just about everything. The villagers were a contented lot, though not without imperfections, but they dealt with things with relative ease and unity.

He realized why the village operated with almost no conflict. After speaking to several of the villagers he learned that many of them, if not all, found their way here after a great deal of suffering and none of them wished to jeopardize the safety and peace they found. And he certainly could respect that.

"Did you find what you were looking for?"

Her question stopped him dead. Had he found what he was looking for?

"Your brother? Did you find out more about your brother?"

He hadn't thought of his brother when she had asked

her question. It had been Zia who entered his mind. He cleared his head as best as possible since thoughts of her continued to flit in his mind. "No, I didn't."

She nodded and dropped down by a patch of ground covering and with her fingers gently snipped off leaves. "Then you will be leaving soon."

Artair hunched down beside her. "You wish to be rid of me?"

"You are welcome here as long as you wish to stay." She continued snipping leaves.

"A few more days should do."

"Only a few?"

She sounded disappointed, so he challenged. "Give me a reason to remain longer."

She dropped the gathered leaves into the basket and stared at him for a moment before reaching out and slowly running her fingers down the side of his face. "Perhaps there is more here for you to discover."

He liked her veiled invitation. And he more than liked her touch. It sent shivers through his insides that landed in his loins, and he had a hard time controlling his reaction, though managed to do so with great difficulty. He prided himself on his control, his sensibility, and while he found Zia appealing, he refused to lose sense of his senses.

"We shall see," he said, and gently, though regretfully, eased her hand away, so her touch could not create more havoc.

She stood with a laugh, the basket looped on her arm. "That we will."

He followed her deeper into the woods, confident that while she controlled the path they took, he controlled the journey.

He was impressed with her knowledge of the woodland plants, warning him of the dangers of some, the benefit of others, and the importance of knowing the difference.

"Your grandmother taught you?" he asked, gathering pinecones at her request.

She nodded. "And her grandmother before her and so forth and so forth."

"What of your mother?"

"She died after giving birth to me," Zia answered, scooping various shaped twigs off the ground.

"I'm sorry."

She placed the few twigs in the basket. "I often wish I could have known her. My grandmother tells me that she was a special woman loved by a special man."

"And your father?"

She shrugged. "I don't know. My grandmother told me that he left before I was born and never returned. I believe him dead, since she said that he loved my mother beyond reason. You can't leave and not return when you love someone that much."

"Perhaps there was a reason he could not return."

"What possible reason could a man have for not returning to the woman he loved?" she asked, bewildered.

"Illness, detainment, imprisonment. It is wrong to condemn him when you don't know what happened."

"I don't condemn him. I believe him dead."

"But what if he isn't?" Artair asked, thinking his sound reasoning might possibly give her hope.

"He better be dead!"

"What?" Artair asked, wondering over her surprising response.

"If I ever found out that my father was alive and never returned to the love of his life, I would hunt him down and tell him what I think of him, which isn't much."

"You'd rather he be dead than alive?" he asked curiously.

"No, I prefer him to have loved my mother beyond reason."

"That makes no sense," he said, shaking his head.

"But it does."

"Why?"

"Because love is what is important."

He shook his head again and hesitated attempting to understand her reasoning but finding it difficult. "Being prudent is important."

"It's nonsense."

"Being practical is nonsense?" he asked calmly.

"When it comes to love it is. How can passion exist if you are always practical?" she asked as if she made perfect sense.

"Love and passion have a time and place."

"Love and passion know no bounds. They cannot be confined or manipulated or reasoned."

"Anything can be reasoned," Artair said.

"Not love."

"Yes, love."

She smiled a bittersweet smile. "Then, my dear Artair, you have never loved."

He felt a pang in his chest, near his heart. Had her remark disturbed him? Could there be a ring of truth to her belief?

Once again he found her hand at his chest, firm and warm and pulsating with life . . . or was it passion that he felt emanating from her?

"You feel love here, deep inside. It churns and burns and rushes out, consuming all of you until you think you are going mad."

"How do you know this? Have you loved someone?" he asked anxiously.

She shook her head and sighed heavily. "No, I haven't loved, though I have seen it in the eyes of the young and old couples alike. I have watched how one suffers for the other, watched one pray for the other and watched them grasp hold one last time. Love consumes the heart and soul and never lets go."

"Love is slow and steady and dependable," he corrected, confident in his opinion.

With a disappointed shake of her head, she stepped away from him. "It is not."

"It is," he reasoned. "And it allows love to survive the difficult times."

"How can you believe that?"

"How can you believe such fantasy?" he asked.

She sighed. "It is not fantasy to me."

"You're not being logical," he said.

She tapped his chest. "Precisely."

He laughed. "You make no sense and are proud of it?"

"I most certainly am."

He scratched his head. "We are of different opinions. I reason with my mind, you reason with your heart."

A sudden frown surfaced on her face and while he thought she would argue with him she remained silent in thought until her expression turned troubled.

"You think little of love," she said.

"I think highly of love. I just approach love differently than you, with more sense and reason."

"You think me a fool?" she asked bluntly.

He was quick to correct her. "I didn't say that."

"But if, as you suggest, I don't speak with reason, then I must speak foolishly."

"You twist my words."

She smiled. "I clarify them."

He grinned. "You are quick-witted."

Her smile broadened. "I am knowledgeable."

"Then perhaps it would do me good to think over your words," he said.

"A wise choice," she said with a nod, and walked off.

He smiled, admiring her opinion on love even if it was unreasonable. Love required sensibility if it were to survive. He saw that with his father and mother. They did what was necessary. He wanted the same, a dependable union.

Artair followed after her. "Are there more plants to gather?"

"You don't need to help me. Take the time to think about love."

"I can do both. Besides, I enjoy helping you. Just tell me what to do."

"Truly?"

He smiled at her teasing glint. "Within reason."

She sighed and shook her head, though the glint remained. "Too bad."

"For you or me?"

"For both of us." She turned and walked away swallowed by the dense foliage.

She taunted him and it worked, and made him follow her yet again. He disappeared after her and found her near a stream, harvesting another plant with her tender touch.

"Pudding grass," she said without looking up at him.

He noticed the change in her before he hunched down beside her. She was focused intently on her chore and working as usual with a delicate touch.

"It makes a good stuffing mixed with honey and has good healing properties when brewed, though caution must be taken with it."

Following her directions, he helped her pick the hairy leaves and after they finished they sat by the stream beside each other. There was so much he could say to her and yet he chose to say nothing. He simply enjoyed sitting beside her in silence.

"What is it you are looking for here?" she asked.

He glanced over at her and wondered himself. Was he remaining because of his brother or because of her? He couldn't answer, and that disturbed him. He turned and focused on her eyes, always so passionately bright. "I'm not sure."

"Then you should remain here until you are."

"I was thinking the same myself."

Chapter 8

Zia yawned and attempted to stretch the exhaustion out of her body. After a lovely supper with her grandmother and Artair, she had hoped for some quiet time alone with him. She had no idea why she was attracted to Artair. She liked that he was considerate and intelligent and also charming, but she believed he reasoned more than necessary.

How could anyone rationalize love? The idea still had her shaking her head.

Another yawn reminded her why her plans had changed. The barbarian developed a fever, and it had taken hours of constant care to make certain he didn't succumb to it. He was resting now, spent from his ordeal.

Zia wandered outside the cottage, the late summer night cool and the dark sky clear, every star sparkling as if it had just been polished. The waning moon seemed to blink awake from a peaceful slumber, and she heard the occasional sound of nocturnal animals that prowled the night.

She took a deep breath, drawing in the peace and beauty of the late night.

"Tired?"

Zia jumped, startled by the unexpected but familiar voice, then watched Artair emerge from the darkness. He was bare-chested, his dark green and black clan plaid wrapped smartly around him. His dark hair was tousled, which had Zia assuming he'd just rolled out of bed.

"What are you doing here?" she asked curiously.

"I woke, saw your bed empty and grew concerned," he said, stepping closer.

"Concerned for whom?"

"You know full well who. I could care less what happens to the barbarian."

He cares about me.

The thought yanked at her heart strings and filled her with joy.

Oh, dear, is that good or bad?

"The barbarian does well," she said.

"It's you I wish to know about."

"I am fine."

"But exhausted." He moved in closer and reached out to gently caress her cheek with the back of his hand. "I can see it in your face."

"A lass can't be expected to look good all the time," she teased.

"But you do. You always look beautiful."

"Now you tell tales," Zia said, though she smiled.

"You believe me trustworthy, remember. So therefore I do not lie. When I say you always look beautiful, I mean it." He cupped her chin. "Your loveliness plays havoc with my senses."

"Now you surely tease, for I am far from intoxicating."

He brushed his cheek faintly against hers. "I am besotted by your scent alone."

She pressed her cheek against his and could almost hear the sizzle of his coolness meeting her warmth. It sent tingles racing through her, and she knew at that moment that she wanted him to kiss her. She actually hungered for the taste of him, knowing his flavor would be tangy and bold and oh so delicious.

"And what of taste?" she invited.

He kept hold of her chin and stared into her eyes. "Spicy and audacious."

"Are you sure?"

"There is only one reasonable way to find out."

"Reasonable?" she repeated curiously. "You reason a kiss?"

"Damned if I didn't put my foot in my mouth," he mumbled.

"You don't reason; you just kiss," she said, as if speaking to a young child who needed instructions. "It happens—no planning, no reasoning, no wondering." She sighed. "You simply kiss."

Zia was suddenly grabbed and yanked into Artair's arms and his mouth captured her open one and within seconds he demonstrated his prowess. Good Lord, he knocked the breath out of her and she went limp in his arms.

Her mind reeled, her lips pulsated, her tongue mated with his and her legs trembled. Heavens, could the man kiss.

Her head fell to rest on his naked shoulder after the kiss ended, with reluctance on her part, though necessary since she needed to reclaim the breath he had so expertly stolen from her.

When she was finally able and he certainly didn't rush her since his arms remained firm around her as she lifted her head and with a soft smile said, "I liked that."

"As did I."

"It wasn't planned. It just happened."

"Actually," he said with a grin, "I realized that if you didn't stop talking—"

Zia stepped away from him and covered her ears with her hands. "Please don't make it seem planned. It will ruin it for me."

"Why?"

She pressed her hands tighter to her ears.

He grabbed her hands, yanking them away from her ears. "Don't be ridiculous. The kiss was fantastic. What difference does it make whether it was planned or spontaneous?"

"Ridiculous? You think how I feel is ridiculous?"

"Did you hear the part about the kiss being fantastic?" he asked, befuddled.

"I agree it was fantastic."

"Then what is the problem? We shared an absolutely thrilling kiss. Nothing more needs to be said."

"That seems sensible," she said softly.

"Of course it does," he said, reaching out for her.

"One problem." She stepped out of his grasp. "A first kiss shouldn't be sensible."

Then she turned and walked into the cottage, closing the door behind her.

Artair swore beneath his breath. She certainly wasn't sensible; she was pigheaded and foolhardy. Their kiss was incredible, like none he had ever tasted in his entire life. It had nearly buckled him at the knees, not to mention the punch to his gut and the heat to his loins.

A first kiss . . .

It had been their first kiss, or had she meant her first kiss ever? Were his lips the first to ever touch hers? He grew excited at the thought. Maybe she was right. It was about the kiss and nothing else. No rhyme or reason, just pure passion, and he had certainly tasted that on her. Zia's zest for all she did could prove to make life more interesting. Besides, as he got to know her, he'd be able to determine her nuances and deal with them in a more reasonable fashion.

He laughed as he walked away. Reason would win over passion. It was inevitable.

"Be careful. She is more of a handful than you think."

Artair jolted to a stop as Bethane appeared from the shadows, Nessie close to her side. "You saw?"

She shook her head slowly. "No, but your look tells me all I need to know—slightly dazed, but still confident."

Artair nodded. "That's how I feel, thanks to your granddaughter."

Bethane wiggled two fingers at him. "There are two of you."

"Admonishment or advice, which are you giving me?"

"Which do you need?"

"Zia is very much like you," he said.

"Then you are a lucky man." She smiled.

"I'm beginning to think that."

"Keep that thought strong and it will never fail to help you."

"I'll do that," he said, aware that she offered wisdom. "Where do you go?"

"It's where I have come from," she said, and pointed to the woods.

"The woods are so dark at night. Why go there?"

Bethane pointed to the night sky. "There are medicinal plants that can only be harvested under the waning moon or they lose their potency."

"You should have asked. I would have gladly gone with you."

"Nessie kept me company. Besides, you would have only slowed me down."

"I meant no disrespect. And as for my dog, it seems she favors a new master."

"I know it's the warrior in you always looking to

protect. As for Nessie," she added, with a pat to the dog's head, "she doesn't require a master."

"You understand far more easily than your grand-daughter, and far more than I do," he said with a nod toward Nessie.

"I have lived far more years and have gained far more wisdom."

"Then I can safely assume that Zia's passionate nature will soften with age."

Bethane chuckled. "Now you're asking for a miracle."

Artair laughed. He liked Bethane. It didn't take long to realize that she was a remarkably wise woman, and obviously loved her granddaughter very much. He also was aware that she served as leader of the village, and did so with distinction and honor. Not that she would admit it, but it was her who the people turned to, not only when ill, but to settle grievances and to lend an ear when necessary.

"The sun is only a couple of hours from rising. You should get some sleep," Bethane said.

"And you?"

"I go to see if Zia needs help."

"You both could use some sleep. Are you sure I can't help?"

"No, though thank you for asking. Zia and I are ac-customed to getting little sleep. I will see you in the morning," Bethane said, and with a pleasant smile, walked on, Nessie keeping step with her.

Artair drifted back toward Zia's cottage. He didn't

feel sleepy, his mind overrun by their kiss and his limited time here. He couldn't stay much longer. He had to return home and discuss with Cavan what he'd discovered. But he didn't want to leave Zia. He'd love her to come with him and meet his family, but she wouldn't leave here, unless—

The thought struck him like a lightning bolt. It was a perfect solution, actually, a very sensible solution. He had mentioned to Zia that his brother Cavan had not joined him due to his pregnant wife not being well. If he requested she return with him to tend Honora, she probably would agree and then they would not only have more time together, but his sister-in-law would have the benefit of an excellent healer.

There was another benefit of her returning with him, though it troubled him to even suspect that Zia was keeping something from him about his brother. Regardless, he did suspect he wasn't being told the whole of it. With her at his home, he'd have more time to discover what she *wasn't* telling him.

He turned around excited over the prospect and not wanting to wait until morning to ask her. When he neared the cottage he stopped and remained in the shadows as he watched Zia and Bethane talking on the side of the cottage.

Zia was tucking a cloth over the basket that hung on Bethane's arm. Then she kissed her grandmother's cheek and the older woman disappeared into the woods, along with his dog, and Zia returned inside the cottage.

What was going on? Why was Bethane returning to the woods And with a basket full of what? Where was she going? What were they hiding?

Perhaps there were more secrets to this quiet little village than he realized, which meant he wasn't leaving just yet.

Chapter 9

Artair began his inquiry the next morning at the breakfast table. "I'd like to speak to the friend who brought Ronan here."

"He's not here," Zia said.

"When will he return?"

"He doesn't live here."

"Tell me where he lives and I will go see him," Artair said.

"He travels. He has no one set place he calls home," Zia explained.

Artair remained persistent. "Tell me of the places he frequents and I will find him."

"We cannot do that," Bethane said.

"Why not?" Artair asked.

Bethane explained. "The person you seek helps those in need. His identity is known to only a chosen few. He risks his life helping others."

"I will tell no one of his honorable deeds," Artair insisted, feeling there was more to this person than Bethane was saying.

Bethane shook her head. "I am sorry, but I cannot, nor will I betray his trust."

"Is that who you went to see in the woods last night?"

"Do you accuse us of hiding something from you?" Zia challenged.

"Do you?" he snapped.

Bethane raised her hand to stop the sparring before it could escalate. "I understand your need for answers, Artair, but you must realize by now what this village is all about."

"It's a sanctuary for those in need," he answered.

"In desperate need," Bethane corrected. "There is no one to help them, no place for them to turn, and some are being pursued unjustly. We welcome them to remain here if they wish; some do, while others feel compelled to move on."

"And the person in the woods?"

"A visitor who has long since gone," Bethane said.

Artair's response died on his lips when she raised her hand.

"You search for your brother, and these questions you ask will not help find him. He chose to leave. I wish I could tell you why, but unfortunately I do not know. As for the secrets of this village? They pertain to us alone."

Artair sat back in his chair, crossed his arms over his chest and gave an abrupt nod, accepting her explanation for now. But this was far from the end of his inquires. He wanted answers and he intended to get them.

Zia leaned forward, and her grandmother placed a firm hand on her arm. "I believe Artair understands what I say."

Artair almost smiled at the fire that raged in Zia's eyes. She was ready to argue, and he couldn't deny that he felt like a fight, but not with her. It was his own frustration that he needed to battle.

"You have been more than generous with your information and hospitality. And you are right about your secrets. I would not care for a stranger demanding secrets from my clan."

"You have secrets?" Zia asked, the fire continuing to dance in her eyes, though playfully.

Her mischievous glint began to melt his irritation. He leaned closer to her. "Be nice and I may just tell you some."

She walked two fingers rapidly, though lightly, up his forearm. "I bet I can get you to reveal a few without being nice."

"I've heard enough," Bethane said with a laugh, and stood. Nessie, who had been sleeping at her feet, stood also. "I'm going to check on the barbarian."

"I'll be there shortly," Zia said.

"Take your time. He's been resting comfortably and I have some potions to blend." Bethane walked out leaving the open door as it was so that the late summer air could drift throughout the cottage. Nessie as usual trailed after her.

"I meant no insult to you or your grandmother," Artair said.

Her fingers danced slowly up his arm this time. "We know that, for if you did you wouldn't be sitting here right now."

He grabbed hold of her seductively wandering fingers. They were doing much too much damage to his senses, and if he didn't stop her soon, he wouldn't be able to think straight.

"Where would I be?"

"Where I really don't want you to go yet," she said softly.

"Where is that?"

"On your way home."

"You like me." He grinned and tapped her nose.

"That's obvious, but you feel the same," she said bluntly.

"I do, and have no problem admitting it."

"So you will stay here for a while?" she asked excitedly.

"I was hoping you might return to my home with me and meet my family and tend to Honora, my brother Cavan's wife who is with child. If you recall, I told you she wasn't feeling well."

She hesitated, and he thought he knew why. She had obligations here, and yet, Honora was in need of a healer.

"That's not the only reason why I want you to return home with me," he said, wanting to be truthful with her. "I feel we would do well together."

That brought a bright smile to her face.

"I believe, given time, getting to know each other more, we would realize that we make a good match."

Her eyes widened. "Match?"

"It takes a good match for a marriage to work."

"Marriage?"

Why did he feel like he had just jumped into a river and found he couldn't swim?

"What of love?"

How did he know she was going to ask that, and why hadn't he realized it sooner? He attempted diplomacy. "Love develops along the way."

"What if it doesn't?"

She didn't challenge; she actually sounded anxious.

"What then? Without love, a marriage is doomed."

"I don't believe we'd have that problem," he assured her, for he felt confident they would indeed make a good match.

"We barely know each other," Zia reminded him. "Passion sparks in both our eyes, and I daresay our bodies as well. But is it the passion of love or simply lust?"

This time he was blunt. "I won't deny I feel lust when I'm with you."

That brought a huge grin to her face.

"But I also enjoy your company. I want to spend time with you. I look forward to it, even if I must collect plants to do it."

Zia laughed. "It is good to know it is not beneath a warrior to stoop to collecting plants."

He grinned. "I'll stoop anytime you want me to."

She laughed again, though softly, and moved closer to him. "What you tell me is that you are willing to do what is necessary—"

"To make this work," he finished.

"I don't want to *make* it work. I want to fall in love."

He threaded his fingers with hers. "In time love will come."

She eased away from him. "Then we will give it time."

"How much time?" he asked.

"As much time as it takes." She bounced out of the chair. "I must tend to my chores now."

Artair wasn't going to let her escape that easily. He caught her before she could race out the door and wrapped his arms around her.

"I can be reasonably patient."

"That is good, for you will need it."

"Will I, now?" he asked, and with a wicked grin stole a wicked kiss.

He felt her arms go around him and her fingers trail up his back to grasp the top of his shoulders. He crushed her against him, her breasts pressing hard into his chest, her taut nipples poking even harder and making him grow hard.

The gentle sway of her hips against him nearly did him in, and he knew he had to end the salacious kiss or there might be no stopping either of them. He eased them apart, his body almost rebelling when he saw how plump and ripe her lips were from their kiss, and the way her nipples remained taut beneath her blouse.

At the moment, they were both full of lust.

He took her hand and led her outside into the sunlight. She blinked several times as if waking herself, looked around surprised, then smiled at him.

"You don't trust yourself," she teased.

"You are absolutely right."

She chuckled. "That is good to know."

"Damn, I gave away a secret," he said playfully.

"See, I told you I could get secrets out of you without being nice."

"I could be more vigilant, though I like it when you're not nice."

She tapped him on the chest, turned, and with a provocative sway of her hips said, "Ahh, but what about reason?"

Her lighthearted barb made him laugh, and made him think that he might not be as patient as he first thought. They suited each other and he could offer her protection. Only the very foolish would dare accuse a Sinclare bride of witchcraft.

He would get her to return home with him, and once she did, it would be easy to convince her to remain and become his wife. He felt pleased with himself as he turned and walked away. His trip might not have been successful in finding his brother, but he had discovered that Ronan was still alive, and that would give the family hope. And he had found an appropriate woman to take as a wife. All in all, it was a good trip.

He would return with good news about Ronan, and do it with his bride-to-be.

Zia and her grandmother sat in wooden chairs outside the cottage door, quenching their thirst with cider. It had been a hectic morning. Several villagers had arrived with various complaints, and two of them needed stitches to close deep wounds. The barbarian also demanded attention, asking endless questions as Zia changed his bandages.

"I think he will remain with us," Bethane said, resting her head back against the rim of the chair. Nessie curled comfortably beside her.

Zia hesitated briefly. "He's already asked me to go with him."

Bethane smiled at her granddaughter. "I wasn't speaking of Artair."

Zia returned the smile and nodded. "I agree the barbarian will choose to stay here."

"But Artair will not."

Zia sighed. "He told me that his brother Cavan's wife is with child and not well, that she could use my skill."

"He knows you will not refuse to help someone in need," Bethane said with a nod. "But there is more, I think."

"He believes us well suited and thinks we would make a good 'match.'" Zia stood, leaving the empty tankard on the chair, and paced in front of Bethane. "He talks of marriage when we barely know each other.

He says in time love will develop." She stopped pacing and stood starring into the distance.

Bethane waited.

Zia finally turned around. "It is a practical decision for him. It has nothing to do with love, and it is too soon to tell whether it's just a passing attraction or something more." She threw her hands up in the air. "What do I do?"

"Let it be. Time will handle it for you."

"Do I go with him?"

"I think you have already decided that," Bethane said.

"If his sister-in-law does need help and I don't go, I'd never forgive myself."

Bethane eased herself out of the chair. "I think if you don't go and see how things develop between you and Artair, you would never forgive yourself."

Zia hurried to her grandmother's side. "But you need me here."

"There are many good healers here. We will survive in your absence," Bethane assured her.

"Then you believe I should go?"

Bethane shook her head. "I cannot nor will I decide for you. The choice must be yours and yours alone."

"Part of me wants to go, and part of me . . . " Zia sighed.

"Part of you fears going," Bethane said.

Zia bobbed her head. "Yes, yes, but why? I've always faced my fears with courage. What makes this different?"

"Love. Love makes all the difference."

"What if—"

Bethane placed a gentle finger to Zia's lips. "Let it be, just let it be."

Artair knew he had a problem as soon as he saw James present a bouquet of flowers to a woman and she responded with a bright smile. That James had picked the flowers was amazing in itself, but that he had washed up and made himself presentable was even more amazing.

James was first and foremost a warrior. But at the moment he looked more like a besotted fool, which made Artair smile, and worry.

The woman, short and plump and oh so pretty, smiled at James as if he were the handsomest of men. He had never seen a woman look at James with such adoration.

"I think Mave fancies James."

Artair smiled as Zia hooked her arm with his.

"They look to suit each other," he said.

She smirked and shook her head. "Take a closer look. I'd call that love."

"They only met."

"Just met or not, just look at them."

He looked at the couple again and had to admit that it wasn't lust he saw in their eyes, but a sparkle that he couldn't quite define, though it made him smile.

"You see it," she said with an excited tug to his arm.

"I admit I see something." Actually, he couldn't believe his eyes. James was most attentive to the young woman and it seemed he couldn't help but smile. In fact, James rarely smiled, and when he did, it was a short burst that passed quickly.

"The poor man is completely love-struck."

Artair cringed, and joked, "She's given him a love potion."

"Mave hasn't asked for a love potion."

Artair turned wide eyes on her. "I was teasing."

Zia gently squeezed his arm. "So am I."

He shook his head. "You could get into trouble if someone heard you."

"Not here I wouldn't, but then none here would believe such nonsense. They would know it isn't our way."

"But you do concoct potions."

"To aid in healing. That's what we do here—we heal."

"Broken hearts need healing," he said with a smile.

They strolled off together arm in arm as they continued their conversation.

"There is no potion to heal a broken heart. Only time will heal it."

"True enough," he said sadly. "I see how it has been for my mother since my father died. She tries to appear strong, but I know how much she misses him, and that she sheds tears more often than she lets anyone know."

"Tears can be cathartic, and time will lessen her tears."

Artair guided her to a bench under a nearby tree, its huge branches providing a shady canopy. "I know, but it still hurts me to see her suffer."

"Perhaps she will find love again."

"She will not," he said emphatically. "She loved my father and will never love another."

"That's nonsense. I bet your father would want her to love again."

"He would not."

"I can't believe it," she said with a smile.

"Believe it. My father would not want my mother to love again."

Zia shook her head. "No, what I can't believe is that you're actually being unreasonable."

"I am not," he said defensively.

"Oh yes, you most certainly are. If your parents loved so strongly, then your father would not want to see your mother alone and mourning for the rest of her life. He would want her to be happy."

"She has her sons and will soon have a grandchild, and more to come in the future."

"She's a woman with needs."

He bolted to his feet. "She's my mother."

Zia smiled up at him. "She's still a woman with needs, especially if she and your father—"

Artair's hand shot up. "Don't say another word. My mother has all that she needs."

Zia got up and entwined her arm with his. "I'll have to speak to her about it when I meet her."

"You most certainly will not."

"Meet her or speak to her?"

Artair shook his head, though he smiled. "Perhaps I was too hasty in inviting you to my home."

Zia grinned. "Too late! I've already decided to return home with you."

Chapter 10

Artair woke the next morning feeling refreshed and eager to return home. He hadn't been surprised, though he was relieved, that Zia had consented to return with him. At least he wouldn't be arriving completely empty-handed.

His family, Cavan in particular, would be pleased that he returned with a healer. Though their clan had women who helped heal, none could truly be called a healer. And his mother would surely be pleased, for she had done her share of healing over the years and often wished she had known more. She would be delighted to work with Zia, and that would keep her from feeling lonely.

Zia believed wrongly that his mother would even want to love again, let alone need to love. But she would see that for herself.

He sat up, stretching, and swung his legs off the bed. He was eager to make preparations to return home. He and Zia had spoken with Bethane last night at supper. He didn't want to just snatch Zia away from her. That wouldn't be right. Not after Bethane had been so kind to him.

The three agreed that within a week's time, Zia and he would leave. He looked forward to their departure, though he had to admit that he enjoyed his time at the village and wouldn't mind returning now and again.

He stretched himself off the bed and slipped on his shirt and plaid and tied his sandals. He drew the curtain back and wasn't surprised to find Zia's bed empty. He had thought he was an early riser, but Zia had him beat. She was always up before him. He usually caught up with her at breakfast. She always made a point of sharing the meal with her grandmother and he had grown accustomed to the same. He quite enjoyed it.

Morning greetings were called to him as he meandered through the village to Bethane's cottage. It was a beautiful sunny day and he'd never felt so alive. Life had suddenly become more potent and more pleasurable.

He entered the cottage and stopped abruptly. It was empty. In the few days he had been there, he always found Bethane and Zia at the table sharing breakfast. What had happened?

He began to worry.

He walked around to the side of the cottage, certain he would find either of the women. He didn't.

Tara, a healer-in-training, was there, and she didn't know where they were.

Without hesitation, Artair began searching the village, but no one, not a single soul, could tell him their whereabouts.

He decided to see if his men had seen Zia or Bethane.

James shook his head at Artair's approach. "Patrick has returned with bad news."

Artair had recently sent Patrick to the main road to see if there were any signs of John, the warrior he had sent to inform Cavan of their whereabouts.

"Tell me," Artair said, prepared for the worst.

Patrick stepped forward. "The village that thought to burn Zia as a witch has contacted the church council claiming that Zia practices witchcraft. The council intends to investigate the accusation."

The news shocked and frightened Artair. How would he ever keep Zia safe? And how could he keep her safe if he didn't know where she was?

"Be prepared to leave," Artair ordered, and his men nodded.

He then continued his search of the village, and as before, no one could tell him where Zia or Bethane was and no one seemed concerned.

By early afternoon he was beside himself with worry and wanted to rush and grab Bethane and hug her when he finally caught sight of her entering her cottage.

He hurried to her, his silhouette filling the doorway. "Where have you been?"

Bethane turned with a flourish. "Artair, you startled me."

"I have been looking for you and Zia. Where is she?"

"Is something wrong?" Bethane asked.

The older woman was perceptive; he should have known she would sense his concern. However, he couldn't hide it. He was worried about Zia's safety.

"Where is Zia?"

"What is wrong, Artair? Tell me," Bethane demanded.

Artair recounted the news he had heard from Patrick, and watched Bethane pale. He reached out and helped her to sit, and she took his hand.

"Before sunrise an urgent message arrived from the village Holcote pleading for a healer. A difficult birth, we were told. Zia packed her basket and went to her aid." Bethane shook her head.

"Tell me."

"Holcote is not far from the village Lorne, which accused her of witchcraft."

"I'm going after her."

Bethane grabbed his arm. "She will not leave the woman in need regardless of her own safety. She will remain with her until the babe is delivered and both mother and child are safe."

"She'll leave," Artair said firmly.

Bethane shook her head. "You know better than that. It will do you no good to force her, especially if you have feelings for my granddaughter."

Artair ran a frustrated hand across his chin. "I don't know what feelings I have for Zia. All I know is that she won't leave my thoughts and she frustrates the—" He took a deep breath and plopped down in the chair beside Bethane. "I need to keep her safe."

"You need to let her be who she is."

"That will only get her into more trouble."

"You know her better than I thought," Bethane said.

"I hope to know her even better."

"Then go and keep her safe."

"Nessie, come," Artair ordered, and the dog plopped her bottom down next to Bethane.

"I will look after her, go," Bethane urged, and he did.

Artair and his men made their way to Holcote with haste. He arrived at the village half expecting, or perhaps half fearing, that he would again find her tied to a stake. Instead he found a village in need. The cottages were in disrepair and the fields ravished, and not by the inhabitants, for most looked half starved. These villagers were vassals to a feudal lord whose only interest was his own prosperity.

Several women lingered around one particular cottage, and Artair felt it safe to assume they were there to help in the delivery if necessary. Before dismounting, he spoke to James and Patrick.

"Go hunt game for these people, and if anyone attempts to stop you, tell them it's by order of the laird Sinclare."

Both men nodded and grinned. The Sinclare name was respected throughout the Highlands, and few would dare oppose them. Artair also knew that Zia would refuse to leave the village people in dire straits, but then neither could he. These people needed help, and he was capable of giving it to them. He could not just ignore them.

The door to the cottage was open, and as he approached he heard the suffering moans of a woman and Zia's comforting voice.

"It won't be long," he heard her say, and hoped it was true. He wanted to get Zia out of there as soon as possible.

"Zia," he said, entering the cottage cautiously.

She turned, and while her eyes brightened, she didn't smile. "I don't have time for you right now."

"We need to speak; it's urgent."

Zia handed a mug to one of the two women in the room with her. "Make sure she drinks this. It will help dispel the babe."

Artair walked outside with her and kept his voice low. "You need to leave here."

Zia looked appalled. "You can't expect me to leave this woman now."

"You are in danger."

"So is she, and what danger?" she demanded.

"You are being investigated for witchcraft thanks to the village of Lorne. I need to take you somewhere I know you will be safe."

"I cannot nor will I leave this woman."

"How long?" he asked, having expected her response and prepared to do whatever was necessary to keep her safe until she was ready to leave.

"Two maybe three days."

He nodded, not believing it a problem, since it would

take time for someone to be sent to investigate. He believed he would be able to get her safely to his home before then. In the meantime, he and his men could protect her.

"We will leave for my home when you finish here," Artair said.

"Are you certain?"

He took gentle hold of her face. "Why would you ask that?"

It bothered him that she stepped away as if she wished to distance herself from him.

"I do not wish to bring trouble upon your family."

He smiled, reached out and drew her into his arms. "My brothers relish a good fight."

"But this is a different type of battle."

"A battle nonetheless, and one we will win," he assured her.

An agonizing scream ripped through the air and all but ripped them apart.

"I must go," she said, already turning away.

"Can I help?"

Zia stopped at the open door. "Can you find a way to feed these people? They are starving."

"Already done," he said.

She smiled then, and it overwhelmed him, but not near as much as when she declared, "You're my hero."

He never considered himself a hero, but he liked the idea of being *her* hero.

*   *   *

His men were welcomed with tears and cries of joy when they returned with sufficient game for the whole village. It wasn't long before the scent of roasting meat peppered the village and smiles decked most faces.

Artair spent his time between helping his men and checking to see how Zia was doing. She worked tirelessly, limp curls plastering her perspiring brow. She encouraged the laboring mother with soft words and assured her repeatedly that all would be fine.

Artair found the husband camped out on the side of the cottage, face in his hands, sobbing. He was barely old enough to be considered a man, but a man he needed to be.

"Crying will not help her," he said, reaching his hand down to the lad.

The scrawny young man looked up, startled, wiped at his tears, then hesitantly grabbed for the offered hand. "I am Albert."

Artair yanked him to his feet. "Albert, you're a man who is about to be a father. You must be strong for your wife and child."

"She suffers and I can do nothing," he said.

"She needs your strength." Artair grasped his shoulder. "Come eat and strengthen yourself. Then clean up and be ready to go to your wife a man."

The lad nodded and stood a little taller as he walked with Artair to the roasting pit.

The villagers feasted, laughed, and offered prayers for mother and child and the healer who had brought them such fortunate luck.

That is until the feudal lord arrived with six of his men.

The villagers grew quiet and huddled close to each other when he and his men rode up to the roasting pit and stared at what was left of the carcasses.

His dark narrow eyes warned that he was not pleased and the tight set of his thin lips showed he fought to hold his tongue. He and his men looked well fed and their garments freshly woven. They obviously lived well off the sweat of others.

Artair stepped forward before any could be accused of theft. "I am Artair, brother to Cavan, laird of the Clan Sinclare of Caithness."

The man's eyes rounded and his demeanor immediately changed. "I am William, laird of the Clan MacWalter. You are most welcome on my land."

Artair knew the Sinclare clan would be recognized and respected, actually feared by some. His clan was known for its fierce and noble warriors, and many paid homage to them in hopes of earning them as friends rather than foes.

"I appreciate your hospitality, William, though I am more than willing to reimburse you for the game my men hunted."

"Nonsense," William said with a dismissive wave. "Sinclares are welcome to hunt on my property whenever they pass through."

"Your generosity is appreciated. I will be two, perhaps three days. My healer is seeing to one of the villagers."

"Someone is ill?" he asked sharply.

Artair knew it wasn't out of consideration that William asked, but rather, fear of catching a deadly illness. He set his mind at ease. "A difficult birth."

William sneered. "These pagans whelp their babes in the field and continue working. Do not waste your healer's time on them."

"My healer helps all those in need," Artair said firmly, knowing an altercation with this man would only provoke suffering for the villagers.

William gave a curt nod. "As you wish." He sent a stern look at the villagers. "This man is my honored guest; make certain you see to his care."

The villagers bowed their heads and kept them bowed until their liege lord had disappeared out of sight. Their frightened expressions showed that they feared reprisals. There was little Artair could do to help them since they belonged to another's clan. He could, however, make certain that the village was supplied with enough game to smoke and dry for the winter.

Nightfall arrived, though the babe didn't. The longer it took, the more worried the women in the village became, and soon whispers were predicting that mother and child would not survive.

Albert trembled with fear, and Artair walked him away from the gossiping tongues.

"Zia is an excellent healer," he said, hoping to reassure the lad, though wondering if there could be any truth to the chatter.

"It has been nearly a full day my Ciley has labored to deliver our child. She must grow tired."

Before Artair could continue to reassure him, Zia stepped out of the cottage, a solemn look on her weary face.

Albert rushed over to her. "Ciley?"

"Is resting, go see her."

Artair waited until Albert was out of sight and joined Zia. "What's wrong?"

"I fear the babe is somehow stuck. I've seen it happen before."

"And?"

Zia rubbed the back of her neck. "I'm not sure, but if I don't deliver the child soon, neither of them will survive the night."

Artair wrapped his arms around her, and she immediately rested her head on his chest. "You're tired."

"That doesn't matter."

"It does to me."

She smiled up at him. "It's nice to have you here with me."

"I'm not much help."

Zia placed a hand to his cheek and a kiss to his lips. "You have helped more than you know." She turned to reenter the cottage, but stopped and looked at him. "Keep Albert away until I come for him."

Artair nodded, and when the young man joined him again, he placed a supportive arm around him and walked Albert to the roasting pit to sit and talk with him.

As the night wore on, Artair became more concerned for mother and child, but he did not let Albert see it. He kept him talking, even suggesting that Albert might find a better home elsewhere for his family, and telling him he'd be welcome in Caithness with the Sinclare clan.

The young man had no chance to respond. Zia stepped out of the cottage and walked toward them. Artair stood along with Albert, intending to help the lad however he could, though he hoped it would be congratulations that he offered.

Zia sighed and ran a hand through her choppy hair as she approached. With hands on her hips, she settled a hard glare on Albert. "So, are you ready to meet your son?"

Albert broke out in a grin. Laughed, then cried. "A son?"

"A big boy for sure, which is why you can have only a few minutes with Ciley and then she must sleep. She is exhausted." Zia smiled and pointed at the cottage. "Go, they both wait to see you."

"Thank you. Thank you," Albert said, bobbing his head as he ran past her to the cottage.

Artair went to Zia, slipped his arm around her waist and ran a gentle finger under each eye. "You're worn-out. You need to rest. A cottage has been prepared for you."

She nodded. "The women told me."

"I'll take you there when you're ready."

"I just need to give instructions to the women who

will watch over Ciley throughout the night." She rested her warm flushed cheek next to his cool one. "I won't be long."

"I'll be here," he said, running his hand down her arm and lacing his fingers with hers, only to reluctantly release her and feel her fingers slip one by one from his grasp.

He stood waiting where he was, and though she returned in mere minutes, it felt like much longer. He took her hand, lacing his fingers with hers once again, and again not wanting to let go, yet knowing he would soon have to. Even with slow steps, they would be at the cottage much too soon.

They strolled to the entrance and when they reached the door he planned to kiss her good-night. She surprised him and turned around, took hold of his other hand and hesitantly brushed her lips over his. "I want to kiss you," she whispered as if seeking permission.

"I want you to kiss me," he said.

She brushed her lips over his once again. "I want to keep kissing you."

A low groan rumbled in his throat. "I want you to keep kissing me."

Her lips kept brushing, teasing and tasting his until she pushed the door open and pulled him inside.

Chapter 11

Zia loved his arms around her, the strength of his kisses, the warmth of his body, but most of all his kindness. Artair might be a mighty warrior, but he was a compassionate man. He had helped the young father find courage, made certain the hungry were fed, and come after her, concerned for her safety. And more important, he was patient with her.

She pressed her cheek to his and rested there, wishing nothing more than to remain close to him, feel his arms strong around her and know this moment was for them alone.

She would kiss him again; she knew that, but for now this was enough. This was what she wanted, to simply be close to him.

He obliged her by not moving, though he ran his hand up and down her back and it felt so wonderful that she could have remained there all night wrapped in his arms.

However, her yawn interrupted them.

"You need to sleep," he said.

Slipping her arms around his waist, she prevented him from leaving her. "Not yet."

"If I stay too long, I will not want to leave."

"Then stay," she whispered in his ear.

His inquisitive look questioned her motive.

"Lie beside me and hold me, just hold me all night."

She saw reluctance in his eyes.

"Do I ask too much?" she asked.

He traced a finger around her lips. "To lie beside you and not touch you might prove difficult."

She retraced his path with the tip of her tongue, then said, "Am I that appealing?"

He kissed her quick. "You are that wicked."

"I can be wicked," she teased with a sigh, "but alas I'm too tired."

He coiled his fingers around the back of her neck and massaged the stiff area, and she all but melted in his arms.

"Now you take advantage," she said.

"Don't tempt me."

She smiled and saw desire rage in his eyes, but tenderness remained in his touch. "You are a good man."

"You truly tempt my honorable nature."

"Ah, but that is what I count on." Her smile faded and she pressed closer, his hands falling away from her neck to slip around her, and as he embraced her, she leaned in and kissed him.

It was a good thing he held her, for her legs grew weak as he took control of the kiss, and she eagerly surrendered. She didn't realize that he had picked her up or that he walked with her in his arms to the bed. She knew nothing but the kiss. It overwhelmed her senses and befuddled her mind.

She hadn't realized she was lying on the bed until he gently pried her arms from around his neck and eased away from her.

"You will not hold me?" she asked, her arms outstretched to him.

He stared at her for a moment, his look stern and unpredictable, and she waited.

He quickly unlaced his sandals and stepped out of them, but left his shirt and plaid on. Then he slipped over her outstretched body, giving her a quick kiss as he went, and settled alongside her. Before she could turn to face him, he tucked his arm around her and drew her back against his chest.

"Sleep," he whispered in her ear, "before I forget that I'm an honorable man."

She almost chuckled but instead yawned and settled comfortably against him. She remained still, not wishing to tempt him any further. At least not now. She was simply too exhausted.

There would be another time; she would make certain of it.

She drifted off to sleep with dreams of the future dancing in her head.

Artair planned to leave as soon as she fell asleep. He didn't think he could last the night without touching

Zia. Her teasing alone fired his loins, not to mention her kisses.

This feeling he had for her was strange. He had assumed that when he found a suitable bride, he would simply wed her. Passion would follow; he never expected it to precede it.

And as for a bride? He never expected to find such a suitable one. He believed that he would have to make concessions, as he had done when a marriage had been arranged for him with Honora. She had been sweet and obedient, but not what he truly hoped for. She was, however, the perfect woman for Cavan.

Zia might just prove to be the perfect wife for him, and with that thought in mind, he fell asleep, the future invading his dreams.

Artair woke with a smile and a stretch, then suddenly recalled where he was and bolted up in bed. He was alone. No doubt as soon as Zia woke, she hurried to see how the new mother and babe were. And if all proved well, they could take their leave from the village of Holcote sometime today.

He refreshed himself with a splash of warm water that most likely Zia had left in a bowl on the table for him. She hadn't woken long before him, for if she had, the water would have cooled by now. That was good; at least she'd gotten a good night's sleep.

He'd be glad when he could get her home. With his family's influence he might even be able to have the investigation dismissed before it started.

Feeling confident, he left the cottage in search of Zia.

The sun was bright and the villagers busy masking a storehouse that would hide the meat his men had hunted since before sunrise, and which was now being dried and salted. They would survive the coming winter, and with some suggestions from his men, learn how to hide a portion of their harvest so they would not starve.

Artair took his time walking through the village relieved he would, in a small way, leave these people better off. He headed to Albert's cottage and once near saw Zia standing outside staring in the distance, her hand at her chin. She didn't even notice him approach and startled when he stopped beside her.

"What's wrong?" he asked.

She shook her head. "You're not going to like it."

"Tell me," he said, standing beside her. Though he had known Zia only a brief time, he realized that it was more than likely he would hear the unexpected from her.

"First," she said with a smile, "mother and child are doing well."

"Good news," he agreed. "Now the bad?"

"Another village is in need of help."

"Have your grandmother send another healer," he said, relieved that he could dispatch the problem so easily.

"My grandmother wasn't contacted—I was."

"How?"

"The liege lord of this village requested assistance for his friend. He felt that since he extended his hospitality to you here, in Holcote, you certainly wouldn't mind sharing your healer."

"How long do you think a healer will be needed?" he asked, her safety foremost in mind, though meanwhile he was annoyed at himself for having made mention of her to the liege lord.

"I'm not sure. It depends on the severity of the illness."

"How far is the village?"

"That isn't the problem," she said.

A chill raced through him, and he knew he wasn't going to like what she had to tell him.

She continued. "The village Donnan where I am needed is a brief walk from Lorne."

He shook his head, and kept shaking it, unable to think of anything but Zia tied to the stake in Lorne. "You can't go," he finally said.

"I don't have a choice." She held her hand up before he could interrupt. "From what I'm told, the illness is spreading and one person has died already. If I don't get there as soon as possible, more deaths are likely."

"And what of you? You could possibly grow ill yourself and die, and if not that, the village of Lorne might discover your presence and attempt to burn you at the stake yet again."

"It's a chance—"

"I'm not willing to take," he finished. "I'll send word to Black and request that another healer be sent to Donnan."

"I can't allow that."

"Allow?" he snapped, and realized he was close to losing his temper, which he rarely did. A clear and sensible mind was needed to handle this situation.

Her hands went to rest firmly at her hips. "It's *my* choice."

"You're right," he said calmly, and watched her eyes grow wide. "But it's my responsibility to keep you safe."

"You are not responsible for me."

"I'm afraid I am. I and my family not only owe you for taking care of Ronan, but we would appreciate any help you can give Honora. Therefore, it is my responsibility to see to your safety."

"A reasonable explanation," she said and he wondered why she sounded perturbed. "You can do only so much. After all you can't guarantee my safety."

He stared at her, her words having set his thoughts churning. "Actually," he said with a grin, "that might be possible."

"What do you mean?" she asked, curious.

"The Sinclare clan is well-respected and has many influential friends. If you were to wed a Sinclare, your security could be guaranteed."

She stood stock still. He wondered if he had shocked her silent, and intended to file that fact away for future reference. It just might come in handy.

"You can't be serious," she finally said.

"It's a logical solution to a serious situation. If the village Lorne hears that you are at Donnan, there could be grave repercussions. But if it is learned that you are the wife of one of the Sinclare brothers, no one would dare threaten you."

"And this is a good reason to wed a stranger?"

He took her hand and laced his fingers with hers. "You cannot claim us strangers. After all," he grinned, "we slept together last night."

She tugged her hand loose. "We are presently friends."

"That's even better. A friend would make a good wife."

She shook her head, and he persisted.

"I admire your skills and your intellect, and I believe we are a good match. Given time, I am sure we will learn to love each other."

"Learn?"

"People learn to love."

"Because they have no choice. I plan on having a choice," she said.

"If you had the luxury of choosing, that would be fine. But with the present situation?" He shook his head. "Consider your safety first."

"My healing comes first," she said sharply.

"That's fine. Then let me protect you so that you can do your healing without worry."

"I don't have time to debate this now."

"No, we don't. Let's be done with it. Marry me,

and it will afford you the protection you need to continue your work," he said, hoping she would finally see reason.

She sighed, running her fingers through her cropped hair. He loved the way the short blond strands stood out afterward and how they glinted like fine gems in the bright sunlight.

"I cannot marry you. I look for love and passion and will settle for nothing less."

He was prepared to argue but she quickly continued.

"But I do see the wisdom in your suggestion. So I believe the best thing for us to do is *pretend* to be husband and wife while we are at the village of Donnan."

"That won't do," he insisted. "Someone will want proof of our union."

"I doubt anyone at the village will suspect. Their only concern will be for their well-being."

"But there is the village of Lorne nearby, as you said," he pointed out, "and they will certainly suspect our vows. Someone there may demand proof."

"Lorne will claim that I bewitched you into marrying me. So proof won't matter."

"You are being stubborn," he said.

"I am being true to myself. I wish to fall in love and wed, and I refuse to settle for anything less. It will be my way, Artair, or not at all."

He would have argued further with her but knew it would be senseless. She would not budge, and they would only waste time. Time better spent preparing a cohesive story that everyone would believe. He would need both James and Patrick's support with this plan, and would have to send word to Bethane so she could verify the story if asked.

He finally nodded, reluctantly accepting her suggestion.

"We will need a consistent story about how, where, and when we were wed," she said.

"I thought the same myself. If I'm correct, it will take us at least a day to reach our destination. How long before we can leave here?"

"It will take at most a day to reach Donnan, and with mother and child doing so well, I think we can leave by late afternoon."

"Good. We will discuss our wedding while traveling, and share the news with James and Patrick when we stop for the night."

Her face brightened with a smile. "I'm sure they'll be overjoyed for us."

He leaned closer to her. "You got your way this time. Don't be so sure about next time."

She laughed softly and slipped her hand inside his shirt, to tickle his chest. "Believe me, Artair, I will always have my way with you."

Chapter 12

Zia found Donnan in worse shape than she had expected. About a quarter of the village suffered from a low, persistent fever accompanied by aches and pains. The least resilient suffered; the very young and the elderly were forced to remain abed.

The story she and Artair had concocted concerning their recent marriage didn't matter to the villagers. Their only thought was for the healer who had come to help them. Zia hadn't spared a moment once she arrived. She quickly deposited her personal items in the cottage made ready for her and, with her healing basket, began making rounds of the village.

Within a few hours she knew she had a problem on her hands. She had seen this ailment before, some resulting in dire circumstances, while on other occasions it proved less severe. Try as she might, she couldn't find the source.

She had been recording her findings in her journal, where she kept a wealth of information. Old ways mixed with new ways on the pages, helping her to better understand illnesses and cures. Now, in the cottage of a young couple whose two-year-old little boy suffered from the mysterious ailment, she pored through the journal.

She knew, without a doubt, that she wouldn't be leaving Donnan until all in the village were healed. Artair would not want to hear as much, since to him her safety came first, but there was no way she'd leave these people to suffer, or perhaps die.

"What is this?" Artair asked, peering over her shoulder at her journal, while holding the rocking chair she sat in so it remained steady.

"My secrets," she whispered.

He arched a concerned brow.

She shook her head, her expression grim. "You think it is a book of spells?"

"Quiet," he urged in a harsh whisper, and cast a quick glance around the sparse room.

"It is only young Andrew, you, and me here. His parents have gone to a friend's cottage to get some much needed rest. They are worried senseless over their only child." She shook her head. "Do you think me a wi—"

Artair pressed his finger to her lips. "Do not even speak such nonsense. I worry more what others will assume if they saw your book. To you it is an accumulation of knowledge; to the less wise, it would appear arcane writings meant to hurt and destroy."

She reluctantly agreed with him. "Unfortunately, you're right, which is why I call it my secret book.

The knowledge within is best kept for my eyes alone."

"But you let me see it?"

She smiled and patted his hand where it rested on the chair. "You are my husband."

He nodded with a grin. "It is a wise wife who does not keep secrets from her husband."

"I would never keep secrets from my husband. There would be no reason to."

"You are a good wife already."

She chuckled. "Don't speak too soon."

They both laughed softly, and he pointed to the open pages of her book. "Can you find something that will help?"

"I'm trying a combination of things, but I have found that with an illness such as this, sometimes the only thing that can be done is to let it run its course."

"Then the village will survive this strange outbreak?" Artair asked with concern.

"I can't be sure. It seems the very young and the elderly have the hardest time battling the sickness."

"Those with strength survive?" he asked.

"It seems that way, which is why I try to strengthen the less hardy."

"There is nothing more you can do?"

"Patience is a big part of a healer's strength," she said.

Artair leaned down and whispered in her ear. "Patience and passion, not a harmonious match."

His warm breath felt like feathers tickling along her

neck, and her flesh instantly prickled. She shuddered as she turned a smile on him. "It takes patience to know true passion."

"I never thought of it that way."

"That's because you're too practical. But you'll learn," she said.

"So confident."

She stretched, reaching up to kiss his cheek. "In you? Always."

His hand caressed her neck. "I knew you would make a good wife."

"Of course I would," she whispered. "But will you make a good husband?"

The young lad woke crying, and Zia jumped out of the rocker, closing her book and handing it to Artair. "Keep it safe."

She didn't hear his response, or perhaps was too focused on the lad to have heard it. She needed to get more of her brewed broth into him and to make certain he got as much rest as possible.

The lad took the broth without a problem. Zia had prepared a tasty brew so the ill wouldn't refuse to drink it. However, Andrew didn't want to go back to bed, so she returned with him in her arms to the rocking chair.

After a short time he fell asleep, and as she stared at him, his full cheeks flushed with fever, she thought of how much she looked forward to having her own children, lots of them.

With her free hand, she reached in the basin near the

chair, squeezed the cool cloth, and gently caressed his feverish brow. He squirmed and cuddled in her arms. She held him close and comforted with soft words and the cool cloth.

"You'd make a good mother," Artair said, stepping out of the shadows.

"You didn't leave?" she asked quietly, noticing he still held her journal.

"I thought you might need help, but I saw how easily and gently you handled the child. I amend what I said before, though I believe it a quality you alone possess. You have the patience to heal and the passion for healing, which makes you an amazing woman and healer."

Zia was glad that the arrival of Clare, the lad's mother, interrupted any further discussion. Artair's compliment had overwhelmed her, and she wasn't certain how or if she should respond.

"Is my Andrew all right?" the young mother asked anxiously.

"He's fine," Zia said, and motioned her over. "Why don't you put him in bed; he needs his rest."

Clare nodded as Zia placed the sleeping lad in her arms. She hugged him close and kissed the top of his head.

"He's such a good son." She looked to Zia with tears in her eyes. "He'll be all right, won't he?"

"I believe so, though he needs to rest and drink the broth."

Clare nodded. "He hadn't wanted to eat, and barely drank anything until you gave him that broth."

"It helps heal," Zia assured the worried mother.

Clare rested an anxious hand to her cheek after placing Andrew in bed. "Good Lord, I almost forgot. You're needed at old Mary's. She isn't doing well."

"You know what to do," Zia confirmed with Clare, and as soon as the woman nodded, Zia hurried out the door.

Artair followed her.

"Please put my journal in my garment sack."

"Then?" he asked, keeping pace with her.

"Then you're on your own," Zia said, and sped off.

Artair roamed the village after doing as Zia asked. He had instructed his men to become familiar with the layout of Donnan and with its people and to report any change in talk or behavior to him immediately. And to be wary of any strangers who arrived, especially with word spreading that a sickness had hit the village. No one would dare come there unless . . .

Someone was interested in the healer.

He kept close watch over Zia, following her from cottage to cottage, and after a few hours wondered how she kept up her frantic pace. She no sooner got finished with one ailing person than another summoned her, and then there were those whom she revisited more often—whose fevers had spiked and who appeared to be losing the battle. But like any courageous warrior, she refused to give up. She fought on.

While he admired her tenacity, it also worried him. Zia constantly put the well-being of others before herself. No matter how tired she was, she kept going and didn't complain. She seemed to thrive on it.

Passion.

He had known passion with more than one woman, and on more than one occasion. But that was different. Or was it that Zia was different? She seemed to embody passion in everything she did. It was a significant part of who she was, and he doubted she could ever do without it, though he did wonder if in time it might dim or burn out completely. After all, it wasn't reasonable to think that her extraordinary passion could last forever.

By late afternoon he realized that Zia had eaten nothing all day. Between tending people, she'd been busy crushing leaves and brewing broth, and was now baking bread to distribute among the ill. And it was only their first day in Donnan.

He caught up with her in old Mary's cottage—Mary being the oldest and weakest of those ill.

He stood in the open doorway, his hands braced overhead on the wooden frame. "You bake bread but have eaten nothing."

Zia looked up from her task, smiled, and dusted her hands on the faded and stained white apron that hugged her waist and protected her dark blue skirt. She walked over to him and slipped her arms around his waist, resting her head on his shoulder.

"I'll have a rest right here," she said with a sigh.

His arms coiled with a gentle strength around her. "Rest as long as you like."

"I wish it could be for . . . "

A heavy sigh followed, and he wondered if she wished as he did, that they could remain this close forever.

"You need rest and food," he said, caressing her back.

"There's no time."

"We'll make time," he insisted, her welfare his only concern.

"There are many who need me."

"If you are too tired or take ill, you will do them little good," he said.

She rubbed her face in his shirt and took a deep breath. "I love the scent of you. It reminds me of woods and earth and fire." She sighed again. "And you are right. I should eat."

His only thought for a moment was that she liked the scent of him and he liked the way she snuggled her face into his chest. He almost had to shake his head to clear it and he had to tame his stirring passion. This was about her, not him. "You also need help. There are too many ailing villagers for you to look after."

"Once I have enough broth and bread made, I can distribute it to the families who have ailing relatives and they can help see to their care."

"You can take a few moments and eat first."

She glanced up at him with a smile. "Is that an order, husband?"

He liked being addressed as her husband, and smiled. "No, a concern."

"A thoughtful husband. I like that." She patted his chest. "I just need to set the bread to baking and then I can spare a little time to eat, though I would prefer to remain close to Mary." She turned and looked at the old woman asleep in the bed. "I'm worried about her. She's so frail."

Artair nodded. "I'll get us some food and we can eat right outside. It's warm and the sun is bright. I'm sure you can use some fresh air."

Besides, part of him was selfish; he wanted some time with her, even if it was only a short time. He knew she'd be back to healing the sick soon enough, but for now he'd have her to himself.

He sat on a bench just outside the cottage door. When he requested some food for the healer from the villagers, he was given more than he needed, but accepted it with appreciation. These people were grateful for her help and they showed it.

When Zia joined him and quickly dug into the basket of food, he wasn't surprised. "I told you that you were hungry," he said, laughing.

She nodded, her mouth full.

He didn't interrupt her meal with senseless chatter. He enjoyed sitting in silence watching her take pleasure in every morsel she put in her mouth, and the way she tilted her head back now and again so the sun could kiss her face. She relished her life; whether healing or simply sitting, she found pleasure in it all, and suddenly he wanted some of that enduring passion. He wanted her.

"You are beautiful," he said.

Her smile and eyes brightened simultaneously. "You really mean that."

"Why wouldn't I?"

She shook her head slowly, the brightness in her face never fading. "It's just that I could see it your face." She stretched her hand out, her fingertips grazing along the corner of his eye. "Here. I see the depths of truth here, and it touches my heart."

He would have kissed her then and there if an anxious woman hadn't interrupted them.

"Another young one has fallen ill," the plump, tired-eyed woman said, twisting her hands fretfully.

Zia stood and without a word went off with the woman. Just when she almost disappeared from sight, she turned and waved at him. He understood her well enough now to not take it as an afterthought. It pleased him that he had entered her thoughts and that she had acknowledged him.

He wasn't sure about what was happening or certain of the feelings stirring inside him, though he knew that he wanted Zia in his life, and not just as a brief interlude. He sat there for a while thinking that only a few days ago he hadn't even known her, and now thought of her as a permanent part of his life. He most certainly must be foolish.

Foolishly in love.

He would have laughed if it wasn't so serious. He couldn't possibly believe he was in love with Zia. That he was attracted to her, cared about her, admired her—

yes. But love? That was something else that took more than a few days to determine.

He continued to sit there as the sun wilted in the sky, luscious scents drifted out of the cottage chimneys, villagers meandered to their homes, and evening settled around them. And still . . .

He continued to think of Zia.

Chapter 13

Zia rubbed the back of her neck and down along her shoulder. The stiffness would grow worse but it couldn't be helped. There were too many ill people who continued to need her. She worried that if she didn't get the illness under control it would infect the entire village. She had worked endlessly, and prayed that she would soon see good results.

Now and then, when she could, she caught a wink of sleep. In the three days she had been there, she had managed only a few hours. Artair had made certain that she ate, bringing her food when she hadn't even realized she was hungry.

His attentiveness had caught the attention of the village women, and many remarked to her how considerate and patient her husband was. They were right. Artair was patient. He didn't grow angry with her or make demands. He would reason with her and of course he would make sense and she would do as he suggested.

She had realized soon enough what a good man he

was, but it startled her to realize the full depth of his genuine character. And she actually felt a sense of luck that he should be the one to rescue her, though perhaps fate had something to do with that. Or could it have been love that brought Artair to her?

What most fascinated her about him was the way he controlled his passion. It sparked in his eyes now and again, though he never let it flare. And she felt it in his touch, especially when he held her and caressed her back. He was careful where he touched, never going beyond the proper boundaries. She reminded herself that they had only met and she shouldn't expect more And yet?

She smiled and hugged herself. She wanted much more from him. She wanted to taste deep passion, kisses that ignited, touches that demanded. And, eventually, if he proved the right man?

Intimacy.

She was glad that her healing skills had allowed her to learn about intimacy without actually experiencing it. She'd been forced on many occasions to ask personal questions in order to treat a woman, and often the women provided more than she needed.

So now it was easy to understand why her body heated just at the thought of their naked bodies rolling around in bed together.

It was sheer anticipation.

"Are you feeling all right?'

She turned from the table where she had been mixing crushed leaves to see Artair enter their cottage.

He hurried toward her and reached out to feel her forehead.

She ducked under his arm after grabbing a handful of leaves off the table, dumping them in the cauldron of water hanging over the flames. "I'm fine."

He pressed his hand against her forehead as soon as she turned around.

"You are warm," he said.

She heard the concern in his deep voice, felt it in his tender touch, and her traitorous body flushed with desire for this man who seemed to stir her soul with a simple touch.

She stepped away from him, returning to busy herself at the table. "Of course I am. I've been working too long near the hearth, that's all."

"Are you sure? Your cheeks are flushed." He rested the back of his cool hand against her hot cheek.

How could his simple touch stimulate her senses so very much? She wanted to sigh and surrender and beg for a kiss, a touch that would ease the ache inside her. Instead she turned away again and proceeded to mix leaves that were already well-mixed. And to convince herself that she had more important matters that needed her attention. There was no time for this nonsense now.

"I'm a healer," she said, reminding herself rather than him.

"Healers can fall ill. I do not want that to happen to you."

"It won't," she said, and a yawn rushed out of her mouth.

He grabbed her chin. "You will come to bed tonight."

Her insides tingled from the innocent demand.

"We've been here three days and you have yet to sleep in our bed."

Our bed.

Did he have to remind her that they played at being wed? And also remind her how wonderful it had been to sleep in his arms that one night? They fit each other as if made for one another.

"You will sleep in our bed tonight," he said.

"Will I, now?" she asked, her desire for him sparking frustration.

Instead of arguing, he slipped his arms around her and cuddled her close to him. How could she get annoyed with a man who hugged her rather than fought with her?

"A few hours away from your healing will not hurt anyone. And everyone knows where to find you if you are needed." He hugged her tighter and rested his cheek next to hers. "Besides, what kind of husband would I appear if I did not try to get my wife into our bed?"

She was grateful for the rap at the open door that drew their attention.

"I'm sorry to bother you," Clare said, appearing embarrassed that she had disturbed them.

"You're not bothering anyone. Is Andrew all right?" Zia asked, slipping out of Artair's arms.

Clare stepped into the cottage with a smile. "That's why I came. To tell you that he's much better. He wants to eat more than just the broth and the bread."

Zia clapped her hands together, a sense of relief rushing over her. "That's wonderful, but one more day of bread and broth to make certain, and then he can eat other foods."

Clare nodded. "I hear old Mary is feeling better as well, and that no one else has turned ill." Tears pooled in her eyes. "I was so afraid—"

Zia hurried to her side and took hold of her hand. "Don't even think about it. Andrew is well and will stay well."

"Because of you," Clare said, and hugged Zia. "You truly are a *special* healer."

"My wife is a *skillful* healer," Artair corrected.

Zia turned a curious eye on him and was surprised to see concern in his eyes.

After Clare left, she turned to him. "What disturbs you?"

"She called you a special healer. No one else has taken ill. No one has died."

Zia realized what he was suggesting and was about to argue when she realized that was how her problems had started at Lorne. People began thanking her, praising her, and then accusing her.

"You understand what I'm saying?" he asked.

"Yes, I do."

"A day or two more is all we should spend here."

"As long as no one else turns ill," she said, and stopped his protest with a shake of her head. "I will not leave if I am needed."

He held up two fingers. "Two days, and if everyone has improved and no one else turns ill, we leave."

"Agreed," she said, knowing that if in two days time all looked good, she could depart without worry.

He walked over and took her hand. "I will leave you to your work, but if you are not in our bed tonight, I will come find you and bring you there."

She had to smile. "That sounds like an interesting prospect."

"I can heft you over my shoulder and cart you off, if that is what you want."

"Telling me takes all the passion out of it," she complained.

"Being carried off like booty from a battle isn't passionate," he said.

She slipped her hand out of his. "When you put it like that it isn't."

"Like what?"

"Booty from battle?"

He shook his head. "It expresses it perfectly."

"Perfectly practical," she shot back. "Why even bother suggest it?"

"I didn't," he said. "I simply stated—"

"It wasn't simply. You made it appear as if you'd drag me to your bed."

"I would never drag you to my bed."

"Why not?" she asked curtly.

"I prefer you willing," he chortled.

"And what if I'm not willing to come to bed tonight? What then?"

He leaned in close. "I'll see that you do."

"How?"

He tapped the tip of her nose. "Don't challenge me."

She poked him in the chest. "I love a good challenge."

"You may get more than you bargained for."

"I can handle it," she said confidently.

"Why must you always prove your courage?"

His question startled her, and she took offense. "I don't need to prove my courage to anyone."

"No, you don't, but it appears you need to prove it to yourself.

A call from outside the cottage prevented the reply stuck in her throat. Zia hurried outside to discover that she was needed at old Mary's cottage. After returning to grab her healing basket, she stopped and stared at Artair.

"I'll be waiting for you," he said.

She nodded and rushed off, running from his question or the answer, she wasn't certain. Or was she running because he was waiting for her? And he would indeed wait, and with patience, damn him.

She tried in vain to keep him from her thoughts and concentrate on her work. Old Mary had developed a rash on her arm, but once she took a look, she knew it wasn't anything serious and began putting a generous layer of salve on it.

The older woman was recovering nicely, with color highlighting her thin cheeks and her green eyes lively. She might look frail, but Zia could see she was far from it. She had a tenacity about her that couldn't be missed.

"I heard you got yourself a good husband," Mary said as Zia applied the salve.

"Artair is a good man."

"How did you find him, or were you just lucky?" Mary winked.

"I believe a little bit of both," she answered, ready to tell the story she and Artair had concocted, but only if necessary.

"Make sure you hang onto him. A good man is not easy to find," Mary said, nodding slowly. "I know. I had one, and we had twenty-five wonderful years together. He's been gone five years now and I still miss him terribly."

"So you had all good times, no fights?"

Mary laughed till her thin body shook. "Good lord, lass, fighting comes right along with marriage. You're going to fight. You need to fight. The trick is not to hold onto the anger. Spit it out and then forget it or it will eat your marriage up, and worse, it will eat you up."

Zia chatted for awhile, then made to leave when Mary started nodding off.

But before she stood, Mary took hold of her hand

and said, "Love that husband of yours every day. You don't know how long you'll have him."

Zia didn't know what to think and didn't have time to ponder this advice. She was summoned to several cottages, where people praised her healing skills. Fever lingered in a few, but it remained low, and with vigilance and healing broth she was certain they would recover as well.

She made her rounds of the remaining cottages, and when finally done, realized that night had nearly fallen and Donnan had grown quiet. Standing in the center of the village, she could almost feel the calm that had been restored.

It was what she enjoyed most about healing—restoring hope and peace.

Why do you always have to prove your courage?

Artair's words reminded her that it sometimes took a tremendous amount of courage to enter villages, and even more courage to try and heal, for when she failed, it hurt her heart. Her grandmother had told her that time would teach her how to deal with such loss, but she feared she'd never learn.

What then?

She sighed and shuffled along, going nowhere in particular and not in a hurry to go anywhere.

Not only did she have her healing work to concern her, but she now had a make-believe husband. She thought she would have been married long before now. At twenty and two years, most women were married several years already, but she had been so involved with her healing work, a husband simply never materialized.

Now she had a good man, but he lacked passion. He was practical about every single solitary thing he did. You couldn't ruffle his feathers. He remained calm and in control even when passion sparked in his eyes.

It was a good quality, so why then did she question it? Why did it bother her?

Zia.

It sounded as if her name drifted on the warm night air, coming from far away. She looked around and saw no one.

Zia.

She smiled and knew her grandmother thought of her.

Artair is good for you and you for him.

Her grandmother must have thought she needed reminding. She smiled, realizing that perhaps she did.

"Zia."

She tilted her head to listen more closely. Had someone actually called out her name?

"Zia."

She turned, and seeing Artair, smiled. He was such a handsome man, she thought, watching him approach, so confident in his stride, his muscular body so deliciously appealing. Damn, if her body didn't tingle just looking at him.

"Have you come to collect your battle booty?" she teased with a laugh.

He knocked her laughter out of her when he scooped her up, flinging her over his shoulder. "No, I came to sweep you off your feet."

Chapter 14

Artair hadn't planned on scooping her up and carrying her off, but when he saw her standing alone, and with such a concerned look on her face, he didn't hesitate. He snatched her up, wanting her in his arms where he could heal *her*.

Zia needed someone to look after her. She pushed herself until exhausted and barely ate enough to keep her going.

And yet?

Her zeal for her work kept her going regardless of anything else.

But it was different now. She had him, and he would be more sensible than Zia was. He'd see that she was taken care of, whether she liked it or not.

He had expected her to complain, but she remained quiet after he scooped her up. He wondered if she was just too tired to voice her opinion. He smiled and almost shook his head. Zia would never be too tired to give her opinion.

Yet she hadn't said a word to him since he hefted her over his shoulder.

He entered the cottage and kicked the door shut behind him. Walking straight to the bed, he gently lowered her down onto it.

He rested her head against a pillow and ordered, "Stay."

She made a move to bolt off the bed, and he pointed a finger at her. "Stay where you are. I'm going to fix you the brew that you favor."

"Really?" she asked with a tender smile, and leaned back against the pillow.

He fussed with the leaves, hoping he'd watched her enough to know how to prepare the concoction the way she liked it. "How is everyone doing?"

"Much better. Old Mary has improved greatly, and most have no fever. I think the illness is finally under control."

"That's good to hear," he replied.

"It's a relief for all concerned," she said.

He brought the mug to her and after handing it to her, he nudged her legs over so that he could sit down beside her. "Tell me about you."

She sipped then shrugged. "There's not much to tell."

He smiled warmly. "I beg to differ. There's more to you than anyone can see. Or should I say, that you *allow* anyone to see."

"Isn't that true of us all? To an extent, we all keep something of ourselves secret."

He ran the back of his fingers down her cheek. "I want to know all your secrets."

"And will you share yours with me?"

"I keep no secrets."

She laughed. "We all keep secrets. Some large, others small, but they are there, tucked safely away where no one will ever find them."

Artair smiled sadly, her remark reminding him of an incident when he was young.

"See, you recall one of those tucked away moments," Zia said. "Tell me."

"I haven't thought about it in years," he said, shaking his head. "I suppose I wanted to keep it so safe that I forgot about it until this very moment."

"Please," she said, taking hold of his hand. "Share it with me."

Her hand was warm from the mug, and he watched her slowly lace her fingers with his until their hands were wound together snug and firm, a perfect fit. Would their joining be as perfect?

He chased the lustful thought from his head and returned to the memory she had inadvertently stirred. "I was just a young lad of five and my brother Cavan and I were playing in the woods. He was seven, old and knowledgeable to my young mind.

"Cavan had a wicked imagination and would create a world where we were mighty warriors fighting hordes of all manner of imaginable enemies. Cavan would have us gather fallen branches and use them as weapons. He told me that we must always be prepared. One day while I was supposed to be gathering branches, I got lost in my own imaginary world and started tracking a hare. Slow and steady the little beast moved, and I inched right along with it, thinking it an enemy I had to keep in my sights.

"I lost track of time while tracking the hare and didn't bother to gather any weapons when I heard Cavan yelling. I ran to him and stared in horror as he tried to fight off a wild dog with what sticks he had. He saw me and called out for me to use my weapons. I had none, and Cavan saw that."

Artair shook his head. "Cavan continued to battle, and after I finally got my wits about me, I picked up stones and started throwing them at the dog. Together we chased him off. Cavan never asked me why I didn't have any weapons. Instead, he claimed me a brave warrior.

"I did not feel like one. I felt ashamed that I had not followed his orders. I wasn't prepared to help him defend against an enemy."

"And you never told him that you were tracking a hare instead of gathering weapons," she said.

"I was too ashamed and I didn't want him to be disappointed in me, so I never told him the truth."

"But he wasn't disappointed, for you didn't fail him. You came to his aid and used weapons at hand. Your brother spoke the truth when he claimed you were a brave warrior."

"Perhaps, but as I said, I didn't feel like one, and from that day on I made certain I was always prepared." He looked at her then. "Now it's your turn to tell me a secret."

Zia sipped at the brew and wrinkled her nose.

"Too many to choose from?" he teased.

"No, I want to share a special secret with you. One I have kept close to my heart."

He squeezed her hand. "I'd like that, and know that your secret will always be safe with me."

"I know, or else I would never chance sharing it with you."

It pleased him that her trust in him was growing stronger. It was a good sign, for trust was important to a marriage, and the more he got to know Zia, the more he realized that she would make him a truly good wife.

Zia began. "There was this place on the hillside I liked to go to pick flowers and just sit and watch the sky. I loved the clouds and the way they would float by in all different shapes. I would talk to them, ask them where they were going and make up answers.

"One day while talking to the clouds, I suddenly got an idea. I asked them if they would go find my father and bring him to me. I told them that I missed him, though I had never met him, and I was sure that he must miss me. I was only five that first time I asked, but I continued asking and only recently stopped."

She handed the empty mug to him. "That was delicious. Could I have another?"

He took the mug from her and raised their joined hands to gently kiss her fingers. "You never shared this with your grandmother?"

She shook her head. "I think I was afraid she would tell me that it was a useless task, that my father was never returning. And as a young child I didn't want to think that I had a father who not only didn't want me, but didn't love me."

He felt her ache, her emptiness, and the fear that goes with not knowing where a loved one was or if that loved one was all right. Ronan's disappearance had taken its toll on him and his family, and it was drawing close to two years since he'd been gone. He couldn't imagine what the pain was like for a child who longed to know her father.

"I will help you find him," Artair said.

"Perhaps someday," she said with a sad smile.

Artair stood, kissing her fingers one more time before releasing her hand and walking over to the hearth to prepare another mug of tea for her. "Whenever you're ready, you just say the word and I will find him."

"You sound so confident that you could," she said, surprised.

"Just as I search tenaciously for my brother, I would search the same for your father."

"That is generous of you. But why? You barely know me."

"Barely know you?" he said in feigned surprise. "We just shared intimate secrets no one else knows about us. I'd say that makes us at least best friends."

Her face lighted with joy. "I'd love to be best friends. You share everything with your best friend."

He handed her the steaming mug. "I want you to share everything with me, and I will do the same."

She placed the mug on the chest beside the bed. "Good, then since you're my best friend, I wish to ask a favor."

"Anything," he smiled. "Within reason of course."

She laughed and shook her head. "What if it's not reasonable?"

"I'll consider it but I can't make any promises."

She bounced off the bed and took his hand. "Come take a swim with me."

"You need food and rest," he argued.

"But I want to take a swim."

"The water will be—"

"Warm and welcoming," she finished, and tugged him toward the door.

He stopped abruptly, jolting her to a halt. "Early morning would be better."

She stood staring at him for a moment, then smiled. "I'll go myself."

She was out the door before he could stop her. He stood for a second, cursing her stubbornness, then went after her. She shouldn't be going off to the river at night by herself. All kinds of danger lurked in the dark.

He had forgotten how swift she was on her feet, and by the time he found her, she had already stripped and entered the water. The partial moon cast a soft glow along the surface of the river, and he watched her swim, her hands and arms skillfully cutting through the water.

She was a vision to behold. Her wet ivory skin glistened in the moonlight and the blond tips of her hair sparkled like stars around her head. She turned, her chest arching as her arms churned in powerful backstrokes, her tight nipples cresting the water just enough to send a flash of heat to his loins.

Join her.

He shot down his wild thought before it could gain momentum. He had no intention of taking advantage of her. She had invited him for a swim, not sex.

Or had she?

Wishful thinking, he told himself. He wanted her, that was a certainty, but he wanted more than just sex from Zia. The more he learned about her, the more interesting and appealing she became, and the more he wanted to know.

She turned again, spotted him and waved for him to join her.

Should he? Was it wise? Could he keep his hands off her?

She bounced along in the river, her persistent wave continuing to urge him to join her.

"Hell," he muttered, and striped off his clothes.

He hit the water in a run and dove in, coming up not far from Zia. With a few quick strokes he was beside her and speechless. Her wet flesh shimmered like the dew on a blooming white rose and gave her a luscious appeal. His only thought was to touch and taste her.

"Warm and welcoming," she said.

"What?" he snapped.

"The river is warm and welcoming," she repeated.

It wasn't the river he wanted to greet him. He stared at the droplets of water that clung to her lips and thought of licking them off one by one. A quick lick with the tip of his tongue and they'd be gone, and he'd want more.

He played it safe and kept his distance.

"It's not wise to swim naked with a man."

"True enough, but you're a safe man to swim naked with."

"Why is that?" he asked, not sure if he should be insulted or pleased.

"You're a practical man I can trust, especially when I'm not being sensible."

"Like now?" he asked, forcing a smile.

"Precisely. I know you will not do anything improper." She reached out and patted his shoulder. "You're a good man."

"That I am, *wife*." His hands shot out and took hold of her waist, dragging her against him.

Their bodies connected with an impact that sent water shooting up between them, and by the time it settled over them, he had his mouth against hers, hot and urgent and looking for more.

She didn't protest. She returned the kiss with even more fervor.

His hands slid up her midriff until they rested

beneath her breasts, and his thumbs began to play against her hard nipples. They felt so good that he had to taste them, and he tore his mouth away as he lifted her up and settled his lips over one nipple at a time.

She dropped her head back with a groan, and it fired his loins to an awful hard ache. He knew if he didn't stop, if he didn't put distance between them, that in the next few minutes he would slip inside her and make her his, and permanently.

Passion had quickly consumed both of them, and he could quickly satisfy it, but he wasn't looking to give Zia a quick romp in the river. He wanted something more with her, something that would last their entire lives and always remain special to them.

He didn't want only sex with her; he wanted love.

He eased her back down into the water, not daring to let her flesh meet his, and pressed his wet cheek to hers. "Another time, another place, and I'll make you mine."

She wasn't only stunned; he saw disappointment on her face.

"Time to go," he said.

Surprisingly, she followed him without protest. She didn't utter a word, not when he stepped out of the water before she did or kept his back to her while he dressed, affording her the privacy to do the same.

Silence went home along with them, even into the cottage. He didn't join her in bed until after she had changed into a linen shift and climbed under the light blanket. With only his plaid on, he climbed in beside her and fitted himself against her back, wrapping his arm around her, his hand resting firmly beneath her breast.

"Rest well, I will be right here," he whispered, and kissed her cheek.

Chapter 15

Zia lay awake long after Artair fell asleep. She couldn't get the strange evening out of her mind. Artair had startled her in more ways than one. First, when he swept her off her feet. She was too shocked to protest, but liked that he'd done it. And then she was shocked again when he fixed her favorite brew.

She had assumed that after depositing her on the bed, he intended to kiss her. While she would have invited it, she thought it endearing that he made her favorite brew, and even knew what it was. And made it so perfectly. She wondered if he had practiced.

And then their tryst in the river. She had realized she was tempting fate, actually tempting him beyond reason. She chuckled. She hadn't really expected him to join her, especially after he suggested that she wait until morning. And once he did join her, she wanted much more than it seemed he was willing to give.

She smiled, recalling his words.

Another time, another place, and I'll make you mine.

Just the thought enthralled her, tingles prickling her skin.

And then, when their brief tryst was over, he'd been such a gentleman. He didn't gawk at her, but instead he respected her privacy.

And finally, she recalled how he wrapped himself so lovingly around her when they were in bed, and assured her that he'd remain beside her.

His body continued to warm her and his muscled arms kept her in a protective embrace. Even his steady breathing soothed her while faintly tickling the back of her neck.

It hadn't been two full weeks since she met this man, yet she thought of him as a friend she'd known since she was young. Someone with whom she could safely share secrets, tell her troubles to, laugh with and when necessary cry with.

She wondered how they had bonded so quickly, but then silently laughed the thought away. Her grandmother had told her that Artair was good for her. Why question it? Why not simply wait and see where it led? He would reason over it enough for the both of them; for her part, she would let fate take its course.

It had been an interesting evening, and she could only imagine, with a flutter of anticipation, what the immediate future would bring.

With exhaustion overwhelming her bevy of thoughts, Zia fell asleep with a smile.

* * *

Their departure was delayed because of a young child whose fever remained constant. Until the fever broke and the child's appetite returned, Zia refused to leave, and Artair remained concerned.

The villagers thought highly of Zia and treated her with respect, and Artair suspected that much of it was because they believed she was his wife. His men had confirmed his suspicions when they shared what village gossip they heard.

James, with Patrick corroborating, told him how the women believed that Zia and he were a good match, and how lucky she was to have a husband who not only allowed her to heal, but was patient while she did. Yes, the women had claimed them an extraordinary pair.

The news concerned him more than pleased him since gossip was more contagious than the pox and could spread with the same speed. He reiterated his order for James and Patrick to remain alert to anyone entering the village.

He worried about keeping Zia safe, especially after last night. She had taken off for the river without even thinking, as if there were nothing for her to worry about. She never gave thought to possible danger. She simply did as she pleased, without considering the possible consequences of her rash actions.

Not that he hadn't enjoyed their night swim, though in truth they hadn't swam much. He grinned at the memory. If he hadn't controlled the situation, Zia would have sealed her fate in becoming his wife. As much as that would have made it easier for him, he'd realized he wanted more from her, a realization that surprised him.

It was still another reason for getting Zia out of there. He wanted to be with her in normal surroundings so they could determine what it was they wanted and expected from each other.

"Artair!"

He looked up from where he sat on the bench of the cottage he shared with Zia. She had left while he still slept, and with James's hurried steps, he suddenly wished he knew where she was.

Artair stood and matched James's rushed steps. "What's wrong?"

James shook his head. "A messenger from the village of Lorne has arrived."

"Damn," Artair said, and ran rough fingers through his hair. "Where is he?"

"He's speaking with the elders of the village in the common shelter."

He could confront them, Artair thought, or wait to be summoned.

His course of action was decided for him when a young lad rushed over to tell him the elders wanted to see him.

As soon as he entered the large gathering room and saw the dire expressions on the elders' faces, he knew trouble was brewing.

The messenger who had arrived in Donnan from the village of Lorne didn't give anyone a chance to speak.

He swung an accusing finger at Artair. "He's no husband to the witch."

"My wife is no witch," Artair said firmly. "And if you continue to spread such lies, I will cut out your lying tongue."

The thick-chested man wasn't swayed by the threat. His pointed finger disappeared into a clenched fist, which he shook furiously at Artair. "She has bewitched you. We warned you and you did not listen and now you have condemned us all."

"What nonsense do you speak?" Artair demanded.

The man lowered his voice, his eyes shifting fearfully. "It is not nonsense. The witch works her magic with her potions and spells."

"Those potions heal the sick. And what spells? My wife cast no spells."

"Then why do you claim to be wed to her? Show me proof," the messenger challenged, though now, at Artair's adamancy, he did show fear, his voice quivering.

It was just what Artair had been afraid would happen. He couldn't help but think that if Zia hadn't been so stubborn, this situation might have been settled without a problem.

Placing his hand on the hilt of his sword, he advanced on the messenger. The man shrank away from him. "You dare call me a lair?" Artair demanded.

"I only wish to protect you from evil," the man hurried to explain.

"My wife is not evil. She generously heals the people of this village."

The messenger spoke up bravely. "She did the same for us and then used her spells and charms to entice the men. If you had let us burn her—"

"The good people of Donnan would be dead," Artair concluded.

His blunt remark had the elders whispering among themselves.

"Don't listen to him," the messenger begged. "He is bewitched. She has him doing her bidding and will have all of you doing the same."

Odran, the oldest of the elders, spoke. "Zia has asked nothing of us."

The messenger cringed and covered his ears. "Do not say her name. I will not hear it and I will not look upon evil."

Artair wanted to beat the man senseless, but he knew that would only serve to reinforce the accusations against Zia. He had to show that he remained in control of himself.

"The only evil here is the evil you speak against *my wife*," he emphasized yet again. "She has tirelessly tended the ill of this village and has healed them."

"He is right," Odran agreed.

The messenger's finger shot out again. "She is casting her spell over all of you. You should burn her now before it is too late."

Once again Artair was incensed. He almost grabbed the man—the blithering idiot—to smash his face in, but stopped himself and spoke with a calm he didn't feel. "You've delivered your message, now leave."

"I will leave after you show me proof of your marriage," the man said boldly.

"It would settle the matter," Odran said.

It certainly would, Artair thought, and silently cursed himself for not insisting that Zia and he wed. But that did him little good now.

"She's tricked him into thinking he wed her," the messenger accused.

The elders mumbled among themselves, no doubt agreeing that proof was necessary for the protection of their village. And he couldn't blame them.

"Artair!"

The men turned to see Zia, smiling, holding a bouquet of wild flowers in her hand. She looked more angel than evil, her blond strands forming a halo affect over her red hair, her cheeks tinged softly pink.

She rushed over to him, holding out the bouquet. "Look what the women give us to celebrate our one week anniversary." She looked from one startled man to another. "I'm sorry. It seems I've interrupted a private meeting."

The messenger raised a quick, outstretched hand to ward her off as he turned his face away. "Don't cast your evil eyes on me, witch."

The elders ignored the messenger, and Odran said to Zia, "How wonderful for you, and how good of you to come to our village to help after being wed for such a short time."

"Illness never arrives at an opportune time," she remarked.

"Proof. Proof. Ask her for proof," the messenger demanded irritably and with his glance cast to the ground.

Zia slipped her arm around Artair's. "Our marriage papers are with my belongings that were sent on to Artair's home. We saw no reason to carry proof with us." She cast a blissful glance at Artair. "Anyone who sees us knows we are madly in love and newly wed." She chuckled. "Did no one see us sneak out of our cottage for a swim last night?"

Odran smiled sheepishly. "Someone mentioned your husband chasing after you."

Artair joined in her game. "I bet that I'd beat her to the river."

Zia grinned. "He lost."

The elders laughed and nodded, recalling youthful follies of their own.

"She lies!" the messenger screamed.

"Enough!" Artair declared with strength that near shook the walls. "Did my wife heal your people?"

"Yes, but—"

"Did anyone die?" Artair asked curtly.

"No, but—"

"Does your village suffer?"

The messenger hesitated, then shook his head. "You don't understand. You are bewitched."

"I do understand," Artair confirmed. "You are ungrateful. Leave now. You are not welcome here with your lies."

The elders agreed with repeated nods.

"You'll be sorry," the man vowed with a raised fist. "My village has contacted the church council and they will decide her fate." He hurried to the door, stopped but didn't turn around. "I will make certain a messenger is sent to Caithness to verify your wedding papers."

He left without looking back.

"We are grateful for your help, Zia," Odran said, and the others agreed. "We thought for sure that many would die, but your *remarkable* skills have saved us."

Was that a flash of skepticism he caught in the elder's eyes? Artair wondered. It worried him. All that was needed was a drop of doubt for problems to start, and the messenger had planted more than a drop. They had to leave the village, and soon.

After exchanging niceties with the elders, he and Zia left the common shelter and walked arm in arm to their cottage, their smiles bright while they spoke softly to each other.

"We can't stay here," Artair said. "Please tell me the child is well enough for you to leave."

"Her fever broke and no doubt will not return. The worst of this is over." She kept her grin steady, aware that they were being observed. "Do you think the messenger will return with others for me?"

"I doubt he's given up. I wouldn't be surprised if he lurks in the woods waiting to talk to each of the elders alone and convince them of your magical powers."

He laughed joyously as if they had just shared a funny tale, slipped his hands around her waist to swing her up in the air and bring her back down for a kiss.

"We need to wed before we reach my home," he murmured as he set her feet back on the ground.

Zia said nothing until the cottage door closed behind them. "You can't mean to wed a witch."

He cringed. "Be careful what you claim."

"There are those who will believe I am, and once the church sends someone to investigate—" She shivered and dropped the bouquet on the table. "I could understand being accused of witchcraft if I made people suffer, but they accuse me because I make people well." She shook her head. "It makes no sense. A true healer would never intentionally hurt anyone."

She pushed past Artair when he tried to embrace her, angry that she needed to defend her skills. "There's no magic to my potions."

"To the less knowledgeable, it appears magic," he said, and reached out to tug her into his arms. "But they have not seen what I have."

"And what is that?" she asked, her anger melting away as his powerful hands kneaded her arms.

"All the hard work you do in preparation of tending the ill. Your healing basket doesn't miraculously fill itself. Your potions don't magically mix. Your healing plants don't grow without care. Your knowledge doesn't expand without study. You don't make a remarkable healer by casting a spell. You work for it."

Zia was stunned by his words. He had noticed how much work it took to be a good healer, and he praised rather than criticized.

"I like watching you work," he said. "You have a caring touch and soothing words to offer the ill, and you do it with patience."

She melted into his embrace. "You do know I don't always have patience."

"Really?" He looked startled, then laughed.

She poked him in the chest. "I have patience when necessary."

"So I've noticed."

"What else have you noticed?" she asked.

"That you don't always see reason, which is why you need me."

She sighed dramatically. "How have I ever managed without you?"

He rolled his eyes upward and shook his head. "Heaven only knows." He kissed her quick. "But you needn't worry any longer. I will look after you."

"I know you will, and that's what worries me."

Chapter 16

Artair kissed her lovingly, wanting to kiss away all her worries. "We will wed and you will be safe."

Zia slipped out of his arms as he tried to hold onto her, and it felt to him like a punch to his gut, a sense of deep loss overwhelming him. He wanted to reach out, grab hold of her and make sure she remained his. Instead he calmed his thoughts and confronted the situation more reasonably.

"It's the best solution to our problem," he said.

"Why do you want to continue to place yourself in harm's way for me?" she asked.

A good question, he thought, and until he had a good answer, she was staying with him.

"Honora could use your help, and you can use mine. I'd say that's a good exchange. Besides, you helped heal my brother Ronan. For that alone I and my family owe you."

"So you wed me to repay me?" she asked with a quick shake of her head.

"It doesn't hurt that we're attracted to each other."

Zia threw her hands up in the air. "You owe me and we're attracted to each other—"

"You're not denying it, are you?"

"No, I'm not, but I've made it very clear why I will marry—"

"Love," he said, and nodded. "And given time—"

"No!" she shouted, and shook her finger in his face. "Love first, marriage second. It's that or nothing."

"You're not being sensible. You need protection, and I can give it to you. I can also give you a good life."

"I already have a good life," she said adamantly.

He folded his arms over his chest and shook his head. "You constantly live with danger. That is no life."

She poked him in the chest. "My life. My choice."

"You can object all you want, and you can poke me all you want, but you *will* marry me," he said confidently.

She stepped back away from him and mimicked his confident stance. "No, I *will not* marry you. We will simply continue to pretend we're wed."

"That won't do. You heard that fool of a messenger say he will send someone to my home for proof."

She shrugged. "We'll address that matter when the time comes."

"Then you're willing to live with me as my wife once we arrive at my home?" he asked with a grin.

"So far our pretense has worked," she answered, with her own wide smile. "I don't see why it cannot continue to do so."

He walked over to her and took hold of her shoulders. "Did you forget the other night in the river? What happens when you share my bed?"

Her face shadowed with doubt. She knew as well as he did that they would be intimate, and soon. And he knew she wanted him as much as he wanted her. So why did she fight it?

"Wed me and be done with it. We are good for each other," he said, trying to make her see reason, though he knew there was little chance of that. She was tenacious, which proved useful at times, and other times simply got in her way.

She sighed heavily and battered her lashes. "Your romantic prose takes my breath away."

"Unfortunately, at the moment there is no time for romance. Reason takes precedence here."

"I will not be bullied into wedding you," she said firmly. "We will continue to pretend to be wed—"

"Until it is necessary that we do wed," he finished.

"If ever," she added with a shrug.

He knew better, but then she would see, given time, that marriage was the best solution. He didn't intend to keep reminding her. She would realize it eventually, and he believed—or was it merely a hope?—that she would see the wisdom in such a choice.

"We leave at first light tomorrow," he said.

"Good. That will give me time to leave instructions with the women and visit with those recovering."

He took hold of her hand, bringing it to his chest. "I think it would be wise if I remained by your side until we leave . . . or rather, until we reach my home."

He watched as her defensiveness melted as quickly as spring snow. "You truly are concerned," she said, easing closer.

"Finally you realize that," he replied teasingly, and slipped his arms around her.

"I realize more than you know. It is you who does not know what you commit to."

She settled herself in the crook of his arm, and he coiled it around her and rested his cheek on her head. Her hair was soft, the scent fresh, and he wished only to linger in the moment.

A rapid knock at the door had them separating quickly, and Artair prayed that no one else had taken ill.

Clare, Andrew's mother, was there with a couple of other women who were concerned by the news they had heard. They wanted Zia to know that they did not believe her a witch and how grateful they were for her help.

Artair retreated from the cottage, leaving the women to talk. He would speak to James and Patrick about departing tomorrow at first light and making it home to Caithness as soon as possible. The sooner he had Zia in the confines of his family's land, the safer she would be.

He didn't want to think about what would happen if the church council decided against Zia and proclaimed her a witch. His family had power and influence, but no amount of influence could combat a judgment of witch-craft. He only hoped that her alignment with his clan could give her at least a degree of protection.

Somehow, he would find a way to circumvent the situation. But that would take time, and making her his legal wife would go a long way toward securing her safety. He would see it all done; he merely had to remain patient.

After firming plans for the next day's departure with his men, he headed back to the cottage, hoping the women had left and Zia would be alone. He wanted her packed and ready to leave as soon as the sun peeked on the horizon.

It annoyed him to find the cottage empty. He as-sumed she had gone to check one last time on those still ailing. He wished that she'd stayed put, but knew she would work until the very last moment, and then only reluctantly mount her horse, still feeling she hadn't done enough.

He browsed through the village, looking for Zia, and not finding her, began to worry.

Then he spotted her in the open doorway of a cot-tage, her cheeks tinged pink and her smile bright. Seeing him as well, she waved and with a light step headed his way.

He caught a swift movement out of the corner of his eye and yelled a warning, "Zia, watch out!"

"Burn, witch, burn," the messenger screamed, and flung the lighted torch he carried at her. Not waiting to see if he hit his target, he kept running until he vanished into the woods.

Zia was holding her arm, her face twisted in pain when Artair reached her. She had deflected the torch with her hand, the brief contact scorching her flesh. He grabbed hold of her and winced when he saw her palm, which appeared charred.

"Tell me what to do?" he asked, swinging her up into his arms.

"You can put me down. It's my hand that has been burned, not my feet."

He smiled at her humorous retort. "I'm sweeping you off your feet."

"Ahh, another romantic moment."

"Tell me how to take care of you," he ordered, though with a smile.

She acquiesced with a nod. "Take me to the cottage and I will see to my hand."

He started walking. "No, *I* will see to your hand."

They laughed while debating who would be the healer, though when they reached the cottage and Zia winced, Artair would hear no more of her protests. He intended to see to her care, and that was that.

After placing her on a chair, he looked at her hand and flinched.

"It looks worse than it is," she said, reassuring him, and stretched for her healing basket on the table.

"Stay put," he said, and brought the basket to her.

"It's just a minor burn. Once I clean it, you'll see for yourself."

She wiped the flesh with a damp clean cloth, and Artair was surprised when the blackened area turned pink. Her skin hadn't been charred; she was right, it didn't look as bad as he had first thought.

"Let me do that," Artair said, and took the cloth from her. He didn't want to imagine what could have happened if the flame had caught her garments.

She touched him lightly in the spot between his eyes. "Frown lines. Something troubles you."

"You could have gone up in flames, and if the village Lorne has anything to say about it, you will." He threw the cloth aside, the pad of her palm a shiny pink.

He was ready to order their immediate departure when she smiled softly and handed him a small crock of salve. He didn't know if it was her tender smile that said "I trust you" or the fact that she gave him the salve to put on her injury that attested to her trust. Perhaps it was a combination of both.

"Thinking on it, I agree with you."

He stared at her, startled.

"I may be stubborn, but I'm not ignorant. I realize that at the moment it will be far better for me, and those I care for, if I remain with you."

Relieved that she would battle him no more, he almost reached out to hug her, but restrained himself. Instead he applied the salve to her palm with a gentle stroke.

"All are well?" he asked, wanting her to leave the village without worry.

"Yes," she answered with a sigh, closing her eyes as he finished with the salve.

He watched her body relax, her shoulders slumping, her head waving from side to side as a gentle yawn slipped from a nearly closed mouth. He was glad she trusted him. It would make things easier for them both.

"I will send word to your grandmother so that if she should hear of this incident she will not worry," he said, and held up a clean cloth, silently asking if he should bandage the burn.

She nodded. "Thank you. I appreciate you thinking of her."

He wound the bandage around her hand, though her own hand stilled his after a few wraps.

"Let me show you," she said, and guided the hand that held the bandage. "A light touch with only a few twists and turns will be sufficient."

Her delicate touch was like a faint whisper on his flesh, a tingle to his senses. Her hand rested over his, as well as her glance, and it was as if time stood still and there was only the two of them.

She broke the trance, leaned forward and boldly said, "I think I want to kiss you."

"And I you."

He slowly captured her lips, and while he would normally tease a woman into responding, Zia needed no such enticements. She responded with enthusiasm that rapidly turned passionate. Her fervent responses never failed to astound and excite him.

She stopped the kiss abruptly and with labored breathing said, "I don't know why I'm attracted to you."

He was so stunned he had to laugh. "I'm not sure how to take that."

"I'm not sure how it's meant." She shook her head. "I mean, I can't seem to make sense of what I find appealing about you." She continued to shake her head. "I mean—"

He took hold of her shoulders, then ran his hands slowly up and down her arms. "I think the problem is that I'm not quite the man you expected."

She nodded. "You're right. You're nothing of what I expected of the man who I—"

Artair wanted to strangle whoever pounded at the door and interrupted. He stomped to the door, swung it open and instantly calmed himself at James's worried expression.

"We couldn't find the messenger," James said, "but there's another problem. There are some—men, mostly—who are wondering how Zia escaped the messenger's wrath so easily."

"That's how the problem started in Lorne, with the men," Artair said.

"It won't take long to get out of hand," James whispered.

Artair nodded. James was right. Before they knew it, Zia would be in trouble again, and with two villages proclaiming her a witch, the church council was sure to condemn her.

"Be ready to leave shortly," Artair instructed.

"Our hasty departure will raise suspicion."

"Spread word that we've been summoned home immediately," Artair said, and turned to tell Zia.

"I heard everything," she said, "though understand none of it. I have done nothing wrong."

"The gossip will stop as soon as we leave here," he told her. "The people will return to their daily lives and soon forget you."

"The village of Lorne is not going to allow that. They seem determined to see me condemned as a witch."

"Let's get you to a safe place first and then we'll concern ourselves with the rest," he said. "Now gather your things. We leave immediately."

She stepped toward him. "Are you sure?"

"Yes, I'm sure. You'll be safe at my home."

"No, that's not what I meant," she said, annoyed. "As I've expressed before, my presence could cause trouble for your family, and I—"

"Let me worry about that."

He stopped any further protests by beginning to shove things haphazardly into her healing basket. Zia stopped him and took over, continuing the task more carefully. She remained silent, and Artair knew her to be deep in thought. And why wouldn't she be? There was much for her to consider, and this was only the beginning of it.

He walked up behind her and wrapped his arms around her waist. "Once we arrive at my home, I'll arrange a small wedding ceremony for us and—"

She pulled out of his embrace and moved around the table, continuing her task of packing her things while on the opposite side. "I told you I will not marry you, and don't ask me again until . . . "

"Until what?" he asked impatiently.

She threw the pouch she held in the basket. "Until you're finally not reasonable anymore."

Chapter 17

They kept an arduous pace for four days, stopping more to rest the horses than themselves. Zia said nothing. She knew Artair's intentions were to get home to his village as fast as possible. They ate and slept little, and talked even less.

It didn't matter. She knew what he was thinking, and it annoyed her. He had it all planned and truly believed it would turn out *his* way. She might presently require his protection, but that didn't include marriage.

Besides, how many times did she have to tell him that she would marry only for love? He was thick-headed and much too reasonable, about which she had reminded him often enough. The man just wouldn't listen. He could be so frustrating. But he could also be kind and loving.

She sighed as they stopped once more to give the horses a rest. Her backside and thighs were sore and she was hungry.

"A brief stop," Artair commanded. "I want to reach home by nightfall."

Zia dismounted, and while her mare drank from the stream, she grabbed a couple of apples from the sack that hung from her saddle. Before biting into one of them, she took off her sandals and dunked her feet in the cool water.

It felt so refreshing that she sighed aloud.

"Feels that good, does it?"

She smiled, turning to face Artair, and threw him an apple. "Join me."

He obliged, shedding his sandals and walking into the stream. He smiled broadly. "It does feel good, and even better, tonight you will sleep in a comfortable bed."

"And whose bed will that be?" She raised her brow in question as she took a last bite of the juicy apple.

He hesitated, then said, "I must assume that my family has received news of our marriage, and if not, they would hear of it soon enough, so it would be sensible for us to arrive home as husband and wife."

She shrugged. "I'll continue the pretense until it is no longer necessary."

He tossed the finished apple aside. "And then?"

"I'll decide when the time comes."

He stared at her while he called out orders to his men, then said to her, "We leave now."

Zia splashed out of the stream and walked past him.

He grabbed hold of her arm. "Be sensible about this, Zia."

She laughed. "Actually, I am."

She hurried into her sandals and mounted her horse, and they were soon on the road again. Artair resumed their swift pace, and she had no doubt their arrival home would be as he predicted.

Dusk covered the land as they passed through the village and approached the keep. Those who were out and about called out greetings and congratulations to Artair. Zia could see that news of their union had reached the people of Caithness, so she knew the pretense of their marriage was necessary. She would do her part, but for how long? She decided not to put a time limit on it. She would know, would feel it when the time was right. Until then she would look after Cavan's expectant wife while seeing—she chuckled—just how sensible Artair could be.

Every part of her body ached as she climbed the few steps to the keep. What she truly wanted was food, bath, and bed, in that order, but there was his family to meet and Honora to look after, if necessary. She would do what she had to, as she always did.

A yawn escaped her just as they reached the door.

Artair's arm went around her. "Tired?" he asked.

"No," she said, dropping her head on his shoulder. "I'm exhausted."

The door abruptly swung open and a man with similar features to Artair—not as handsome, but with a charming smile—regarded them.

"We heard your approach," he said. "I was just coming to welcome you home."

"Zia," Artair said, "my brother Lachlan."

Lachlan smiled and reached out to snatch Zia from Artair's grasp. He wrapped his arm around her. "Come meet the family, sister," he said cheerfully, and walked her into the great hall.

Boisterous cheers rang out, and she almost sighed in resignation. She always enjoyed celebrations, but not when exhausted. The hall was filled with people waving raised tankards in the air and calling out congratulations. Tables were covered with platters of scrumptious looking food that she wouldn't mind digging into, and wine and ale were flowing freely.

Artair slipped her out of Lachlan's grasp, though his brother protested.

"Wait a moment, I wanted to introduce my—"

"*My wife,*" Artair said. "Get your own." And with a grin he guided her through a welcoming crowd. He leaned over before they reached a large table in front of the hearth and said to her, "I'll let them know you're tired and—"

"No," she said quickly. "They wished to show and share their joy for you. I will not deprive them of that; besides, I'm starving and the food looks delicious."

"Thank you," he said, squeezing her close up against his side, the many onlookers smiling wide at the loving show of affection.

Zia immediately knew who Cavan was. Taller than Artair, broader and ruggedly handsome, he had a confident stance and a warm smile. His arm was around a very beautiful, pregnant woman whose smile matched his own.

Before the loving couple could greet Zia, a woman stepped in front of them, beaming. Though sadness lurked in her lovely green eyes, she stood with grace and beauty that age had not marred.

She spread her arms wide, tears glinting in her eyes, and Zia stepped aside so Artair could greet his mother with a hug.

"I am so happy for you," Addie Sinclare said, her arms tight around her son. When she finally loosened her grip, she looked past him to Zia. "Another beautiful daughter. How lucky I am."

Zia went to her and gave her a hug. "I'm happy to meet you. Artair has told me much about you."

Addie turned to Artair and teasingly said, "What gossip do you spread about me?"

"The truth," Artair replied with a smile. "That you are a loving and wonderful mother."

A tear spilled from Addie's eye. She brushed it away and looked at Zia again. "Artair is a good man. I am proud of him. He will make you a good husband."

Zia squeezed Addie's hand. "I know. A man who respects and treats his mother well will do the same for his wife."

Addie nodded. "You were taught well."

"As you taught your son," Zia said, and kissing the woman's cheek, she whispered, "Thank you."

Addie wiped another tear from her cheek. "Meet my oldest son Cavan and his wife Honora."

Introductions were made, hugs and kisses exchanged, and finally Zia was able to sit and enjoy the feast that had been prepared for them, while getting to know Artair's family.

"I am glad Artair wed a healer, and one whose skills precede her," Cavan said. He and Honora sat across the table from Artair and Zia. "My wife hasn't been feeling well of late," he added, and his arm went protectively around Honora.

"Give Zia time to rest," she protested. "She must be exhausted after her long journey."

"Husbands usually worry needlessly," Zia said, noting that Honora's cheeks were ripe with color, her violet eyes sparkled, and her lips were flushed pink. She looked healthy, which was a good start.

"You but appease me," Cavan said with concern.

Artair laughed and shook his head. "If it's one thing Zia doesn't do, it is appease."

Zia leaned into the crook of her believed-to-be husband's shoulder. "He's right about that."

"I think I'm going to like you," Cavan said with a firm nod.

"You looked to be someone I could get along with," Zia replied with her own firm nod.

Honora laughed. "You will fit well with the Sinclare clan."

The festivities continued, food and drink devoured at a steady pace, with accompanying shared laughter and smiles. The celebration did not dwindle for several hours.

It was Addie, to Zia's relief, who suggested that the new bride needed rest.

"Bless you," Zia said with an uncontained yawn followed by a generous smile when she heard Addie order a bath prepared for her. "You know my thoughts. How wonderful."

Addie stood. "I'll help you."

Zia shook her head as she dislodged herself from Artair. "No need. I can see to it myself. You stay with your sons." She gave Artair a peck on the cheek and followed the young lass who had been directed to help her.

She was relieved that no one had insisted and followed her. She wasn't accustomed to so much attention, and preferred the peacefulness of solitude. It gave her time to think or simply empty her mind and relax. At the moment, her body and mind screamed for rest.

The bedchamber she entered reflected Artair's practical nature. It was orderly, with everything in place, and she laughed softly knowing it wouldn't remain that way for long with her around. It might not be fair, but he wanted to play at husband and wife so he would have to suffer the consequences.

Her small sack was on the bed, and she opened it, shaking out the only other skirt and blouse she had brought with her. She hung them on a peg near the door, then shook out her plain linen nightdress and laid it on the bed.

Zia couldn't discard her garments fast enough once the tub was filled, and shooed the young girls away with a wave, insisting that she preferred to tend to her own needs.

It didn't take long for the steaming water to penetrate her flesh and soothe her weary and aching bones. She washed her hair and body quickly before the water cooled, and barely rested her head back on the rim when she began to doze off. She jolted awake and told herself to get out and go to bed. She was bone-tired, and if she didn't get out would fall asleep there, which wasn't a good idea. It wouldn't do having her pretend-husband find her like that, naked in the tub.

After the hall emptied, Artair was left at the table with Cavan. He thought his brother would want to wait until morning to speak with him, but when Honora had gone to bed without her husband, Artair knew that Cavan wished to talk.

"You have made a good match," his brother said. "And one that will benefit our clan. I am happy for you and proud of you."

"Thank you," Artair replied, though knew soon enough he would have to confide the truth to Cavan. "It would have been better if I had returned with Ronan."

Cavan didn't agree or disagree. Instead he asked, "What did you learn of him?"

Artair shared the news, and Cavan shook his head.

"Why would Ronan leave the place that saw to his care and safety?" Cavan asked.

"I don't know, and neither does Zia or her grandmother Bethane."

"Are you sure of that?" Cavan asked skeptically.

Artair took no offense to his brother's question. After all, it was a practical one. "I asked the same myself, but from what I learned of the village Black and the people, I couldn't see any reason for anyone to keep the truth from me." He shook his head. "Though . . . "

"You feel you weren't told the whole of it?"

"There remains a nagging doubt," Artair confirmed.

"And the other question that remains is, if Ronan left the village of his own volition, why hasn't he returned home?"

"I've wondered over that myself. Perhaps wherever he went, he continues to heal, and once fully healed he'll return to us."

Cavan shook his head. "Something about the whole thing doesn't sit right with me. I feel as you do. We haven't been told the whole of it. Someone is leaving something out—and on purpose."

"Do you refer to my wife?" Artair asked, again not taking offense. His brother's duty was to protect the clan.

"I like your wife, and after telling us of the troubles she has faced due to her healing skills, I'd say she's a brave woman."

"Sometimes foolish," Artair said with a laugh.

"What woman isn't?"

"I wouldn't let your wife hear you say that."

Cavan laughed along with his brother before his tone once again turned serious. "I am truly grateful that you have wed such a gifted healer, though it is selfish on my part. I worry about Honora. She continues to not feel well and has fainted twice since you've been gone. I feel better with a skillful healer being here."

"Zia is a remarkable and diligent healer. I've seen it with my own eyes, which is why she has been accused of witchcraft."

"The clan will keep her safe, though it is better she remain on Sinclare land until the whole matter is settled," Cavan said, then lowered his voice, though no one was about. "It makes no sense that Ronan left the village where he was cared for."

"I thought the same myself. Why leave a safe place?"

"Something forced his departure," Cavan said.

"I do not think Zia or Bethane had a hand in it. Their concern is to heal."

"Then as it seems you suspect, there is more to Ronan's departure from the village Black than you have been told."

"True enough, but what reason could there be for keeping any pertinent news of Ronan from his family?"

The answer struck him before Cavan could answer.

"Zia is trying to protect us from something."

Chapter 18

Artair entered his bedchamber quietly, not wanting to wake Zia, who he was certain was sound asleep. He stopped short when he saw her in the tub, her head back, a snoring purr coming from her lips. An arm and a leg were hanging over the rim, as if she had fallen asleep while getting out of the tub.

He had to smile. She looked sweet and delectable, and he'd love to devour her, but not yet. In time she would come to understand that their union would benefit them both, and commit to a proper one—the marriage he had suggested to her more than once.

Until then?

He shook his head and wondered how he'd survive.

He walked over and hunched down beside the tub. She was a beauty in every sense. Her body was curved to perfection, her breasts and hips molded just right. He ached to reach out and touch every bow and arch.

He closed his eyes, hung his head and took a deep calming breath. If he continued to look at her, he'd continue to want to make love to her. He needed to get his soaring desire under control, get her out of the tub, dried, and in bed.

"Lord, give me strength," he muttered, then gently tapped her shoulder. "Zia, wake up."

She didn't budge. He muttered several incoherent oaths and tapped her shoulder more firmly while raising his voice. "Wake up."

Her eyes drifted open and the tip of her tongue slowly licked at her bottom lip.

He muffled his groan with a hard swipe of his hand across his mouth and this time spoke louder than he intended. "Wake up!"

Zia catapulted forward, splashing water over the sides, and glared at him wide-eyed. "I'm cold."

"No doubt," he said. "You're sitting in a tub of cold water."

Zia looked down, and a moment later her arms rushed to cover her naked breasts. "I fell asleep."

Artair grabbed a towel from the nearby bench. "So it appears." He stood and spread the towel wide. "Now stand up."

She didn't hesitate; he doubted she would, since her hands were shriveled, gooseflesh prickled a good portion of her skin, and there was a noticeable shiver to her.

He wrapped the towel around her and began rubbing her dry. As he ran the towel over her, Zia's shivers began to lessen. Scooping her up, he carried her to the bed and set her down on the edge.

"Arms up," he ordered, grabbing her nightdress and slipping it over her head. Then he hunched down in front of her and, when she finished wiggling the gown onto her body, snatched up one foot at a time and dried them with the towel.

Even her feet were beautiful, toes neatly shaped, a soft arch, smooth skin. When he realized that the towel had slipped from his grasp, he caressed her foot with his hand instead, and damned if he wanted to stop.

He didn't. It was Zia who slipped her foot away from him and crawled under the woolen blanket, pulling it up to her neck.

"All settled?" he asked.

She nodded, her fingers over the edge of the blanket and her eyes intent as she watched him.

He turned and walked to the door.

"Where are you going?" she asked.

He didn't look back. "I need a cold bath."

She chuckled. "There's one right here."

He spun around. "Want to see me naked, do you?"

He had his clothes off before she could respond, but she didn't disappoint him. She continued to watch him. She even propped herself up on her pillow to get a better look.

He wasn't shy. Once naked, he took his time getting into the tub. With one foot in, he almost changed his mind, since the water was colder than he expected.

"Coward." Zia laughed.

"I was giving you time to enjoy the view."

"I've seen enough."

"Like what you see?" he asked, his chest puffed broad.

"You're passable."

He turned too quickly to protest her witty response and lost his footing, plunging down into the tub. The water splashed up and over the sides as he plopped down on his backside.

Zia fell forward with a burst of laughter, holding her stomach as she came up to laugh some more at him.

"This is all your fault," he said, rivulets of water running down his grinning face.

She controlled her laughter, though it slipped out between words. "*I* maneuvered the tub just fine."

"But you failed to get out, didn't you?"

"Better than falling in." A yawn interrupted her laughter.

"Go to sleep, you're tired."

"I'll wait for you," she said, snuggling down beneath the blanket once again.

He wanted to ask why, since she certainly didn't intend for them to make love, and luckily she answered without him asking.

"I want to know what your brother thinks of our marriage, and with the water so cold, it shouldn't take you long."

She was right about that. He hurriedly washed his hair and his body and was out of the tub and dried in rapid time.

Then he approached the bed, the towel wrapped snug around his slim waist. "I sleep naked."

"I don't," she said. "And stay on your side."

"I'll try," he teased, released the towel and hopped into bed.

After he was settled, she asked, "What did your brother say? Oh, I do like him and Honora. They make a wonderful couple, and your mother is perfect; I do feel so sorry for her, though. You can see the sadness in her eyes. And Lachlan . . . " She chuckled. "He's a charmer and hides what a truly caring man he is."

"I'm pleased that you like my family and are so perceptive when it comes to Lachlan. As for Cavan? He's pleased with our union, though he has questions concerning Ronan."

He lay next to her, on his back, and felt her tense as she turned on her side to look at him.

"I imagine he would. Though only having met your family, it is obvious how close you all are. Ronan's absence must weigh heavy on all your hearts."

He heard the sincerity in her gentle voice and thought that since she empathized with their pain, she might tell him more of Ronan. Instead she changed the subject.

"I thought you would have confided in Cavan and told him the truth about us."

"Not at the moment."

She smiled. "I know why you didn't tell him."

"Enlighten me," he said, turning on his side to face her.

"You hope to convince me to marry you before it becomes necessary for you to tell everyone the truth."

He scratched his head in confusion. "You know, you may be right."

She poked him playfully. "You're not going to get your way."

"We'll see about that." He tapped her on the tip of her noise. "After all, you are in my bed."

Her yawn defined her response. "For sleep only."

He leaned over and gave her the faintest of kisses. "Then sleep, *wife*."

She poked him again. "Remember to stay on your side, *husband*."

"You too."

"Don't worry. I won't budge."

Artair woke for the third time with Zia's head plastered on his shoulder. Her arm was thrown across his chest, her leg hooked over his, and her knee resting much too close to his groin. He'd moved her twice already, and she was back again. And *she* had been concerned about him encroaching on her side, he thought with amusement.

He would have left her where she lay, except that she was so warm, smelled so sweet, and felt so good that it would be tempting fate. Actually, the temptation would be too much for him.

Reluctantly, he eased her off him, but this time she blinked a few times and groggily said, "Stay on your side."

Before he could inform her just how wrong she was, she turned on her side and promptly fell back into sleep.

In seconds she was snoring, that soft purr he was getting so very used to.

He wanted to snuggle up against her, wrap his arms around her, bury his face in her neck and nibble at her soft flesh. Instead he turned on his side, away from her, and after laying there for what seemed an eternity, fell asleep.

Zia woke with a yawn and a stretch and recalled that she was in Artair's bed. Looking around, she saw that not only was he gone, but that she was on his side. She lay there thinking back on the night and wondered if she had been the one who had not kept to her side of the bed. If so, as it appeared, Artair had remained a gentleman nonetheless, which spoke much for his character. Or was it his never-ending logic?

She bounced up in bed. He was a good man, but one question continued to nag her. What of passion? Didn't he ever surrender to it? So far as she could tell, he always kept tight rein on himself. What would happen if he let loose? She realized she would like to find out.

With much to do, she was out of bed and dressed in no time, slipping into her common attire of plain skirt and blouse and worn sandals. She didn't have to concern herself with her short hair since a run of a comb or her fingers through it usually had it looking presentable.

She hurried out the door, her thoughts crowded with

all she had to do. There was Honora to see to, and the keep garden to look over; she hoped it had a bevy of useful herbs. She also had to find a place where she could work, to explore the woods, and much more.

When she entered the great hall, only Addie and Honora sat at the table. With a smile, she joined them.

"I slept much too late," she said, glancing around the empty room.

"Nonsense," Addie said. "You were exhausted. You had a right to sleep all day if you wanted to."

"Oh my no," Zia protested. "I have much too much to do."

Honora, with her hand resting on her protruding stomach, said, "Artair says you are to enjoy the day. Tomorrow is soon enough to work."

"Artair is not—" Zia almost bit her lip, realizing she'd been about to say that Artair wasn't her husband and had no right to dictate to her. She grinned. "—to worry about me."

"He will anyway," his mother said, nodding. "It's his way. He believes he knows best, and he usually does."

Zia didn't intend to argue the point, mostly because she had discovered it was the truth. Artair was usually right, damn it. "Yes, Artair is considerate, but he need not worry about me. I'm fine and wish to resume my work immediately." She turned to Honora. "I'd like to talk with you about how you're feeling and the coming birth."

"That can wait until tomorrow," Addie assured her. "Take time for yourself today."

"I am. I'm doing what I love." Zia grabbed a piece of bread from the platter and stood. "Show me around, Honora?"

Honora looked to Addie, who responded with a congenial shrug. "If that's what Zia wants then by all means show her around."

"Perhaps we can talk later," Zia said to Addie.

"I'd like that."

"Good. Then I can have a look at that cut on your hand."

Addie glanced down at the red abrasion. "It's nothing."

"But it could turn poisonous if not treated properly."

"Take care of Addie first," Honora said, clearly upset as she struggled to stand.

Zia had reached out to help her when strong arms reached past her and took hold of Honora.

"What's wrong with my mother and why is my wife upset?" Cavan demanded, his arm going around Honora.

Honora rushed to answer, only worsening the situation. "Mother's hand is filling with poison."

"What?" came the startled cry behind her.

Zia cringed, hearing Artair's voice, and swore silently for losing control of the conversation.

"Stop!" she said, holding her hand up.

"Got yourself in trouble already?" Artair asked with a laugh, and slipped his arm around her waist.

Zia had to smile. Sides had been drawn. Artair was protecting her, as Cavan protected his wife, while Addie remained neutral.

"There's nothing wrong," she said, attempting to explain. "I'm doing what I always do—"

"Getting into trouble," Artair teased.

She elbowed him in the gut. "Hush up."

Cavan raised a pointed finger at Zia, and Honora grabbed hold of it. "Cavan will take a walk with me while you tend to mother."

"Good idea," Artair said.

Zia saw the two brothers exchange a look, and without another word, Cavan and Honora left the room.

She turned around with a flourish to Artair, and out of the corner of her eye saw Addie slip out of the room. "I can look after myself."

Artair scratched his head. "Which is why I've already rescued you two times?"

"This is a misunderstanding, and it's your fault," she said.

"Me?" he asked with shocked laughter. "I wasn't even here."

"No, but you left orders for me to—"

"Enjoy the day, which is far from an order," he said. "I've watched you work yourself exhausted, and then I forced you to endure a rough pace to return home. I felt you deserved time to rest and recoup before you again spend all your time helping others. I was concerned for you and only you."

Zia sighed with a smile. "How wonderfully romantic."

He took hold of her hand and kissed the back of it. "I can be romantic."

"You know what follows romance?" she asked, stepping closer to him.

He kept hold of her hand and lowered his face near to hers. "Tell me."

"Love."

"Then passion follows," he whispered in her ear.

"Is that an invitation?" she asked.

"I think we should discuss this in depth later tonight."

"Discuss which, love or passion?"

Lachlan interrupted any further talk between them when he rushed into the hall yelling, "Honora has fainted."

Chapter 19

Artair stood while Cavan paced outside his closed bedchamber door. He understood that his brother was more worried than angry, though moments before, that could have been debated. When Zia told Cavan to leave the room while she looked after his wife, he bluntly told her no. Artair had to give Zia credit for dealing patiently and calmly with Cavan, until he gave her one too many orders, and then she ordered him out of the room.

That's when he had gotten involved, convincing his brother that it was better to let Zia work and better that Honora wasn't further upset by the squabbling. Cavan had reluctantly vacated the room after informing Zia he'd stay right outside the door, waiting for news, which she was to deliver in due time or he'd return—and this time not budge from his wife's side.

Hence, the endless pacing, scowl lines, and concerned creases on his brother's face.

Cavan stopped abruptly. "That wife of yours has a strong personality."

"I like to think of it as passion."

"Then you're asking for trouble," Cavan said, and resumed his pacing.

Artair defended Zia not merely because it was expected of him as her supposed husband, but because he had seen for himself the depths of her commitment to her healing work, and he admired her for it.

"Zia's passion is what makes her the remarkable healer that she is," he explained. "Her only thought when she heals is for the person she is healing. Right at this moment, she is concerned only about Honora and what she must do to help her, even if it means offending the laird of Clan Sinclare."

Cavan stopped pacing. "I guess I needed reminding of who this was about. Your wife does what she knows best, and for that I am grateful, though her outspoken nature will take some getting used to."

Artair had to laugh, and he then realized that he had laughed and grinned more since he met Zia than he ever had, and he was pleased that she brought such consistent pleasure to his life.

"She grows on you after a while," he assured his brother.

"It's certainly obvious how much she has grown on you."

"It's disgustingly obvious," Lachlan agreed, appearing from around the stairs and walking toward them. "Love is written over every inch of him. What did you do? Fall hard like a complete and utter fool when you first met her?"

Artair was struck silent. All he'd heard was the word *love*, and it continued to reverberate in his head like a tower bell that refused to stop tolling. He had thought it a practical decision to wed Zia, but could the decision truly be perpetuated by love?

Lachlan smacked him on the back. "I'm right; the poor fool is dumbstruck by love and doesn't even know it—much like you, Cavan."

"Just you wait. I'm going to enjoy watching the bittersweet agony of you falling in love," Cavan said with a sneer.

Artair finally found his voice and joined in the teasing. "I agree with Cavan and look forward to the same for you."

"Too bad you'll both be disappointed," Lachlan said with smug confidence. "I intend to be wise when it comes time to choose a wife."

Lachlan went on to explain how he would not suffer any pains or pangs of chasing after a woman. He would make it known he was interested in acquiring a wife, and would then choose between the viable candidates and it would be done—he'd have himself a dutiful wife.

Artair and Cavan laughed so hard it brought their mother to the door.

"What seems to be so amusing?" Addie demanded.

Cavan and Artair couldn't contain their laughter enough to explain, so they both pointed to Lachlan, who reiterated to her what he had told them.

Addie burst out laughing herself, before shutting the

door in their faces. A minute or so later peals of laughter echoed from inside the room, which only caused Artair and Cavan to laugh harder and Lachlan to walk away in disgust.

After the two brothers' laughter subsided, the door to the bedchamber opened once again and Addie summoned them inside.

Cavan went directly to his wife, who sat in a chair by the window. "You're feeling better?"

"Much better after speaking with Zia," she confirmed.

Relief brought a huge smile to Cavan's face. "No more fainting, then?"

"Zia assures me there will be none if I follow her instructions," Honora said.

Cavan looked at Zia. "We'll do whatever you say."

She grinned. "It is Honora who will need to follow the prescribed diet."

Cavan turned an anxious look on his mother.

"I'm already prepared to see that she eats as Zia has suggested," Addie said. "Which is why I'm going to get her a little something to eat right now. And, Artair," she added, turning in his direction. "You need to find a nice cottage where your wife can work. I'm sure many in the clan are going to seek her healing skills."

"That would be nice," Zia said. "I could use a place where I can prepare my brews, mix potions, and blend salves while seeing to ailments."

"Timmin's cottage," Cavan said to his brother. "You know the one. It's been empty for a few months."

"That's at the far end of the village. I'd prefer my wife closer to the keep." He slipped his arm around Zia's waist. It was something he found himself doing often and without thinking. It was as if he felt empty without her in his arms, like a part of him was missing. Whatever it was, he knew he felt whole when he felt her there, pressed close to him.

"There's Biddie's cottage," Addie suggested. "It's more in the middle of the village, though it is small. Good enough for one, as Biddie said many a time throughout the years. I believe she would be pleased that her home became a place of healing."

Artair nodded, familiar with the place and the woman who had passed three months now. "I'll take Zia there and see if it will suit her."

Zia leaned her head back to look up at Artair. "Let me see to your mother's hand first, and then we can go."

Love.

The thought smacked him suddenly between the eyes, hit him in his gut, and caused his heart to thump madly. Is that what he felt—love? Did he see the same in her eyes? Could love's arrow have struck them simultaneously?

"Artair?" Zia said.

He shook his head, regaining his wits.

"It's not all right?" she asked hesitantly.

He went from shaking his head to nodding while trying to recall what he was agreeing to.

"Good," Zia said with a smile. "Give me a few minutes and I'll meet you outside the keep."

As he walked to the door and he fought to remember why he was meeting Zia outside, Cavan slapped him on the back and said, "Thanks for waiting with me." Then, in a hurried whisper, his brother said, "Biddie's cottage."

It all came rushing back then, along with the color to his face. He could feel his cheeks blotch red, and was glad no one could see his discomfort.

"Love really has you by the . . . " Cavan did not finish the thought, but laughed as he walked away, to return to his wife.

Artair didn't find Cavan's teasing amusing, and in an effort to further pull himself together, left the keep, intending to camp beneath a large pine tree. The needles it had dropped provided a cushion for him to sit, but he hadn't sat there in thought for long when Zia plopped down beside him.

"That was fast," he said, taking hold of her hand. He liked the warmth and softness of her skin, and he loved when their fingers entwined, locking together, keeping hold of each other.

"It was a minor abrasion and should heal well now."

She didn't appear in a hurry to see the cottage, and neither was he. He preferred to take a few moments and sit here under the shade of the tree with her and talk.

"I can see there is something on your mind," she said.

She waited, not insisting or pouting or demanding

that he tell her what it was. She simply waited to see if he wished to share it, a reasonable approach that left him confident in discussing the matter with her.

"You have repeatedly told me you wish to marry for love," he finally said.

"Yes, I have, and that has not changed," she replied.

"What if I loved you? Would your thought on wedding me change?"

She appeared startled. Was it because he had shocked her silent, or that she wasn't sure how to answer him? Either way, he didn't think it boded well for him.

"If you loved me?" she snapped. "Are you trying to decide if you could love me? If there's even the remotest chance?"

"You misunderstand me."

She yanked her hand free of his. "I think it is you who misunderstands. Love comes from deep in here," she said, resting her hand to her chest. "It can strike in an instant or develop slowly, but whichever way it arrives, it comes from the depth of the heart, and nothing—nothing at all—can stop it, not even logic."

"Let me explain—"

"No," she said curtly. "I will ask someone to show me Biddie's cottage, and get busy staking my claim on it while I'm here."

She stumbled to her feet, and he quickly stood to help her. He knew her stubbornness had taken hold and if he wasn't careful he would make the situation worse, though he wondered how much worse it could get. He did not want to find out.

"I will take you," he said.

"No, I prefer to go alone."

"How will it look to others if I let my wife find her healing cottage on her own?" he asked.

"That your wife is angry with you, and deservedly so."

Artair kept his patience. It would do him no good to argue with her; that would only fuel the disagreement. So he did what was necessary and sensible. "I am sorry."

"Why?"

"Why am I sorry?"

She nodded. "Yes, why do you apologize? Do you truly mean it or is it the logical thing to do?"

Her intuitive response caught him unprepared and he hesitated.

"I knew it," she said, throwing her hands in the air. "Your apology meant nothing. You simply did it because it appeared the logical course of action." She grunted angrily. "You are impossible. You wouldn't know love if it struck you straight in the heart or punched you in the gut. You see only reason, and being in love is far from reasonable. I doubt you will ever fall in love."

She turned and marched off, and he almost followed, but stopped himself. She needed time to calm down, and then he would speak with her.

His brother Lachlan approached. "You should go after her. She's very angry. She didn't even acknowledge me when she passed."

"That's why I will wait until she calms down."

Lachlan chuckled. "You can't be practical when it comes to women, Artair, because women aren't practical. Zia wants you to follow her. That would show her that you care."

"She'd continue to fight with me if I went after her."

"Of course she would—that's what she wants."

"To fight?" Artair asked, and shook his head. "That makes no sense."

Lachlan placed a firm hand on his brother's shoulder. "Back to lesson one—women aren't sensible."

"Then how can anything ever be settled?"

Lachlan chuckled again. "It can't, because women never forget. They'll remind you of something you did years after you long forgot it."

"And you know this how?"

"I learned it firsthand from every woman I've gotten to know."

"You mean every woman you've bedded," Artair said.

"Women love to talk, especially after sex. That's when I find out a lot about them." He grinned. "And oh how I look forward to every lesson."

Artair shook his head. "I prefer my own approach. It's more sensible."

Lachlan chuckled some more. "You better keep lesson one in mind or you're going to find yourself in deep trouble, especially with a woman as passionate as Zia."

Artair smiled broadly. "I admire her passion."

"That's because you have none of your own."

"I do so," he said, insulted.

"No offense, brother, but passion isn't your strong suit—reason and dependability are, which is great because you can always be counted on to do the right thing. And nothing stops you from doing it. Look how it helped you rescue Zia before she was burnt at the stake. When you told us the story, I thought how I might have considered that she was a witch and let her burn."

"Even when you knew she had information about Ronan?"

Lachlan shrugged. "I'm not taking chances with a witch."

"But Zia is no witch."

"I know that now, but I would have had doubts once I heard that the whole village condemned her."

His brother's words angered him and he was about to argue when he realized what Lachlan was saying. "You warn me that most think like you and trouble still brews for Zia."

"True enough, the clan will need to look out for her, but I was more concerned with your response to my even suggesting that your wife could be a witch. Your response was sensible."

"You would have preferred for me to knock you on your ass?"

Lachlan grinned. "That would have been passion."

Chapter 20

Two days had gone by since Zia made use of Biddie's cottage. No sooner had she gotten the cottage cleaned and ready than people started arriving, most of them with minor ailments that could be taken care of easily enough. When word spread about how much better Honora was feeling, the pregnant women in the village descended on Zia's doorstep.

She focused on her work while immersed in it, but otherwise couldn't help but think about Artair. It was an effort then to push such thoughts away so he wouldn't plague her every moment of the day and night.

She had been disappointed when he didn't follow her to the cottage the day they'd argued. She had hoped he would, even if it meant continuing to argue, but he hadn't. And that night, again to her disappointment, they had no time to discuss love or passion, because she was summoned to deliver a babe that in the end decided it wasn't time to be born after all.

Artair's approach to their situation remained sensible. He kept to his side of the bed, while she didn't. He acted like a dutiful and attentive husband, while she did as she pleased. It was not an intolerable situation. On the contrary, it was fast becoming comfortable, safe, and loving, as if the two of them had been together for years rather then months.

"I've come to walk you home," Artair said, ducking as he entered the short, open doorway and easing around the table. "Are you certain this space is not too small for you?"

"It will do. I won't be here that long." She was glad to see him, but then, she was always glad to see him.

"Still, I would prefer that you were comfortable and had sufficient room," he said, and moving behind her, inched his arms slowly around her waist until they hooked in front of her, then he settled her close against him.

He was forever affectionate, his arms always going around her, his lips pecking her cheek, her neck, or stealing a kiss. The other night, when she was kept late at the cottage of a young lad with an ailing stomach, he had waited outside for her, and afterward they walked to the keep hand in hand. He had stopped, and under the brilliant moonlight kissed her, and she'd welcomed it. She had actually ached for it.

It had been an amazing kiss, and it lingered on her lips for hours and tingled her senses far longer.

Now when he took her in his arms, she thought of that kiss, deep and lazy and loving, and she wished for more.

"The cottage is fine for now," she said, wishing he would remark on her obvious intention to leave.

Didn't he care? Didn't he want her to stay? He hadn't mentioned love again since they'd argued. And she was too stubborn to be the one to broach the subject. He was the one who had asked the question, after all. If he cared enough, he would pursue it. Wouldn't he? She wanted to cry out in frustration. She had no experience when it came to falling in love. She only knew she had these crazy feelings rushing and twisting inside her, and that they grew more maddening whenever she was with him.

She felt Artair blend against her as if becoming part of her, and she hoped he would kiss her. Good heavens, but she wanted him to kiss her.

He is good for you.

Her grandmother's voice reminded her, and while grateful for that, she didn't need it. She knew as much herself. Artair demonstrated his considerate nature every day. It was his unbridled passion she wished to see. Or was she looking for a hint of love? Just once she wanted him to do something completely illogical, when it came to her.

Suddenly feeling the need to demonstrate her own passion, she turned in his arms and whispered across his lips, "I want you to kiss me."

Without a word, he obliged, sweeping her mouth with his in a kiss that made her legs tremble and toes tingle as she melted in his arms. Lord, but the man could kiss. His kiss consumed and completed and made her want more, so much more.

She rested her cheek to his chest and splayed her hand over his heart. She thought she felt it thump strongly. Could it be thumping loudly for her?

"I love your kisses," she said softly, and thought she felt a quickening of his muscles. But it was only for a mere second, and she dismissed it, thinking her mind played tricks on her, while wishing that it hadn't.

"I love kissing you," he said, and gently skimmed his lips over hers. "Whether tender or passionate, every kiss stirs my soul."

Her heart soared along with her smile. "There you go being romantic again."

"One reason I would make a good husband."

She inched out of his arms reluctantly and could feel that he let her go with reluctance. She walked around the table, gathering items as she went, and when she stood opposite him, said, "Tell me other reasons you would make a good husband, and not the obvious ones."

"Protecting you, then, would be one of the obvious ones."

She nodded. "I've heard it enough. Tell me something different."

She waited, thinking he was stumped and feeling a sense of disappointment when he finally replied.

"You fit perfectly in my arms. I feel complete when I hold you, as if part of me has returned and I am finally whole."

He expressed beautifully what she felt herself, and it stole her breath away.

"A good reason?" he asked when she didn't respond.

She nodded and in a bare whisper said, "Another reason."

"We make good bed partners," he said with a grin. "I love that you can't stay to your side of the bed and that you are all over me throughout the night."

She chuckled, since that morning she woke wrapped around him, and he had made a hasty exit out of bed under the pretense of meeting with Cavan. She recalled how empty the bed felt without him. Or had it been that she felt empty without him?

"Finished," she said, dropping the last of the items she held in a basket on the table. "We can go now." She didn't want to hear any more reasons that he'd make a good husband. The two he'd cited were reason enough, besides loving his kisses, and the way he held her, and the way he worried over her safety, and, damn . . .

She hurried out of the cottage, her thoughts chasing after her.

Damn, she loved him.

She'd known it for a while, though refused to acknowledge it to herself. She had never been drawn as swiftly to a man as she had to Artair. He'd been right— they made each other feel whole. It was simple—they had been made for each other.

Then why was she annoyed? Isn't that what she wanted, a man made expressly for her, and her for him? Even though he was too sensible at times, he'd proved he was romantic, so he surely possessed the passion to love. But was it an everlasting love passion, or merely a random passion?

She jumped, startled, when Artair draped her shawl across her shoulders.

"You need this with autumn in the air."

Zia tied the ends tightly together and took his arm with a smile. She didn't want him to know that thoughts of him and of love disturbed her. She needed to work this out for herself, make sense of it all, and— She almost muttered beneath her breath.

How did she make sense of love? Now she was thinking more like Artair than herself.

"Take me to the grove in the moor," she said, dancing out in front of him while holding his hand.

"Night will fall soon enough. I will take you tomorrow."

"But the fairies come out at night," she teased.

He yanked her to him and she stumbled into his arms. "Don't speak such nonsense."

"I only repeat what others in your village have said," she said defensively.

"They are not accused of witchcraft."

She almost argued, but thought better of it when she saw the concern in his dark eyes and knew he was worried about her. She could not fault him for that. He was right, and it would be wise of her to listen.

"I'm sorry. I should have known better."

He scooped her up in his arms and deposited a quick kiss to her lips. "I promise I will take you to the woods tomorrow."

She closed her arms around his neck. "I look forward to it."

"We'll go early, before everyone in the village descends on your cottage."

"Is that jealousy I hear?" she asked with a twinkle in her eyes.

"I would spend more time with you if it was not for your work, but I know your healing is important to you, so I try to be patient."

"You are—" She stopped, realizing that she'd been about to tell him that he was more important to her than her work. The thought shocked her. Her work always came first, and that he understood as much made him all the more endearing to her. That she had been about to declare him more important, startled her and left her speechless.

"Please finish," he begged with a laugh. "You have me wondering."

She planted a kiss on his cheek; such a handsome cheek, smooth and chilled and all hers and hers alone. She almost sighed aloud. What was the matter with her? Had her realization that she loved him made her aware of things she'd simply taken for granted before?

"Tell me," he pleaded in a whisper.

His warm breath tickled her ear and his anxiousness had her smiling. "You are—very important to me."

"Now, that is another very good reason for us to wed. Soon there will be so many you will have no other choice but to wed me."

That very thought had occurred to her, but it wasn't the many reasons that would lead her to decide in favor of marriage—it would be love.

Artair lowered Zia to her feet, and they entered the hall holding hands. Honora waved them over to the table the family occupied before the hearth. Cavan sat beside his wife, Addie beside her, and Lachlan left space on his side of the long bench for them to join everyone.

"I'm feeling so much better," Honora said, smiling. "And Mother's hand has much improved. I am so happy Artair fell in love with you and that you are now part of our family."

"She worries over the lot of you," Cavan said, glancing from brother to brother. "Though with you married, Artair, she now only needs to concern herself with Lachlan."

"Worry not, I do fine," Lachlan said, raising his tankard of ale.

Zia listened to the now familiar banter between brothers. Addie must have long ago grown accustomed to her sons' teasing, for she paid more attention to feeding her dog Champion scraps than to her sons.

They talked, teased, and laughed through the meal, Addie joining in now and again and getting the better of all of them. Zia enjoyed the family's camaraderie, though it made her grow melancholy for her grandmother and the way they had shared their meals and talked. She wished Bethane had been there so she could talk with her. Her grandmother was a wise woman and had a way of saying just what she needed to hear.

When the brothers' talk turned to the workings of the keep, Honora and Addie spoke quietly with Zia.

"Mother and I thought to plan a larger celebration in honor of your wedding, so your family can share in it," Honora said.

"While that is thoughtful and generous of you both, it's not necessary. The feast you surprised us with upon our arrival was more than enough."

"But we never got to see you exchange your vows," Addie protested. "And I'm sure your family must feel the same. Think how beautiful a winter celebration would be, with both of you once again exchanging your vows in front of family and friends."

Zia almost laughed, thinking that such a celebration would finally and properly unite them. "I have only my grandmother, and while I'm sure the village Black would love to join in such a celebration, many of the villagers could not make the trip."

"Then we should at least have your grandmother here for a visit so that she may get to know us and we may get to know her," Addie insisted.

Zia agreed that it was a good idea, but at the same time reflected to herself that she might not be in Caithness long enough for it to happen.

Growing tired, she was looking forward to bed, and to being in Artair's arms. Realizing that she didn't want to go to bed without him, she wondered if that was not still another reason for them to wed. She almost laughed, but was saved by a wide yawn she covered with her hand.

"Time for bed," Artair announced, turning away from conversation with his brothers, reaching out and bringing Zia along with him as he stood.

"I agree," Honora said, looking to Cavan, who quickly assisted her to stand.

Addie stretched herself up, Champion standing as well, at her side. "I'm ready to turn in myself."

Lachlan laughed. "My night is just starting." He looked around the room, and finding a serving lass he liked, gave her a wink and held up his empty tankard.

Zia's legs protested every stair she climbed. By the time she reached their bedchamber, she flopped back onto the bed with a groan.

"I'm so tired," she said on a yawn.

Artair stood over her. "I can undress you and tuck you in, if you'd like."

She fought the temptation to say yes. It would be so easy to do so, but she knew that once she surrendered, she would seal her fate. He would demand that they wed, and she wasn't ready yet. Or was it he who wasn't ready yet?

Before she could answer him, a pounding rattled their closed door. Artair moved quickly and yanked it open.

It was Lachlan. "There's been an accident," he said. "Zia is needed."

She was up and out of the room in a flash, Artair following her. The frightened wailing could be heard rising up the staircase, and it brought Cavan and Honora out of their room, and Addie a few steps behind.

When they entered the hall, they could see that it wasn't only a woman's fretful cries, but that of a young lad no more then four or five. Seeing the blood pouring down the child's face, Zia immediately took control.

Her first order was to Cavan. "Take Honora out of here."

Cavan tried, but Honora wouldn't budge.

"I'm very good with stitches if you should need help," she said defiantly to Zia.

"Have it your way, and thanks for the offer," Zia replied, then she turned to Artair. "I need my healing basket, the large one, and the sack of cloths." She didn't have to tell him where it was. He was familiar with the cottage and knew where she kept everything.

To Addie, she said, "I need fresh water."

Addie took off.

"And me?" Lachlan asked.

"Help calm the lad while I calm the mother and find out what happened."

Lachlan went straight to the task. "What have we here, a mighty warrior who has been injured?" he boomed loudly, taking the lad's hand.

The child stared at Lachlan, who continued extolling his bravery as Zia took hold of the mother and walked her away from the boy so they could talk.

Between sobs, the mother told her all she needed to know. Samuel and his brother, she said, were playing in bed, and Samuel bounced off, his head catching the corner of the chest that rested nearby.

Zia knew that head wounds could be a problem. It depended how deep the wound was and what had caused the abrasion. Any blow to the head could do damage, and the extent of it would determine whether she would have trouble healing the wound.

Samuel sniffled between a few tears and looked ready to cry aloud when she approached.

"May I look at your wound, brave warrior?" she asked with a soft smile.

"Yes," he said, though held firmly to Lachlan's hand, which enveloped his much smaller hand. Only his thumb peeked out.

Zia noticed that blood continued to drip along his forehead, that the wound had yet to stop bleeding. With a tender touch she probed the area and almost sighed with relief. It wasn't bad, though it would re-quire stitches. Without them, it would continue to bleed and would fill with poison. Three stitches would hold it good, and she would see that the bandage remained clean until it could be removed.

She hadn't realized that the hall had gone silent, and when she looked up, she saw everyone staring at her as if holding their breath. They were waiting for her to save this child, and it sent a shiver through her. She hated the thought of telling anyone there was nothing she could do, and at those times she worked harder, knowing the decision was in hands far more powerful than hers.

But that wasn't the case with Samuel, and she smiled. "A few stitches, no running around for a few days, and he should be fine."

The mother broke into another fit of crying, which sent the lad into tears as well.

"Mothers cry, warriors don't," Lachlan whispered to Samuel, who then sniffled his tears away.

Zia nodded to Addie, who had returned with a caldron of water. She instinctively understood, and after depositing the small caldron by the hearth, wrapped a consoling arm around the woman and led her to a table where she could comfort her and keep her from upsetting the lad.

Honora joined her in consoling the woman, while Cavan stood by, watching Zia.

Artair returned with everything she needed, and with Lachlan's help—the lad refusing to let go of him—she got the blood cleaned off while brewing leaves in hot water. The drink would put Samuel to sleep, sparing him the pain while she stitched his head.

She worked diligently, keeping in mind all that her grandmother had taught her and what she had learned herself through trial and error. She had to cut hair away from the wound so she could see it more clearly. Her grandmother had taught her that the wound was less likely to become poisonous that way.

It took about an hour to finish, and that included washing the lad clean of all the blood and giving instructions to the mother, though Zia would see to the bandage herself, making sure it was kept clean.

Lachlan carried the child back to the woman's cottage. The father was out on sentinel duty and would not return until morning, when the next shift took over.

Cavan approached Zia as she began to clean up. "You are no witch," he said, his tone heartfelt. "You are a learned healer, and I am proud to have you as part of our clan."

"Thank you," Zia acknowledged with a nod, and wished she could tell him she was also proud to be part of Clan Sinclare. Unfortunately, since her marriage to Artair was a fiction, she knew she wasn't truly part of the clan, and felt it wouldn't be right to say anything to imply otherwise.

Cavan reached out for his wife's hand when she approached and their fingers locked. Zia could see how much in love they were. There was no denying it—it sparkled in both their eyes—and she envied the loving couple. She wished it could be that easy for Artair and her.

"You are far better with stitches than I," Honora said. "You keep them so uniform. Your embroidery work must be beautiful."

Zia shook her head. "I don't do embroidery. I haven't the time."

"Then I will do a piece for you," Honora said, and Zia smiled her appreciation.

This was a wonderful and loving family, and she wouldn't mind being part of it. She chased the thought. She was tired and didn't need her mind forever churning with wishes and hopes and dreams that might never see fruition. And it bothered her that she had not shared all she knew about Ronan with Artair.

She got busy cleaning, wanting to chase away her haunting thoughts, but Addie ordered her to stop.

Zia attempted to protest, but Artair prevented it.

"A servant will do that," he said, "and I will have your healing basket returned to your cottage. You've done enough for tonight."

He slipped his arm around her waist and walked her to the staircase, and she went along willingly, bidding Addie a hasty good-night.

Once in their bedchamber she fell on the bed, not even having the strength to undress. She wanted nothing more than to climb beneath the covers and sleep.

Artair loomed over her. "This time I'm not asking. I intend to undress you and tuck you beneath the covers."

Chapter 21

Artair expected Zia to protest—she disputed just about everything—but tonight he could see she was bone-tired and needed to sleep.

She stretched a hand out to him from where she lay prone on the bed. "Hurry, or I will fall asleep while you undress me."

He reached for her hand and gently pulled her to sit up. "Sleep. I will see you tucked safely in bed."

"A husband I can count on," she said, and yawned.

"Another reason to marry me." He untied her blouse and ordered, "Arms up."

She obeyed, though shivered when her breasts fell exposed.

Artair quickly retrieved her nightdress from the chest. He not only wanted to keep her from further chill, but wanted her full breasts and hard nipples out of sight as fast as possible, and her nightdress in place. So that when he took off her skirt, the night-dress would discreetly follow, hiding her alluring body not only from his sight, but from his mind, which was already conjuring too many lascivious thoughts.

What he didn't count on was the softness of her skin and how once he touched her flesh he didn't want to stop. She was soft, her skin smooth and creamy and feeling so very delicious to his touch.

His fingers grazed her breasts and the tips of her stiff nipples, and he felt as if he were struck by lightning, a sizzle racing through him, steaming his blood and tightening his loins. With a silent reproach he warned himself to behave. She was tired. Now was not the time to make love to her.

When then was it time?

The thought struck him hard, and he fought the question that haunted him day in and day out. He wanted to make love to her, wanted to make her his, wanted her as his wife.

He pulled the nightdress down to her waist, his hand catching the slim curve, and ever so grateful that her skirt remained in place or his hand would not have stopped.

She sighed softly. Or was it a passionate moan? Did his hand stir her desires as her naked flesh did his? Or was he merely wishing?

"I'll have you done in a minute," he said, letting her know he intended nothing more than to do as he had stated. Tuck her in bed.

"Take your time," she whispered.

He stilled his hand at her waist. She had told him to hurry, and now told him to take his time. What did she truly want from him?

He pressed his cheek to hers. "I love touching you."

He waited, leaving the decision to her. He would finish dressing her and put her to bed or he would make love to her.

She turned, her lips caressing his with the faintest of kisses. "Then touch me."

He grew so hard so fast that it sent an ache through his loins, but he intended to make sure that she was not dazed with sleep, that she was fully aware of what she wanted.

He took hold of her chin and looked directly in her eyes. "Once I touch you, I won't stop."

She tugged her chin free of his grip and teased his lips with hers while she said, "I don't want you to stop. I want to taste your passion. You do have passion, Artair, don't you?"

He could see that her exhaustion had vanished, replaced by a lustful glow, and that was all he needed to know.

"I'll let you see that for yourself," he said, and whipped her nightdress off her head, her skirt following.

She stretched back on the bed like a lazy cat preparing its limbs before sprinting, and he couldn't take his eyes off her languid movements as he slowly disrobed, preparing as she did—to sprint.

He fell over her naked; his hands splayed on either side of her head, his taut body a breath away from hers, beneath him. He heard anticipation in her gasp when he came to rest so close yet not touching her.

She pushed his long hair behind his shoulders and ran her fingers down along his arms and up again, then over his chest and down to his waist just above his shaft. She played his flesh like a fine instrument until his senses heated beyond reason and he bent his head back and groaned with desire.

He dropped his head back down until his mouth nearly touched hers. "My turn."

His lips took charge, dancing over every inch of her creamy flesh, kissing curves, nibbling mounds, tickling nipples mercilessly with his tongue, and when she groaned and grabbed the blanket tight in her outstretched hands, he laughed wickedly. "I've only begun."

If he thought he'd be the only one tormenting, he was wrong. Her hands quickly learned every sensitive spot on his body, and they were soon locked in a battle of sensual wills, each driving the other wild with touches, kisses, nibbles, licks that drove the passion beyond bearable to the edge of erotic insanity.

When she grabbed hold of his neck and with a heavy breath begged, "Please," he wrapped his arm around her sweat-dampened waist and swung her around until she lay beneath him. Holding back, controlling himself despite his excitement, he entered her gently.

Zia smiled and took hold of his shoulders. "Do not keep me waiting."

He laughed low and hardy, and with a grin of pure pleasure drove into her, and she called out in equal pleasure. They rode hard and steady, each holding on tightly to the other, their moans matching, soaring until she cried out in pleasure but warned him not to hurry— she was not done yet.

It wasn't until her third cry that he released himself, and with a force greater than ever before. It was like riding a never-ending wave of pleasure until finally he was deposited on shore.

Together they lay still, wrapped around each other, waiting for their breathing to ease, until Artair finally rolled off, taking Zia with him to rest against his side.

She rested her hand on his chest and he placed his over hers.

"You do have passion," she said.

"Another good reason to wed me," he teased.

"You should show your passion more often."

He laughed. "That would get us in a lot of trouble. We'd forever be making love."

She tried to poke him, but he kept hold of her hand. "That's not what I meant."

"My passion rears its head when necessary," he teased, giving her a poke of his own.

"And it's a large head at that," she retaliated.

He laughed heartily. "You are not the woman I expected—"

He stopped, about to say, *You are not the woman I expected to fall in love with,* catching himself just in time. He didn't think she would appreciate a declaration of love at that moment. She would think that he said it only to please her, which would not be the truth.

She poked him again, bringing him out of his musing. "Finish what you intended to say."

He took hold of her hand. "You are not the woman I expected in bed."

"Why is that?"

"Making love seems to come natural to you. You are comfortable with it and enjoy it, yet you have never been with another man."

"Being a healer teaches you much, and having a grandmother who will discuss anything with you is a great benefit. I've learned that most women feel that bedding their husband is a duty, and they are the ones with the most complaints, whereas the women who enjoy coupling have far fewer complaints." She chuckled. "But far more children."

"So you decided to enjoy?"

"I did, though my grandmother warned me that the right man was necessary for me to get any enjoyment out of it."

Artair thumped his chest. "I'm the right man."

"Then I must be the right woman."

"No, you are the perfect woman, absolutely perfect in every way," he said, turning and raining kisses over her face. "I love every inch of you."

She stiffened, and he could have kicked himself. Why did he have to mention love at this moment?

"You love the act of making love, not me."

He wasn't sure if she was asking or telling him, and he didn't want to get caught in a trap that would only make the situation worse. But he also couldn't agree with her, since it was far from the truth.

"Let's leave that discussion for another day," he said. She looked ready to argue, and he pressed his finger to her lips. "Please, this one time just agree with me."

To his relief, she grinned. "Just this one time."

"I never get another reprieve, ever?" he asked, feigning shock.

"Only time will tell," she teased, and yawned wide and long.

"You need sleep," he said, and kissed the tip of her nose. "And you can encroach on my side of the bed all you want."

"I just might take up all of it if you're not careful."

"Then I won't be careful, for I want you in my arms, on my side of the bed, snuggled tight against me every night."

"Just remember you asked for it," she said with a laugh.

He cuddled her in his arms, and her eyes closed and her light snore followed. He smiled, content, for there was no way he would let this woman get away from him.

It seemed he'd hardly closed his eyes when he heard a pounding at the door. Within five minutes, Zia was up and out of bed, on her way to deliver a babe. He insisted on going with her, but she advised him against it. He could do nothing to help her. He would just wait around while he could be sleeping.

She kissed him before he could get out of bed, told him to keep it warm for her, and then was gone.

He intended to get up and follow her, despite what she'd told him, but continued to lay there, the scent of their lovemaking ripe on the bedding. The fresh memories had him smiling. Content and satisfied, he fell fast asleep.

The babe arrived with the first light of dawn, wailing his face red, the startling color matching the thatch of bright red hair on the top of his head. It hadn't been a difficult birth, which Zia always gave thanks for, and since it was Teresa's second child, labor was shorter, though not less painful.

Zia had mother and child cleaned up in no time, and while the babe slept quietly in his mother's arms, she prepared a brew and some food for Teresa. The brew would help soothe her, and the food help strengthen her.

"I wondered after the birth of my first son why I would ever put myself through the pain of another," Teresa said, her full cheeks red from exertion and her brown eyes sparkling with joy. "But when I hold my babe in my arms, I have the answer. You'll know the feeling soon enough, having that strong, handsome husband of yours."

Zia's eyes rounded like full moons and she dropped the spoon she held, startled. There was a chance now that she could be with child, and while it shocked her, it also warmed her.

"I'm sorry," Teresa said. "I should not have been so bold—"

"Nonsense," Zia said, and hurried to put the woman at ease. "You just startled me, making me realize that after delivering so many babes, I could very well be having one of my own." She winked. "And my husband is handsome."

Her own admission startled her, for she had always been careful never to refer to Artair as her husband, but it seemed to spill from her lips so naturally.

Teresa giggled. "All the women think Artair handsome. Lachlan thinks he's the handsomest brother, but the women all know it is Artair. And you're the lucky woman who won his heart."

Zia nodded, and was relieved that Teresa asked to see her husband, in order to show him that she had delivered him another fine, strapping son. She didn't wish to discuss Artair any further; she had enough on her mind already. So she was only too happy to oblige, and after making certain mother, father, and babe were settled, she gathered her things and left.

"You must be exhausted."

She jumped, not expecting Artair to be outside waiting for her. "You haven't been here all night have you?"

"You worry about me when you look ready to drop?" he asked, walking over and taking her basket. "And no, I've only arrived. I slept the night through."

"Wore you out, did I?"

He laughed. "Proud of yourself?"

"Very," she said cheerfully. And she was; she was happy they had made love, and though it complicated the situation, it was worth it.

He leaned down and pecked her cheek. "I'm proud of you too."

She kissed him back, though she planted it on his lips. "I'm starving."

"Here I thought you were about to tell me how proud you are of me, and instead you tell me you're hungry."

"You didn't bother to ask what my hunger was for."

He shook his head and laughed. "Lord, am I glad I found you."

"Then you don't mind if it's food I want first?"

"Food first and then sleep," he said with concern. "You must be exhausted, and I'd prefer you full of vigor when you come to bed tonight."

"We have to wait until tonight to couple again?" she asked, disappointed, for her body was already tingling for him.

"After you rest—"

"Before I rest," she argued.

"You're too tired," he insisted.

"That's for me to decide."

They squabbled back and forth all the way to the keep, and just as they reached the steps, Zia said, "I should have known your passion was confined to the bedchamber."

He shook his head, scooped her up, and flinging her over his shoulder, swatted her backside. "And your passion knows no boundaries."

Chapter 22

Artair plopped Zia down on the bench at the table before the hearth, where his family was gathered. She looked ready to give him a good tongue-lashing, but instead clamped her lips tight.

He slipped in along the bench beside her with a smile. "Zia couldn't wait to join the family for the morning meal."

"Yup, it sure looked like she came willingly," Lachlan said with a smug grin.

"You look exhausted," Honora said to Zia with concern, then eagerly asked, "How is the new babe?"

"He is a strapping babe with a generous wail and a thatch of bright red hair like his father's," Zia said.

Honora smiled with glee. "I cannot wait for our babe to be born. I know he will be as handsome as Cavan."

"Better he be as handsome as his uncle," Lachlan said, thumping his chest.

"He should look like his father, for then he will also resemble his grandfather," Addie said, sounding melancholy.

Everyone turned silent, though nods circled the table.

Addie broke the silence. "It will be good to have a little one around here again. I cannot wait."

"And more little ones should follow soon," Lachlan said, raising his tankard at Artair.

"When do you do your share in seeing our family grow?" Artair raised his own tankard in challenge while considering the idea. He had always wanted a large family, and after last night there was now a possibility.

Lachlan laughed. "You and Cavan can see to that for now."

"Coward," Cavan accused with a grin.

"Wise," Lachlan corrected.

"Be careful, Lachlan," Artair joined in. "Fools are made to suffer."

"Then I have no worry," Lachlan chortled.

"Lachlan will do well finding a wife," Zia said, breaking off a piece of bread from the freshly baked loaf on the table.

"Why?" Artair and Cavan asked in unison.

Zia answered quickly. "Because he is attentive and passionate with women."

Lachlan grinned from ear to ear. "Oh dear, sister I love you. You know me so well."

Artair and Cavan disagreed with protests.

"Zia's right," Honora agreed. "Lachlan does know women."

Cavan's head snapped around to his wife. "I know women."

"Oh do you now?" Honora said curtly.

"I did know women," Cavan tried to correct.

"So you don't know me?" Honora asked sharply.

Cavan hurried to explain. "That's not what I meant."

"What did you mean?" Lachlan asked with a smirk.

"Shall we kill him now?" Artair offered.

"You can both try," Lachlan laughed.

"This is my fault," Zia said. "Please don't fight on my account."

"Dear, this has nothing to do with you," Addie said, patting her arm. "They're men; they can't help it."

"That's right," the three brothers declared simultaneously.

The women burst out laughing.

Artair loved family, and he loved that Zia now shared it with him and that they would seed the family and watch it grow. Of course, he had to get her to marry him first, but he didn't think that would be a problem, not after last night. In a way, they had actually committed to each other by making love. The only thing left was to exchange vows.

Zia yawned, and Artair slipped his arm around her. She instinctively rested her head on his shoulder, reminding him that she needed sleep. He intended to see that she got it.

Cavan helped his cause. "You need to rest, Zia."

"She's going to bed right now," Artair said.

Just as Artair stood, one of Cavan's warriors burst into the hall.

"The village Hosack is under attack from marauders," the man announced.

The men immediately got to their feet, and Artair looked to his mother. "Please see that she rests."

"I'll look after her," Addie promised.

Artair leaned over and captured Zia's mouth with a kiss. "Promise me you'll sleep. There may be wounded who will need your help."

Her eyes popped wide. "I'm going with you."

He held her down firmly, his hand to her shoulder. "You aren't going anywhere."

"What of the wounded villagers? Who will heal them?" she demanded.

"She has a point," Lachlan said.

"No one asked you," Artair said, annoyed with his brother for taking Zia's side.

"There's no time to argue," Cavan said with the distinct voice of a leader. "The wounded will be brought here if necessary."

Artair almost breathed a sigh of relief, though never got the chance. Zia broke loose of his grip and stood.

"And your wounded warriors?" she asked sharply, and then didn't let Cavan answer. "My presence could mean life or death for them."

Artair knew that settled it, for his brother would do whatever benefited his men.

"Get your things," Cavan ordered, "but remember, you are to obey my every order—my order, no other."

Artair knew that was meant for him, and he knew what Cavan intended to say next.

"Don't even think of designating me to remain behind. My wife goes, I go," Artair said firmly. "It's Lachlan's turn to stay and protect this time."

To his relief, Lachlan agreed. "Artair's right. I'll stay."

Addie stood. "We'll prepare to feed and help the wounded."

Honora kissed her husband. "I will help Addie, and don't try to tell me not to. And make certain you come back to me, husband."

Cavan hugged her. "Always, wife."

Artair envied them, Honora remaining at the keep safe while Zia would be amidst the mayhem and danger of battle.

When all the warriors were mounted and ready to leave, Cavan rode up to Artair. "Do you have anything to say to me?"

"My wife gets hurt and I'll kick your ass."

Cavan smiled. "Keep that angry thought in mind while in battle."

Zia didn't think or feel. She was too busy to do either. Cavan had designated a safe spot for her to remain until the battle was over, but the screams and cries of agony made that impossible. She knew if she could get to the injured sooner rather than later, they would have a chance of surviving.

Artair had given her only one warning.

"Do as you're told."

She wanted to obey both men, but she was a healer

before anything and had to follow her own instincts. It was what kept people alive. So she found a secluded area closer to the battle and fashioned a spot to care for the injured that she might manage to get there.

Her first rescue was a mother and daughter. The young woman was stumbling, the child held tight in her arms, trying to get away from the carnage. Blood dripped down her face, her eyes rounded in fright, and she couldn't gain solid footing. Zia couldn't see if the child was hurt, but she didn't waste time. She looked around, feeling safely for the dirk she had tucked into her boot in case she needed to defend herself, and rushed out to hurry the woman into the surrounding woods and to safety.

It took only a few minutes to ascertain that the woman had suffered a minor abrasion and was more stunned from her ordeal than anything else. Her child, thankfully, was fine, and when she finished ministering to both of them, she left them safely tucked behind a boulder and went in search of others who were injured.

By her fourth trip bringing injured villagers to the safe spot, she had a group of helping hands, all women. One woman began helping her rescue the injured, while two others stood guard with swords, and one with a bow, in case of attack.

Only two of the injuries were serious, though Zia didn't believe they were life threatening. However, she had seen a badly injured warrior who would certainly die if not given immediate attention.

Neddie, the woman helping her rescue the injured, joined her to help the fallen warrior. They waited on the edge of the woods, the warrior not far from them, blood oozing from his chest, his moans audible even above the noise of battle.

"As soon as an opening occurs, we go," Zia ordered.

Neddie nodded, set to move.

Within minutes a lull in the battle and an opening on the field enabled the two women to rush out. They had pulled the warrior to the edge of the woods when a marauder appeared on horseback, grabbed a fistful of Zia's hair and tried to drag her along the ground. But with her hair short, and with her ripping at his hand as he tried to keep his grip, he finally let go.

She scrambled to her feet and ran for cover, but he descended on her with surprising speed. Realizing she wouldn't make it to the woods, she stopped and reached down to her boot for the dirk. She turned in time to see Artair descend on the man. With one blow of his sword, he knocked the marauder from his horse. The man was dead when hit the ground.

"Do as you were told!" Artair screamed.

Zia looked at him wide-eyed, and threw the dirk. It flew past a startled Artair and settled in the chest of another marauder, who'd come up behind him and had been about to end his life. She froze for only a moment, to see if she'd killed the man.

"Go! Now!" Artair screamed at her.

She obeyed instantly, joining Neddie, who had gotten the wounded warrior into the woods. Between the two of them, they moved him to safety. Then Zia went to work on him as Neddie continued to prowl the edge of the battlefield, looking to rescue villagers and warriors as best she could on her own.

When the battle ended, the warriors chased off those who had been wounded but were able to walk.

Within minutes Artair and Cavan descended on Zia.

She abruptly raised her hand at them. "You can berate me later. Right now this man needs me or he will die."

"There are other wounded warriors," Cavan said.

"Any who need immediate attention?" Zia asked while continuing to work on the man.

Artair answered. "James."

With a swift turn of her head, her worried glance fell on him. "How bad?"

"His arm looks near severed," Artair answered.

Neddie had returned as soon as she discovered that her husband and son survived without any injures and offered her help.

She turned to Neddie. "Can your husband and son help get this man into a cottage where he can rest?"

Neddie nodded, and Zia gave her instructions, telling her what needed to be done for the injured man she'd been working on.

As Neddie moved off with him, Zia cleaned her hands in a bucket of water that had been filled and re-filled throughout the battle by the young children. She grabbed her healing basket, which was seriously depleted, and followed Artair and Cavan. She was concerned about several other wounded men, but their situation didn't sound nearly as dire as what she'd been told about James.

She hoped that Artair's description of the wound was exaggerated, but seeing it, she quickly knew that it hadn't been. She didn't know if she could be able to save his arm, or more important, save James.

James appeared to have the same thought. "I'm done, I'm done!" he yelled to the men around him. "Kill me now and get it over!"

Zia dropped down beside him on the ground. "How dare you survive a battle only to surrender to a wound."

"I've lost my arm."

"Not yet you haven't," she said, and looked to Artair. "Find me a clean enough place to work on him."

It didn't take long to have James settled on a sturdy table in a cottage. Neddie arrived to let her know that the warrior she had worked on now slept comfortably and was grateful to her, and she offered further help if needed.

Zia gratefully accepted her offer.

She could see those who had looked at the wound didn't believe she could save James's arm, but no one said as much. They let her go about her work without interruption.

She took several chances she normally wouldn't, but her grandmother had often told her that if it looked like there was no chance at all, to take all the chances you could.

She gave James a concoction that healers rarely used, since it wasn't safe. It would either make him sleep deeply for hours or kill him. But she had little choice. With the work she had to do on his arm, he could never have tolerated the pain, and she needed him very still; the potion guaranteed both, and alleviated his misery over losing his arm, which she knew could still happen.

As she worked on James, she was aware that Artair came and went from the cottage. He was not the only one. There were also women who came to ask advice about injuries they weren't sure how to handle.

Meanwhile, a fresh group of warriors arrived from the keep, while those warriors who could, returned home. Another group was sent out after the remaining marauders, to make certain they didn't terrorize other villages.

Addie arrived when Zia was nearly finished.

"When the news arrived at the keep, I thought you could use some help and more healing supplies and a change of clothes," she said, holding up two baskets.

"You're an angel," Zia said with relief.

"No, m'lady, you are," Neddie said with a tear in her eye.

"I'm a healer," Zia said, as if it explained everything, then returned to stitching James's arm.

It wasn't until hours later, well past nightfall, with James safely tucked in bed and Addie arguing with Zia that she must sleep, that Artair entered the cottage.

Zia was prepared to argue her point that James

needed her nearby if there was a problem with the wound.

"Your wife is not reasonable," Addie said to her son.

"That she isn't, Mother," Artair said.

"James may need me," Zia insisted.

"There is no more you can do for him except get some rest and be refreshed when he does need you," Artair said, walking over to where she stood by the table.

"But—"

"You can do no more, Zia," he reiterated.

"There's always more—"

"Not this time," Artair said. "You have spent hours on him. What will be will be."

Zia felt tears threaten her eyes, felt her limbs go numb, felt her overworked body giving out, and when he opened his arms, she gratefully fell into them.

He scooped her up, and she dropped her head to his shoulder. "I don't want him to die."

"That isn't up to you. You must think of yourself and the others who need you. Mother will look after James and fetch you if needed. All warriors rest after battle, and you have battled bravely today."

Her eyes began to close. "I am no warrior. I am a healer."

"That you are, dear wife. That you are."

Chapter 23

A week after the battle, Artair and a group of men
saw to bringing the last of the wounded men
home. Zia hadn't allowed the seriously injured to be
moved until she felt they were able to make the brief
journey.

He had not only worked beside her that week, but
watched her work, and as usual was amazed with the
way she gave the injured hope and how her generous
smile made even the most downtrodden break into
a grin. It wasn't only her healing skills that helped;
her enthusiasm for life lifted the spirit and lightened
the heart. He could easily understand why so many
would deem her a witch. The envious and ignorant
would claim she used magic, spells or potions, and that
worried him.

He didn't believe that Zia was now safe, and he intended to remain vigilant. Sooner or later news would
arrive from the church council. It was inevitable, and
he'd be prepared to do whatever was necessary to save
her. He would not see her denounced as a witch or

burned at the stake, and with an eye toward protecting her, was determined to make her his wife, and sooner rather than later.

But how?

That was the question.

He barely had time to talk to her, and when they fell into bed together, they were so exhausted that sleep claimed them immediately. However, now that they were home with more helping hands, Artair planned on having Zia to himself for a while.

"Don't count on it."

Artair turned with a befuddled look from where he stood on the steps of the keep, a strong autumn wind blowing, to see his brother Cavan cracking a smile as he approached.

Cavan laughed. "It takes a married man and one in love with his wife to know what you're thinking even without seeing your expression, though once you turned around I knew I was right. You haven't had your wife to yourself lately."

"Neither have you," Artair challenged.

Cavan continued laughing. "Yes, but I'm laird so I can command."

It was Artair's turn to laugh. "You never have nor will you ever command Honora."

"Damn, you can't even let your brother keep his fantasy."

Talk suddenly turned serious as Cavan placed a firm hand on Artair's shoulder and spoke low so no one else could hear. "Your wife works miracles."

"Which could prove fatal for her," Artair replied, voicing what Cavan would not.

"No one in the village speaks poorly of her," Cavan assured. "All are grateful for her healing skills, especially James."

Artair nodded. "He continues to improve, and Zia keeps his hopes high, though she is honest with him, letting him know that she isn't certain if his strength will fully return to his arm."

"I think James is feeling good because your wife informed him that she sends for that pretty lass he favored in her village to help look after him."

Artair chuckled. "James did brighten considerably when Zia told him she had sent for Mave to help."

"Considerably? He nearly jumped out of bed."

The brothers laughed, though it came to an abrupt halt when they spotted their mother running toward them and waving frantically.

The two ran to her.

"Honora. Honora." It was the only thing a breathless Addie could utter.

Artair helped his mother as Cavan took off toward where Addie pointed.

Artair and Addie followed him in the same direction and came upon a hectic scene as they entered the cottage of one of the healing warriors. Honora had been visiting with him when she was struck with pain. Everyone in the cottage was upset, especially Cavan, who held his wife in his arms as she groaned.

Lachlan entered and began yelling, "Do something for her! Do something!"

Artair took over then. He directed Lachlan to find Zia, while Cavan insisted upon carrying his wife to the keep. Interceding, Artair made him understand that it was better for her to remain in the cottage until Zia could look at her.

Shortly afterward, Zia arrived to take control of the situation. Following a brief examine, and asking questions, she said that Honora had no more than an upset stomach. Zia ordered her to bed and then began to prepare a special brew.

It wasn't until Artair was alone with her as she brewed the potion that Zia confessed to more concern than she'd let on. In fact he had suspected as much, having seen the look on her face earlier, during her examination.

"I'm not sure she will carry much longer," Zia said.

"If she delivers sooner, what of the babe?" he asked

"If I can manage to keep her from going into labor *too* early, then I believe the child can be saved."

"And Honora?"

"I'm not worried about her; it's the babe that concerns me."

"Should you speak to Cavan about this?"

"Honora will see his worry."

Artair nodded. "You're right. What do we do?"

"I will speak with Honora."

"And Cavan?"

"That will be up to his wife," Zia said.

"If it were you, I would want to know," Artair said.

Zia placed a gentle hand to his cheek. "I would confide in you, for you would do what was necessary. Cavan, however, is madly in love with his wife and fears losing her."

Artair almost grabbed his chest, the stab was so sharp. Zia had no idea how he felt about her. But then why should she? He hadn't made his feelings known; he'd only just realized them himself. And if he claimed them now, she wouldn't believe him. What was he to do?

Show her you love her.

The voice in his head was clear, and it sounded just like Bethane, but then, the older woman did give good advice.

Artair took hold of Zia's hand. "Handle this as you will, but later make time for *us*." He leaned down and, before kissing her, whispered, "You are so beautiful."

Her breath caught as he stole a quick kiss. Then he walked off. He had to or he would have dragged her upstairs to their bedchamber and kept her there for the rest of the day and night. They hadn't made love since the battle—no time, no chance—though desire was there, and not only his. He could sense it in the way Zia leaned heavily against him when tired, the way her arm went around his waist to hug him, the way her lips found his at the oddest times, and how she whispered in his ear when least expected, "I want you."

Zia was more of a woman than he had ever expected.

And now that he had her, he wouldn't exchange her for anyone else in the world. She was his and he loved her.

He hurried up the stone stairs to Cavan's bedchamber and entered through the open door. His brother sat on the bed beside his wife. For a moment Artair thought of placing his hand on Cavan's shoulder, but realized if he did that, his brother would know something was wrong.

"Zia will be here in a minute," he said, walking over to the bed and seeing that his mother sat on the edge of the chair in the corner. "How are you feeling, Honora?"

"Better," she said with a weak smile.

He noticed how her eyes darted to the open door, and knew that she waited for Zia.

"Why don't we leave the women to handle this?" Artair said to his brother. "I'm thirsty for an ale or two."

"Make that three or four," Lachlan called from the doorway. "Are you feeling better, dear sister?"

Honora waved to him from the bed. "Much better, thank you. Now take this husband of mine off to drink with you while I tend to woman's work."

"You heard her," Lachlan said, waving at Cavan.

Cavan didn't budge. He looked to his wife. "Are you sure—"

"Go," Honora said, shooing him away. "Your mother is here, and Zia will be here shortly."

Cavan left reluctantly and with a promise to return soon to see how she was feeling.

Artair hoped they wouldn't pass Zia on the way to the hall, but they had no such luck. They met her on the way down as she was on her way up.

"My wife?" Cavan asked anxiously.

"Is fine," Zia said, and Artair knew she answered honestly. He only hoped that Cavan would not ask about the babe, and was relieved when his brother simply nodded and moved on. Her answer was enough for now, though Artair didn't think it would suffice for long.

He lingered behind his brothers, wanting a moment with Zia, if only briefly. Reaching out, he brushed his fingers along her arm. She couldn't respond in kind, since she had a steaming cup of brew in her hands, but he felt her response. It was a sensual shiver that rippled through her body and along his.

"Later," he whispered with urgency, and with a wide smile she nodded vigorously.

He followed his brothers down the stairs, wishing he and Zia were going up the stairs to their bedchamber. Shaking the thought from his head, he kept a quick pace behind them.

Zia entered Honora's bedchamber with her mind far from where it should be. Artair had been in her thoughts far too often. And she found that she wanted to be with him far more often than she'd ever imagined possible. She sighed, knowing she had no time for such thoughts. But later she would . . .

She smiled as she approached the bed in which Honora lay.

"Tell me," Honora demanded sharply, and caused Addie to jump out of her chair.

Zia took charge, handing the brew to Honora. "Drink slowly and we'll talk."

Honora followed her directions, Addie slipping back into her chair, waiting.

The two women were like family to her. She couldn't say when that had happened. Perhaps from the start she'd felt close to them because of Artair. Whatever the reason, she wanted to alleviate their fears while alerting Honora to potential problems.

"You need to rest," she said.

"Why?" Honora asked fearfully.

From experience, Zia knew that many women blamed themselves when something went wrong with their babe, so she answered carefully. "The easiest way for me to explain it is that the babe is restless."

Honora grew upset.

"It has nothing to do with you," Zia assured. "It is the babe who is making his wants and needs known."

"What do I do?" Honora asked anxiously.

"You rest and listen to what the babe has to say."

"How?" Honora asked, near tears.

Zia reached out and took hold of her hand. "You already know. You knew as soon as the babe pained you that it was time to rest. Don't be stubborn. Listen to your babe and he will be born without a problem."

Addie shared her own experience. "Like father like son. Cavan kept me off my feet for several weeks before his birth."

"Really?" Honora asked with relief.

"And look at him now," Addie boasted with pride.

The three women laughed while Honora sipped the brew.

"Tell me what to do and I will do it," Honora said. "And then I will share the news with Cavan. I would not want him to keep a secret from me, and I will not keep one from him." She placed her hand on her rounded stomach. "He is our babe, and we must face any problem together."

Zia settled Honora to rest and promised she would send Cavan to her right away. Addie left with her, and as soon as they were out the door, took hold of her arm and moved her aside.

"Honora will be all right?" she asked in a low voice.

Zia nodded. "With rest and attention to the babe's demands, I believe all will go well."

"But you're worried," Addie said. "I can feel it."

"I always worry when a babe makes demands before he arrives, but we are aware of his demands and will keep a watch on him and Honora."

They continued to walk and Addie continued to question, though not about the babe.

"How are you and Artair?"

"We do well," Zia said, and realized it was true. They were doing better than she had imagined they would, or was it better in spite of what she'd imagined?

"You seem surprised."

"I suppose I am," Zia admitted.

"Why?"

"We are different, Artair and I."

Addie smiled. "Not so much."

Zia looked at her, dazed. Artair and she were like night and day, yet Addie was suggesting that they weren't.

Addie stopped before they reached the hall. "One more thing. I want to know the truth about Ronan."

Zia had been expecting her to ask about her son. However, she wasn't sure how to answer.

"I am confident that my son one day will return home and with what you have told the family, I am sure of it. So tell me the truth. Tell me why he has yet to return when it appears he's free to do so."

Zia took hold of her hand. "There are times when it is best that a question is not answered."

Tears pooled in Addie's eyes and she looked ready to argue.

"Please," Zia begged. "I know how difficult this must be, but let it be for now. You will have your answers soon enough."

Addie stuck her chin up. "Cavan is waiting."

"I envy you your strength," Zia said softly.

"And I thank you for looking after Ronan long after he left your care."

They entered the great hall, and Zia immediately informed Cavan that Honora wished to speak with him. She hoped to talk with Artair; about what, she wasn't sure, she simply wanted time with him, even if it were just a walk and they didn't speak a word. She just felt the need to be with him, hold his hand, touch him, kiss him, or have him there beside her, and his intense glance told her he felt the same.

She was walking toward him when a woman entered the hall asking for the healer. Zia stopped, and for a moment wished she wasn't a healer. She could see that Artair felt the same way.

Surprisingly, it was Artair who made the first move, taking her arm and walking with her out of the hall. He was letting her know that he was there beside her and would support her in whatever she did, and his consideration touched her heart and made her want him all the more.

How could a practical man have captured her heart?

Perhaps there was something she could learn from him? Or could Addie be right? Could she and Artair be more alike than she thought?

The possibility intrigued her but didn't have time to gain substance since she was soon busy tending a wounded warrior who had developed a fever. A mere glance at the man told her that her hoped-for time with Artair might not materialize.

She looked to Artair with disappointment.

He smiled softly and rolled up his sleeves. "Tell me what to do to help."

Chapter 24

Artair and Zia stumbled into the room together, exhausted but charged with passion. It had happened innocently enough, with a brief kiss on their walk to the keep. It sparked a passion that they could not ignore, nor did they want to. Soon their steps were hurried, their hands reached out to touch, and they were kissing, their lips simply not wishing to part.

Clothes were nearly ripped off as they tumbled on the bed. Their need was too great to linger in play. Their passion-charged bodies immediately joined in a frenzied union. It was as if he couldn't drive deep enough inside her, or that she couldn't have him deep enough inside her. It was almost as if they wished to blend as one losing themselves in each other until there was no difference between them.

Their naked bodies were soon drenched with sweat, their breathing more labored than ever before and still they would not relinquish the connection between them that spiraled on forever.

They were one. With each forceful climax Zia grew closer and more deeply in love with Artair and though he never voiced the same, she felt it, for certainly love could be the only driving force that could bring them to the brink of insanity and make it feel so right.

They lay side by side in the aftermath of their love-making, their bodies drenched in sweat and their breathing barely controllable. Their fingertips touched as if they refused to relinquish the connection that had made them feel so utterly whole, so beautifully complete.

Zia wished to express how she felt but could not find the strength or breath to do so, and while she sensed he felt the same, he also remained silent.

She suddenly felt like crying. How could this matter ever be settled between them when she would cry out her love for him in front of the whole village, and he would wait for a reasonable time to admit his own feelings?

Her disturbing thought did not distance her from him, far be it. It made her grasp hold of his hand locking her fingers with his as if letting him know she had no intentions of ever letting him go.

His grasp was just as tight, letting her know the same.

The problem was where did they go from here?

Zia sat at the table before the burning hearth in the great hall alone. She had woken before dawn, her thoughts much too chaotic to return to sleep. She had slipped quietly out of bed, dressed and made her way to the hall, though stopped in the kitchen first. The cook was surprised to see her and only too glad to prepare whatever she wanted.

Zia only wanted to fix herself a soothing brew, but surrendered to the cook's insistence that she needed hardy fare to help her face the day. Though the food was excellent, she had little taste for it.

"Troubled thoughts?"

Zia jumped, startled, so lost in her thoughts that she hadn't heard anyone approach. She smiled, seeing it was Addie, and was glad for her company.

"Confused thoughts," Zia admitted.

Addie sat, Champion taking up his usual stance beside her, patiently waiting for any food either woman would give him.

"Tell me," Addie offered, pouring herself a hot brew and refreshing Zia's.

"I love your son," she said without hesitation or doubt and so relieved to have admitted it to someone.

"I had no doubt of that, but you had?"

She had to be careful with what she said, though she preferred otherwise. "We are different, and I thought those differences would create a problem."

"Only if you let it, and besides—" Addie laughed. "As I expressed to you once before, you and Artair are not all that different."

"But he is so practical."

"So are you."

"I am not," Zia said.

"You tend the ill with an unwavering responsibility."

"Responsibility is far different from practicality."

"Is it?" Addie asked, though didn't allow her to answer. "Artair places his family and responsibility before all else. You place your healing before all else. What difference is there? You both are being practical in your approach and intentions. The two of you are more alike than you know."

Zia let her words soak in.

"And while Artair may be more reasonable than most; he is also more passionate than most, for it is his passion that drives him to place others before himself. The story of how you met proves this—he rode into the middle of a village crazed with burning a witch and rescued you. That takes a passion of courage not many possess."

Zia remained silent, soaking in every word.

"Passion, courage, sensibility come in all different guises, and those with clear vision can see each for its own truthful worth and judge wisely."

Zia smiled. "You sound like my grandmother; she's a wise woman."

"Age usually brings wisdom, though it is often learned through difficulties," Addie said sadly.

"You miss your husband."

Tears trickled down Addie's flushed cheeks. "I miss him terribly. There isn't an hour that goes by that he isn't in my thoughts. But the worst part is my empty bed."

Champion woofed as if to let her know she had him, and she gave his neck a rub. "I hate going to bed alone and I hate waking up alone. My heart aches every day, and while many tell me it will get better, it hasn't. I miss my husband."

Words failed Zia. She could only reach out and take hold of Addie's hand and offer what little comfort she could. She couldn't imagine nor did she want to imagine her bed without Artair in it. His loving arms sheltered her, protected her, loved her, and she would not want to live without him.

"I am so sorry," Zia whispered, needing to say something.

"So am I," Addie said, her tears continuing to trickle, though she took a steadying breath. "That's why you must wrap my son in your zest for life every day and share it with him as he does with you. Don't question it, just do it and love will be forever yours."

"Shall I leave you to your women talk?" Artair asked as he approached.

Zia jumped up, startling Champion to bark, and rushed to fling herself into Artair's arms.

"I love you," she said, and kissed him soundly.

He looked at her, startled, and she looked at him the same way. Had she really just shouted her love aloud for him?

But what did it matter? It was the truth.

"Like none of us knew that?" Lachlan asked teasingly as he passed the embracing couple to join his mother at the table.

Zia could see a flood of emotions wash across Artair's face, but he remained stoic, and she wished—

oh how she wished—that just for a moment he would shout out his love for her as she had for him. But that was not his way; only when it was right for him would he admit his love.

"Come," she said, tugging his arm. "There's honey bread with extra honey. Cook made it special for me and I shall share it with you."

He smiled and caught hold of her hand. "How lucky am I."

"I'd say luckier than you know," Lachlan called out.

"I agree," Artair said, smiling at Zia.

They joined Addie and Lachlan at the table, and soon Cavan and Honora joined them, everyone pleased that Honora was feeling better.

"I'm going to spend the morning stitching. I have several garments I wish to have ready for the babe," Honora said with a gentle smile at Zia.

Cavan kissed his wife's cheek. "I will keep you company if you like."

Honora laughed. "Don't be silly. You have work to do."

"I will look after her," Addie assured.

"And I would love to see the garments you stitch for the babe," Zia said, letting her know she would check on her.

"Could it be that you're ready to start stitching your own baby's garments?" Lachlan asked with a laugh.

"Could it be that you're jealous?" Zia asked. "Wanting a wife, but having none?"

Everyone laughed and joined in teasing Lachlan.

"Enough," he finally said, holding his hands up in surrender. "I will find a wife when I'm ready for one."

"You'll never be ready," Artair teased. "Cavan should find one for you."

"Do not even suggest that," Lachlan said.

"I have had inquiries," Cavan said.

"Not ready," Lachlan said, shaking his head.

Cavan grinned. "A couple look promising."

Lachlan kept shaking his head. "Don't tempt me."

"I think I should have a look at them," Honora said in a serious tone.

"No!" Lachlan yelled. "She'll have me wed before I have a chance to protest."

Honora laughed. "Perhaps, but I would find you a wife who would suit you."

Lachlan sighed with relief. "Then when the time comes, I will seek your help."

Zia wanted to linger and enjoy this time with her newfound family, but she had much to do.

She stood. "I must go. I wish to see James before I start the day."

"I'll go with you. I'd like to visit with him," Artair said.

"Later," Cavan said. "I need to talk with you."

Zia planted a gentle kiss on Artair's cheek. She knew a command from a laird when she heard one, and she wondered over it as she took her leave.

Cavan, Artair, and Lachlan retreated to the solar.

"Is something wrong?" Artair asked as soon as the door was closed.

"Lachlan has heard news about the village Black," Cavan said, and nodded to Lachlan.

"It seems that the village Black harbors barbarians," Lachlan said.

Artair nodded. "I know. I watched as Zia and her grandmother worked to help heal one while I was there."

"And you didn't protest?" Lachlan accused.

"I made my objection known, but it's their village, their rules. I was a guest, and one who sought answers about his brother. If I made demands, where would it have gotten me?"

"Artair is right," Cavan said. "We cannot stop them from sheltering or healing barbarians, but it does raise a question that has yet to be answered."

Artair nodded. "Who brought Ronan to the village Black."

"You never found the answer?" Lachlan asked anxiously.

"A friend, was all that I was told, though I got the impression that they knew the person well."

"I think it's time to speak with Zia about the barbarians in her village, and about Ronan," Cavan said. "You agree?" he asked Artair.

"I find Zia to be an honest woman, and anything she knows, I am certain she will share with us."

"Then see when your wife has free time today to talk with us," Cavan said, though it was more an order.

Artair nodded and left the solar in search of Zia. He had planned to discuss Ronan with her, but at the moment was more interested in her unexpected and outspoken declaration of love that morning. It shocked him, and while he certainly felt the same, he felt unsure about what to do.

He wanted nothing more than to steal her away in order to discuss her outburst with her, to see if it had been real or if she simply wanted to add credence to their ruse of being married.

Now, however, he had this added problem his brother wanted addressed immediately, and he couldn't blame Cavan. He had never truly known how Ronan managed to get to the village Black, and it seemed odd that he should just disappear. The healers there—especially Bethane—knew what was going on at all times. He had a feeling there was more to his brother's arrival and departure than he'd been told.

Artair walked without focus, his mind much too jumbled to pay attention.

"What's wrong?"

Artair jumped at the sudden forceful query and was relieved to see Zia a few feet in front of him, hands on her hips, hair falling in sparse curls around her face.

Damn, but she was beautiful.

"Answer me," she said, having walked up to him to poke him in the chest.

"Is that the way you greet your husband?"

"When he looks upset it is. Now what's wrong?"

"When you have time, Cavan wishes to speak with you."

"About?" she asked.

"Ronan and barbarians at the village Black."

"Ronan, I will discuss with him. Who I heal at my village is none of his business. He is not my laird."

Artair nodded. "Actually, you being my wife makes him your laird."

Zia spoke low so no one would hear. "I'm not your wife and even if I was, the village Black is none of his concern."

Artair could see that this wasn't going to be easy, yet the matter had to be addressed. He had let it go far too long without forcing a discussion. Not that he believed she was hiding any great revelations from him; he didn't. In time he would get his answers, and in the meantime he changed the subject.

"Do you really love me?"

Her eyes rounded in shock.

"You claimed to love me this morning. Did you speak the truth?" he asked and felt his breath catch while he waited for her to answer.

She began to walk toward her cottage, toying with the shawl's knot as she did.

He kept pace beside her, then followed her inside, closing the door behind him and waited as she added another log to the fire and lit several candles around the room. He had hoped for an immediate answer but could understand her reluctance, for he felt it himself.

She turned suddenly to face him. "I will tell you the truth, but I do not want you to feel obligated to reciprocate. I know you think differently than I do and—"

"Tell me," he demanded, more sharply than he'd intended.

"Yes, I love you," she snapped, "though I would have much preferred to admit it with a less biting tongue."

He smiled and went to approach her, but she raised her hand.

"Don't," she warned softly. "Let me say what I must."

He nodded and remained where he was, though he wanted to scoop her up in his arms and shout out his love for her.

"Strangely enough, it was your mother who made me realize your true nature, and I admit you have more passion than I'd thought."

He grinned. "You must known that by now."

She laughed softly as he took quick steps over to her and wrapped her in his arms.

She pressed her finger to his lips. "Don't say a word, not now. Just show me."

Chapter 25

Afew hours later, alone in her cottage, she still continued to recall their fast though passionate joining. Artair had scooped her up into his arms and braced her against the closed door, insisting he would not see them disturbed, and she had agreed. All could wait for at that moment she had wanted nothing more than to feel the strength of her husband inside her.

She had to shake her head to remind her that Artair wasn't her husband, but it felt so right to think of him as such and it felt so right when they made love. He had hoisted up her skirt and drove into her with a gentle force she welcomed. She had been ready for him and he had slipped into her . . .

Zia shivered with the memory of their joining.

"Are you all right?" Neddie asked, entering the cottage.

Zia cleared her head with another shake and returned to the matters at hand. Neddie had been spending time with her, wishing to learn the art of healing. She had always been interested in it, and after the battle realized that such knowledge could greatly benefit her own village.

"You work too hard," Neddie insisted.

"A healer always does," Zia chuckled. "But it's my husband who occupies my mind."

Neddie smiled. "He's a handsome one; I don't blame you."

"He's a good husband and a great lover," Zia admitted with pride.

"Then you are a lucky woman," Neddie said. "I was blessed with a plain husband and a passionate lover, even after all these years of marriage."

The two women continued to chat as Zia taught Neddie how to prepare healing potions for various ailments. It was well past the noon meal when Zia wandered into the keep, her stomach growling and she eager to appease it.

As soon as she spied Cavan standing by the table, she knew he was waiting for her. Artair stood as she approached, held his hand out to her and assisted her in sitting beside him. She was relieved that she would at least have time to eat before the inquisition.

"Do you both wait for me?" she asked, taking bread and meat from the platter in the center of the table.

"Yes, we do," Cavan said directly.

"Can we talk while I eat?" she asked, looking around the empty hall. "No one is about to hear our conversation."

Cavan nodded and sat opposite from them at the table.

"First," Zia said, before Cavan could say anything. "The village Black is a healing village, which means we heal the ill, the injured, the suffering. We do not care whether friend or foe, a person in need of healing receives it at our village, just as your brother did."

Cavan nodded. "Fair enough, though I believe you should be more conscious of who you choose to heal."

"If that were the case, we might not have chosen to heal your brother."

"Why not? Ronan is a good, loyal Scotsman."

"Brought to our doorstep by a barbarian," Zia said, knowing the news would shock them both, but realizing it was time for them to know what she could safely divulge without causing problems for others. They needed to understand that not all those they believed to be their enemies were their enemy.

"What do you mean?" Cavan demanded.

"Just what I said," she confirmed. "A barbarian brought your brother to the village."

"Are you familiar with this barbarian?" Artair asked.

Zia nodded, finishing the bread she'd been chewing, then reaching for the tankard of mulled cider.

"He's been to your village before?" Cavan asked.

She nodded again, knowing she could divulge only so much about the person; after all, she had given her word.

"Why has this barbarian been to your village before?" Cavan asked.

"That's obvious," Zia said. "We are a healing village. He brings to us those in need of healing."

"Barbarians kill without regard to anyone not even their own kind. They do not concern themselves with healing," Cavan said. "Are you sure he is a barbarian?"

"I asked the same myself," Zia admitted.

"And did you get an answer?" Artair asked.

"No, I never did."

"Perhaps he wasn't a barbarian at all but someone who had once been captured by the barbarians," Cavan said, as if trying to make sense of it.

"No, he was born a barbarian, of that there is no doubt," she assured him.

"How would you know?" Artair asked.

Zia recalled first meeting the barbarian. "There was no mistaking it. The strength, the courage, but most of all the fearlessness in the eyes; this person would let nothing stand in his way."

"What did he say when he brought Ronan to you?" Cavan asked.

Zia looked from one brother to the other. "Heal him; he is a great warrior."

The two brothers grew silent, and Zia could see that they fought to contain their emotions. She wished she could ease their pain, for she felt it herself.

"I need to go now," she said, and stood.

"One more question," Cavan said.

She waited.

"Did this barbarian have something to do with my brother's sudden departure?"

Her response was simple and yet so much more complicated. "No."

"You are sure?" Cavan demanded.

"I am sure," Zia said firmly. "Now may I go?"

Cavan stared at her. "There is something you do not tell me."

"Have you ever given your word to someone?" she asked.

Cavan nodded. "Many times."

"And you have kept your word," she said, not for a minute doubting he had.

"Of course. A man's word is his honor."

"Though I am a woman, I feel the same. When I give my word, I keep it," she said, standing tall, her chin high.

"You gave your word to a barbarian and you wish me to honor it?" Cavan asked incredulously.

"It is my *honor* I wish you to respect."

Cavan looked from Zia to Artair, then stood.

"Talk to your wife," Cavan ordered and walked away.

"I have work to see to," Zia said, and turned to leave.

Artair stopped her, taking hold of her arm. "We need to discuss this. While I will always defend you, I cannot defend your keeping information from us about Ronan."

"I keep none that is of consequence."

"That is for us to judge."

Zia slipped her arm from his grasp, his warm imprint still tingling her flesh. "I would do nothing to jeopardize your brother's safety or delay you from finding him. I have confided everything I know that would help you in your search."

"But one thing—the barbarian's identity," Artair said.

She didn't like hearing the disappointment in his voice. She liked even less that he challenged her on it. "You don't trust that what I tell you is true?"

He looked startled. "It is you who does not trust me. Cavan tells me to speak with you for he believes that a good wife would keep nothing from her husband. He has given you a chance to confide in me, and if I deem the information useful, I can share it with him. If not, he knows that it is not significant, and the news remains between you and me."

"I am not your wife," she said sadly, not wishing to hurt him.

"You are in all ways but one," he said. "Exchange vows with me and be done with it."

"I will not wed a man whose proposal holds no passion." She turned and hurried from the keep, not stopping until she was past the village, at the moor. She stopped to look out over the expanse of empty land, and realized that was how she felt at this moment—empty.

If he had uttered one word of love to her, she might

have considered his proposal. After all, she did love the sensible fool. But he'd made no mention of it, and that hurt her heart. She had blurted out her love for him, and in front of his mother. It needed saying or she would have exploded with the joy of it. She needed to say it, hear it spill from her lips.

Of course, she could have waited until they were alone. But no! She wasn't afraid of someone hearing her declare her love for Artair. Why should she? Love should be shouted from the highest hill and echoed through the valleys and over the dales. Love should not be confined or tucked away to bring out at the appropriate time.

"Love is magical," she chuckled. She probably would be accused of casting love spells if anyone heard her. But wasn't it she under Artair's spell, and hadn't that been true from the start?

She had felt the magic between them from the very first moment their eyes met. They couldn't have fought it if they had tried, and she hadn't wanted to. She had wanted to see where it would take her.

She had fallen so easily under the Highlander's spell and she didn't care, because she knew she wove her own spell, like so many women before her. This rift between them could not be allowed to grow. They would have to discuss it, but not now, perhaps later, when they both had time to think and reason. She laughed. Artair reasoned all the time, perhaps she should learn something from him and apply reason to this matter and see what happened.

She would have loved to walk the moor, but had work to do and had to be sensible. She laughed again as she turned and walked to her cottage shaking her head.

Artair's naked chest glistened with sweat, his hands ached, and still he swung his sword, taking down his third opponent.

"Who's next?" he asked, challenging the warriors who stood in a circle around him.

"None are foolish enough to practice with a crazed man," Lachlan called out, and entered the circle to throw him his shirt.

Artair flung the shirt over his shoulder and watched the warriors disperse. "You chase them away."

Lachlan laughed. "It is you who frighten them off. You're like a madman with your sword today, which can only mean that you fought with your wife, and why only the single warriors were fool enough not to recognize the signs and agreed to practice with you."

"Shut up," Artair said and walked over to the water bucket and drank from the dipper.

"I knew I was right," Lachlan said with glee.

Artair dumped a full ladle over his head, feeling a sense of relief as the cool water trickled down his face and onto his chest.

"Good idea. Cool your anger," Lachlan said, braced against a thick tree trunk with his arms crossed. "So what did you do to incur your wife's wrath?"

"You're asking for it, Lachlan," Artair warned, brandishing the ladle like a weapon.

His brother held up his hands. "Don't take it out on me. I'm only trying to help."

"How? By aggravating me even more?"

"No, by pointing out that you're allowing your anger to get the better of you, when you usually handle problems with calm sensibility."

"How can you be sensible with a woman who refuses to listen to reason?" Artair asked, running his fingers through his wet hair.

Lachlan looked ready to laugh.

"Don't dare!" Artair warned, swinging the ladle at him.

Lachlan wisely hid his chuckle.

Artair dropped the dipper in the bucket and shook his head. "I don't know how to make her see reason."

"Zia doesn't strike me as a reasonable woman."

"No kidding," Artair said.

"But you sure can see the passion in her."

Artair shot daggers at him with his eyes.

Lachlan grabbed his chest. "Damn, but if you could kill with looks, would I be dead."

"Watch it," Artair cautioned.

"I'm trying to help, if you'd just hear me out."

"By telling me my wife is passionate?"

"Yes! Zia is passionate about life. You can see it in everything she does. In her work, when she talks, when she laughs—"

Artair grinned though barely. "Her laughter is unbelievably sensual."

"Damn right."

Artair shot him another murderous look.

Lachlan threw his hands up. "Sorry, but you need to really know Zia to deal with her."

"I do know her. She's obstinate, insistent, inflexible—"

Lachlan interrupted. "You're repeating your—"

Artair's icy glare shut him up. "How? How do you deal with a pigheaded woman?"

"You're asking the wrong question."

"Really, almighty know-it-all of women?"

Lachlan bowed. "At your service."

"Tell me what question I should be asking?"

Lachlan obliged. "How do you deal with a passionate woman?"

"And pray tell, how do *you* deal with a passionate woman?"

"Brother, brother, brother," Lachlan said shaking his head and slapping Artair on the back. "Need I detail it?"

Artair curled his hand into a tight fist. "So help me, Lachlan . . . "

Lachlan leaned in close and whispered as if the answer was a secret. "You deal with her passionately."

Chapter 26

Zia thought over the situation and no matter how hard she tried she couldn't find anyway to be practical. It just wasn't in her to do it. She was who she was and Artair had to accept her that way or a marriage could never work between them. She loved who she was and she had worked hard to be who she was in spite of obstacles along the way.

Besides, she couldn't live without the zest that claimed her every day. Sunrise always brought with it a joy, a thrill that she embraced and gave thanks for. Her grandmother had taught her that each new morn was a gift to be unwrapped and cherished. She had never forgotten that, and each day she unwrapped her gift, she appreciated it more and more.

Her grandmother would also tell her that she was being stubborn, that if she wished Artair to accept her for who she was, then why not accept him for who he was? But in a way, wasn't she? After all, she loved him and did not plan to simply walk away because at times he could be a practical fool. She knew that about him and loved him anyway. Just as she knew he loved her, but could he truly accept who she was? She had easily voiced her love for him, and he had yet to voice his. She wondered how he would choose to do so. Or did she doubt that he would?

She chuckled at the question. He loved her—of that she had no doubt—and when the time was right for him, he would seize the moment and claim his love.

Would it be enough?

Her own query startled her.

Why wouldn't it be enough? Was it because he would see the rational side of their union, while she was looking for him to see . . . what? The miracle of it all? He had rescued her from a burning stake, and though he had done it for his own reasons, he had never stopped protecting her from the moment he freed her. He took hold of her and never let go.

To her, he had proven a hero beyond measure and a man she could easily love.

Night was falling and the air grew cold. A storm was brewing off the coast, the waves more vicious than usual, and a constant mist blew in off the sea. She was glad for the warmth of her wool cloak on her walk to the keep. She wasn't looking forward to the evening meal, would much prefer to isolate herself this evening, to tuck herself away from questions and demands and worries of her own. Or better still a birth that would occupy her mind leaving no time to think.

She stopped and stared up at the sky, which had darkened, the mist kissing her face. "Send me a joyful birth so I may have peace this night."

Her wish was granted as she reached the keep stairs, an urgent plea from a young lad to help his mother, who was writhing in pain.

She was familiar with Jonas, barely six, and his mother Dora, who was expecting her fourth child. No amount of reassurance helped the worried lad, and after stopping at her cottage for her healing basket, Zia hurried with the lad to his home.

Dora was doing fine, each of her babes having been delivered without a problem. Zia was more concerned for her young son, who felt sure his mother was dying.

"Your mum is doing fine, Jonas. There is nothing to worry about. But I need a favor from you now that I am here to take care of her."

His little body relaxed in a sigh at Zia's firm reassurance.

"Will you please go find Artair and tell him that I am tending your mother and will not be home until the babe is delivered?"

Jonas nodded and took off.

Zia rolled her sleeves up and prepared for the birth, thanking the heavens for their intervention.

Artair had been lost in his thoughts ever since talking with Lachlan. He should have realized himself that the only way to deal with Zia was through her passionate nature. She would not see reason the way he did, though that did not mean she didn't see it.

He'd never known Zia not to be truthful with him, and the way she had blurted out her love for him should have made him realize that if there was anything she needed to share, she would have never been able to keep it to herself. She would have spilled it out in a zestful flurry.

She was an honorable woman, and he very much admired her for that and felt pride that she would be his wife. How to get her to agree was another matter. He hadn't even told her he loved her yet, and he was certain she would never agree to wed him until he declared his love.

He planned on talking with her tonight, in their bedchamber. He intended to have their meal sent there so they could be alone and somehow work out the problems that plagued them.

"You have a good plan?" Lachlan asked, joining him at the table before the hearth in the great hall.

"I'm going to talk with her alone in our bedchamber."

"You call that a plan?" Lachlan shook his head. "Beg her forgiveness, you fool. Better yet, tell her that you love her so much that love has made a complete fool of you."

"It certainly has," Artair admitted. "I've never felt like such an idiot."

Lachlan grinned and was about to comment when Artair shoved a finger in his face. "I warn you, not a word."

Lachlan's chuckle rumbled in his chest.

Artair shook his head. "I will settle this tonight."

"There's a good start," Lachlan said. "You're finally being unreasonable."

Before Artair could argue, the young lad Jonas raced into the hall and straight to their table addressing Artair.

"Sir, the healer says she will not return until the new babe is delivered."

"Jonas, you look out of breath and chilled," Lachlan said. "Sit and have hot cider and a sweet cake."

The lad's eyes brightened and he climbed over the bench beside Lachlan.

Artair stood. "I'm going to see if Zia needs anything."

"She only needs one thing," Lachlan said softly, placing another sweet cake in front of the lad.

"What's that?" Artair asked.

"You!"

The birth took longer than Zia had expected, but the delivery went smoothly, without any problem, and mother and daughter were doing fine.

She settled them both, Jonas having fallen asleep hours ago, though he'd tried to remain awake. She promised to look in on them tomorrow. It was well after midnight, the village silent as she left the cottage. The mist had grown heavier, the wind more biting, and she wrapped her cloak more closely around her.

"You need this."

Zia jumped and swung around. "You near scared me to death."

Artair swung a fur-lined cloak around her. "You should have expected me."

"Why?" she asked, hugging the cloak closed, grateful for its warmth.

Artair curled his arm around her shoulder and started them walking toward the keep. "Because I've always been there for you when you've finished late and are alone."

Zia thought about it. "You're right." She rested her head to his shoulder snuggling her face past the cloak he wore to rest her cheek to his shirt and take in the familiar scent of him; fresh pine, burning hearth logs and pure male. It made her feel safe, secure and loved.

She tilted her head up and smiled. "I love you." She didn't know what made her say it at that very moment; she only knew she wanted to. It felt right and good.

He hugged her tighter, and when they reached the keep, swung her up in his arms and carried her to their bedchamber. Not a soul was about, not a sound stirred. It was just the two of them and when he shut the door she felt complete solitude surround them.

She sighed when she saw that a bath waited for her, steam rising from the water, and quickly shed her clothes, as did he. He stepped into the tub first and held a hand out to her. Zia waited a moment, for she wanted to drink in the sight of him, his body so strong and fine, and all hers.

He settled them down together; she resting on top of him, her head nestled on his shoulder and tucked in the crook of his neck, their legs entwined and their arms around each other. She was more comfortable than she had been in a long time.

"Thank you," she whispered.

"Whatever for? This is pure pleasure for me. I should be thanking you."

She wondered if he knew that his words hinted at his love for her and paved the pathway to her heart.

"Zia—"

"Please, no discussions, no questions. I just want to enjoy this quiet time with you, just you and me, nothing else."

She was grateful he obliged. But why stop him? Did she fear hearing him admit his love? For when he did, decisions would need to be made. Was she ready for them?

All troubled thoughts quickly vanished when he took the soap and ran it over her body, slipping and sliding over every curve, valley, mound, and down the length of her. His strokes were lazy soft caresses that covered every inch of her.

She sighed, though it sounded more like a moan, and when his touch turned intimate—firing her body, her very soul—she reciprocated until they came together, she sitting on top of him, her legs around his waist as he glided into her.

The cramped space left little room for movement, but his firm hands grasped her waist and set them in motion. It didn't take long, though they were far from done, for he dried them both with hurried hands and had them on the bed in no time, where he proceeded to kiss her entire body.

They were tender kisses that drove her wild and soon had her begging for much more, and he obliged time and time again until they both could stand it no more and he took her in his arms and entered her for one last ride that left them both utterly breathless.

Sleep claimed Artair fast enough, and she was glad, for the night had been perfect and she didn't want it spoiled by talk that would irritate either of them. Her eyes fluttered closed and she smiled. It had been a good night—no, a magical night—and tomorrow was a new day, a new beginning, and she would greet it with joy and deal with whatever it brought her.

Zia dressed, not surprised that she was alone. She hadn't felt Artair stir beside her and he probably chose not to disturb her feeling she needed sleep. He was considerate that way, but then, Artair was always thoughtful when it came to her. He put her feelings and needs before his.

Her grandmother was right. He was a good man. So how did she keep her word to someone and not hurt her husband in the process?

Husband?

She kept making that mistake, thinking of him as her husband. But wasn't she feeling that way? More and more she thought of Artair as her husband. More and more she referred to him as so.

She smiled. "This all will be settled soon enough. I'm sure of it."

And she was. She knew that she and Artair would settle it agreeably, and it would be done. After all, he was reasonable and she was trying to be.

She was smiling broadly when she hurried down the stairs into the great hall. All the Sinclares were at the table before the large hearth, where they usually sat, and a few tables were occupied by warriors deep in conversation and the morning meal.

She weaved her way around the tables greeting the warriors, having gotten to know most of them when suddenly she heard her name shouted and she stopped dead when she saw that it was Artair.

Her mouth dropped open and her eyes rounded wide when she saw him standing in the middle, on top of the table where his family sat.

"I love you, Zia!"

She was too shocked to respond but everyone in the hall did with claps and cheerful shouts, a few stamping their feet.

"I love you with all my heart!" Artair shouted, grinning, and placed his hands over his heart.

She continued to stare, dumbfounded, and when it quieted and everyone stared at her, waiting, including Artair, who remained standing on the table like a centerpiece—she did the only thing she could.

She ran as quick as could be out of the hall.

Chapter 27

Zia ran past villagers who called out greetings to her, though she was in too much of a hurry to reciprocate. She kept her frantic pace, it taking her on the moor with a stitch in her side that finally forced her to stop running.

She leaned over, splaying her hands on her thighs and taking in laboring breaths while her rampantly beating heart felt ready to explode. But was it from exertion or did her heart pound because of Artair's most impractical declaration of love in front of everyone?

"Stand up straight and don't fight your breaths."

Zia stood and turned though paid no attention to the warning of fighting her breathing, which only made it worse. But Artair had followed her and now stood staring at her. Expecting what?

"I didn't expect you to run, but after the initial shock I realized why you did," he said. He yanked his fur-lined cloak off and handed it to her.

She took it, realizing she was shivering, and wrapped it around her. "Why did I?"

An easygoing smile surfaced across his face. "Your honesty is one of the things I love about you."

"Do you love that I ran from you when you declared that you loved me?"

His smile turned to a chuckle. "I could be insulted, but I'm not."

"Why? It wasn't very nice of me. I should have flung myself in your arms, especially since you didn't care if you made a complete fool of yourself in front of everyone." She giggled at the memory.

"Someone reminded me that love makes fools of us all, so I decided to let love have its way with me."

"Why, then, did I run?" she asked with a confused shake of her head.

"Because you're afraid."

"Of what?"

"Of us being in love," he said.

"But that's a wonderful thing."

"Yes," he agreed nodding and approached her slowly. "But it also means that now you can marry me for we marry for love."

She gasped and jumped back. "That's it. As soon as you declared your love I knew my fate was sealed."

"You make it sound like a death sentence," he chortled.

"No, no," she hastened to explain. "I have thought often of how right it feels calling you my husband."

"That is good," he said with a pleased grin. "For it feels right calling you wife."

"I only wish to know that you can accept me for who I am, what I do, and the passion with which I live."

Artair reached out again and gently guided her into his arms. "That woman you describe is the woman I love, and I wouldn't have her any other way."

She brushed her lips over his. "It is you who are the witch, for you cast a spell over me from when we first met."

"Damn, I was hoping you didn't notice, but since you did—I intend to keep you under my spell forever and always."

Zia poked him in the chest playfully. "You might have to refresh that spell every now and again."

He kissed her softly, though lusciously. "I do, every time we make love."

She sighed. "That you do. I have never known such magic."

"We make magic together and always will," he said, and kissed her quick. "We will marry immediately."

"No!"

Artair shook his head. "Why not?"

"I want my grandmother to be here when we exchange our vows."

He nodded with a smile. "You're right. Bethane should be here to share in the celebration."

"Your family will not think it odd that we wish to wed again?"

"I will explain that we wish to refresh our vows in front of both our families. They will be pleased and ready to celebrate."

Zia cuddled in the warmth of his arms, pleased that

this was settled and she would wed for love, as she'd always wanted to. "This is good; I am happy."

He hugged her tightly. "I will try to always make you happy."

She ran a tender finger over his lips. "You don't have to try. I am happy just seeing your face when I wake in the morning, or when you wait for me to finish my work, or when you argue with me over a point which we both know I'm right about." She laughed joyously then sighed. "You are happiness to me."

"Damn, but I love you, Zia."

"And that makes me the happiest of all, hearing you say you love me. I will never grow tired of hearing it."

"Good, for I will never grow tired of telling you."

"We are made for each other. A perfect fit."

They kissed on the windy moor, impervious to the chill and the fine mist that began to fall. They were in love, and lost in that love. Nothing else mattered, nothing would.

Artair stopped with Zia at James's cottage. He was doing better, not a complaint from him. The only thing he talked about was Mave's impending arrival. He had received a message from her expressing her concern and letting him know she would take good care of him.

Zia examined his wound, which was healing much better than she'd expected. "You are moving it like I told you?"

"I better," James said quietly. "If I don't, Addie's in here making me work it even harder, and Neddie's been stopping by as well, not to mention all the other women who remind me while dropping off food. Everyone is surprised I still have the arm or that I'm still alive. I think most thought I'd never make it." He shook his head. "For a while there I didn't think I would either."

"Nonsense," Zia scolded gently. "You're a strong, determined man and you fought to live." She walked over to the fireplace to prepare a brew for him.

Artair leaned over James. "I'd say Mave had something to do with you wanting to live."

James grinned. "She's been in my thoughts since we left the village Black, though I've been wondering . . . "

"Speak your piece," Artair urged, sensing the man's reluctance.

"What if I wanted to return to the village Black with Mave?"

"I would wish you both a long and happy life together."

James sighed with relief. "Thank you, Artair, though know I would serve you if ever you should ask."

"I had no doubt of it."

Artair took Zia's hand when they left the cottage.

"I heard," she said. "It was good of you to release him to live elsewhere."

"Actually, it is up to Cavan, but I know he would do the same, which is why James asked me first."

"Your brother is a good and fair laird."

"Yes he is," Artair agreed.

"Has he asked if you've spoken with me?"

"Not yet. He waits, for he knows I will have an answer for him."

"You expect me to change my mind?" she asked.

He tapped her head. "I expect that I understand my wife and trust her word."

Zia threw her arms around him and kissed him soundly.

"Be careful," he whispered in her ear, "or I will carry you into your healing cottage and brace the door so no one can enter until I have had my way with you."

"Promise?" she begged breathlessly.

Artair shook his head as he pointed at her cottage. Five people were already waiting outside her door.

"Later," she whispered, before rushing her lips across his and hurrying off to tend the ailing.

Artair entered the keep with a sense of relief and joy, hoping to find his mother and tell her all about Zia and his plans. He was certain she would be thrilled and get busy immediately with the preparations, which in turn he hoped would alleviate her sadness, if only for a while. He knew his mother felt lost at times without her husband, and while she kept her spirits up in front of everyone, suffered when alone. He worried about her, but then so did his brothers. If only Ronan would return, that would surely make all the difference to her.

"You're wanted in the solar," his mother said as soon as he entered the great hall.

Artair could tell by her serious expression that something was wrong, and he hurried into the solar, to find Cavan and Lachlan waiting for him.

Cavan held up a paper with an official seal. "The church council will arrive in a few days to speak with Zia in regard to claims of her being a witch."

Artair felt as though an arrow had struck his heart. He grabbed hold of the top of a chair and took a breath. "Who do they send?"

"Bishop Edmond Aleatus," Cavan said.

"He leads the witch hunt in this region," Lachlan said. "Many say he is a fair man."

"Fair to whom?" Artair asked.

"Bishop Aleatus knew Father and respected him," Cavan said. "Once the bishop realizes it is the Sinclare family he deals with, I am sure there will be no problem."

Artair nearly swore aloud. He knew this farce of a marriage would return to haunt him. He should have forced Zia to wed him from the start.

"Have your marriage papers ready to present to the bishop," Cavan said to him.

"The villagers will be a help since they speak highly of Zia," Lachlan said.

Artair listened to them talk, though he barely heard their words. He could arrange for Zia and he to exchange vows secretly, but what of the documents? The date would need to be forged, the cleric bribed, but if he learned or knew of the claims of witchcraft against Zia he would never agree. He would report the matter immediately to the church.

"Though her remarkable healing talent could work against her," Cavan said. "For instance, James's recovery. None expected him to survive. Many claim it a miracle."

Lachlan shook his head. "That's all the bishop needs to hear."

"Artair and Zia being wed will probably do her the most good. The Sinclare name is a respected and honorable one. I doubt there are many who would go against it," Cavan said. "And with the bishop having known father, I believe all will work out well."

"I don't think Artair is feeling the same way," Lachlan said, looking at his brother.

"Don't worry, Artair, all will be fine," Cavan reassured.

Artair shook his head. How could he have ever been so stupid to get not only Zia but his family into such a serious situation? Reason had warned him to wed Zia, and yet he'd allowed her to have her way. And now look at the dangerous mess they were all in.

"It can't be that bad," Cavan said once again, trying to reassure him.

In fact, his brother's confidence and support made him feel worse. He had always been the sensible one, the one to do the right thing. No one ever had to clean up after him. He had made sure of it.

"Cavan's right," Lachlan said. "It can't be that bad, and besides, we're in this together. We won't let you down."

That made him feel even worse, for he had certainly

let them down and all because he had allowed a woman to enchant him. He shook his head. He was even making it seem that Zia was a witch and that this was all her fault and it wasn't. He had created this mess, and he would need to find a way out of it. But first he needed to be honest with his brothers.

"Have your say, Artair, and we will work this out together," Cavan said with the confidence of a powerful laird.

Artair spit it out before he changed his mind. "Zia and I are not married."

Chapter 28

Zia received an urgent summons to the keep. She finished tending a minor burn on a child's arm and quickly glanced over the three people who waited to see her, dispensing salves and a potion and advising the last one to return to his cottage and she would come see him as soon as she could. Feeling better that there were no serious ailments, she hurried to the keep.

A knot tightened in her stomach with each step she took and caused her to grow apprehensive. Something was wrong; she could feel it.

Patience.

Her grandmother's strong voice resonated in her head and she halted her rushed steps. Bethane sensed something as well, which meant she needed to keep her mind clear and remain alert. Her grandmother would help guide her; she wasn't alone.

And she had Artair, but most importantly she had his love.

She entered the keep just as a clap of thunder sounded and the ominous warning caused her to shiver. A servant directed her to the solar and when she entered she knew without anyone saying a word that their marriage ruse was known.

They were all there, brothers, their mother, and Honora, and they looked alarmed.

She walked straight to the middle of the room and looked to Artair. "I sense that it was somehow necessary that you tell them the truth."

He nodded. "The church council sends a bishop to investigate."

"We need to get you two wed immediately," Cavan said, standing beside the chair where his wife sat.

Zia noticed that Honora seemed more pale than usual, and restless, shifting as if uncomfortable in her seat. She should have been more concerned with her own predicament, but it was Honora who worried her.

"Cavan has sent for a cleric," Addie said.

Zia didn't like seeing their worried expressions. Addie's few brow wrinkles seemed more pronounced from her worried thoughts and Cavan wore a continuous frown, while the usual joyful Lachlan had not made one joke of the situation. That they were all worried was obvious, and Zia didn't like being the reason for their distress.

"You and Artair will wed as soon as the cleric arrives," Cavan said, though it sounded more like a proclamation.

"What of the date?" Zia asked. "The clerics are most precise about a document they affix a seal to."

"The cleric we have sent for is faithful to the Sinclares," Addie said. "He will record whatever date we request." She smiled sadly, though with pride. "My husband saved his life when he was young and he feels indebted to the Sinclare clan."

Zia listened while keeping an eye on Honora. Something was definitely wrong and she didn't like what she was sensing.

"You'll need to temper your enthusiasm while the bishop is here. It would be better if you appeared pious," Cavan said.

Zia would normally have argued. The thought of her remaining pious was simply ridiculous. But it wasn't she who presently mattered. She had brought her problems down upon the Sinclare family, and she would do whatever was necessary to protect them, as they attempted to do the same for her.

"I apologize for the trouble this has brought to your clan," she said to Cavan.

"Your apology is not necessary, Zia," Cavan assured her. "Artair explained everything. Now it is just a matter of doing what should have been done."

She simply nodded, and actually felt a pang of guilt. If she hadn't been so stubborn and had listened to Artair, all of this could have been avoided. And Artair probably confided the truth to his family, telling them how he had wanted to wed and she had refused, making her feel guiltier.

Artair joined her, slipping his arm around her waist and gently drawing her to his side. He leaned close, kissing her cheek and whispering, "We will have *our* ceremony, the way you wanted it; you have my word."

She swelled with love for him, but her smile never surfaced. As soon as she saw Honora cringe she was at her side. "What's wrong?"

Cavan hunched down beside his wife and took hold of her hand. "What is it, Honora?"

"Pain," she answered both, while cradling her protruding stomach.

"Has it been steady?" Zia asked, hoping the babe wasn't demanding to be born. It was too early. Another week and the babe would have a better chance to survive.

"No, but I haven't felt right since I woke."

"Why didn't you tell me?" Cavan demanded.

"That doesn't matter," Zia said with a gentle squeeze to his arm.

He got the message. "Zia is right. What matters are you and the babe. You need to rest."

Zia smiled. "Now Cavan is right. Rest is what is best for you at the moment. So let's get you settled in your bed."

Cavan lifted his wife gently and carried her to their bedchambers while everyone tried to follow.

Zia turned to Artair. "Please, keep Cavan busy for a while so that I may examine his wife without interference. Your mother will help me, and she'll bring word when it's all right for Cavan to return."

"Zia is right," Addie said. "He will worry about Honora and she will worry about him and—"

"Say no more," Lachlan said. "Artair and I will keep him entertained until you summon him."

"Will Honora and the babe be all right?" Artair asked.

Zia knew that question was on everyone's mind, and she tried to reassure them. "If the babe can wait at least one week, he will have a better chance, and with rest, Honora should be fit for the delivery."

"This is going to be a *long* week," Lachlan said.

Surprisingly, Honora did well and listened to everything Zia told her. She remained abed, and everyone took turns keeping her occupied, while at other times she preferred to do her stitching, sewing garments for the babe.

Zia spoke with Cavan about his wife every morning and evening, letting him know how well she was doing and keeping him from worrying more than necessary. With only three days until a full week passed Zia was hopeful all would go well.

The cleric would arrive in two days. No word had been heard from the bishop, and Zia sensed that her grandmother was close. She had hoped that when word was sent for Mave to come help James, her grandmother would also come.

Zia desperately missed her and their conversations especially about healing. Such discussions helped her to learn and to solve problems. Artair would listen to her talk about various ailments but he hardly had the knowledge to respond with suggestions, though of late she had to admit he had impressed her. He had actually suggested a treatment that worked though he credited her. He had recalled her using it for some other ailment at one of the villages and thought that it might suffice in the present case as well and it had. So he did truly listen with sincere interest when she spoke with him and that pleased her very much.

Things would be good, all would be well.

Then why did a feeling of foreboding hang over her?

"You're deep in thought," Artair said, sitting on the bed beside her. "And you look much too tired."

Zia laid her head on his shoulder with a sigh. "I am, but it is late and everyone rests well, which means that I can also rest well."

He slipped his arm around her and rested his cheek on the top of her head. "This will all pass soon enough and life will be good for us."

"I just thought the same myself."

"We are of one mind, that is good," he said.

She lifted her head. "Do you worry at all?"

He eased her gently down on the bed and leaned over her. "Know this . . . I would enter hell itself to see you safe. I will never let anyone harm you, and never—ever—would I let anyone take you from me."

Zia had never seen such a vicious scowl on his face. It actually distorted his handsome features and made him appear more feral than human. This was the warrior who resided within him, the one who would fight to the bitter end, and would fight for her.

She smiled softly and spoke from her heart. "I do not want to leave your side."

"You're not going anywhere," he assured her with a lingering kiss.

He needn't do any more, for her body responded instantly. "It has been too long that you have been inside me."

He smiled. "It's only been two days."

"Much too long," she said, ran her fingers up the back of his scalp and drew his mouth to hers. She tasted him with a hungry need, and he responded in kind. Their last joining had been slow and gentle, but this time they both were in no mood to take things slow. Or perhaps they feared that at any moment someone would knock at the door and their precious time together would end.

They were naked and rolling on the bed in no time, their limbs entwined and their lips locked in a heated kiss. Zia rose over him and hurried him inside her, but he allowed her only a few minutes before grabbing hold of her waist and swinging her beneath him so he could take command.

"I love the feel of you," he whispered on a kiss.

She could only moan a response lost in the feel of him as he moved powerfully inside her. They were one and would always be, and the thought made their joining all the more powerful and her climax all the more potent as she cried out her pleasure.

He finished along with her, and wrapped in each other's arms, they fell into a deep sleep, both of them exhausted.

An agonizing scream tore them apart, and in seconds and they were both up and dressed flying down the stairs to Cavan and Honora's bedchamber. They came upon Addie on the way, and Lachlan was already in the hall, wearing only his plaid and looking terrified.

Cavan threw the door open for them, a look of pure fear on his face. "You have to help her." He grabbed hold of Zia and dragged her into the room, over to the bed.

Honora was crying and she reached out for Zia. "The babe. There's something wrong."

Zia took hold of her hand and tried to calm her, but the tension in the room was palpable and not good for Honora.

"I need all but Addie to leave," she said, and placed a gentle hand on Honora's stomach. "We have a babe to deliver."

"I'm not leaving," Cavan said.

Artair went to his side and put a hand on his shoulder. "Yes, you are. You need to let Zia do what she does best."

"He's right," Lachlan agreed. "So please don't make Artair and me drag you out of here."

"That I'd like to see."

Everyone turned to see Honora grinning.

She nodded to her husband. "Go, I promise if I need you or just want you with me, I will send for you."

Cavan bent over her and gave her a kiss. "I love you and I will wait for your summons."

"I am strong. I can do this," she assured him.

He nodded and kissed her again, then leaned next to Zia and whispered, "I don't care if you must use witch-craft; don't let my wife and child die."

Zia was shocked. Did he really believe her a witch or was it his fear talking?

"I will do all I can," she promised, for that was all she truly could do. Sometimes it didn't matter how hard she fought to heal, to save lives, in the end it wasn't her choice.

The men left the room, and Zia got busy along with Addie.

Servants were summoned so that cauldrons of water could be kept hot in the hearth. Artair retrieved the healing basket kept specifically for deliveries, and stacks of towels and fresh cleaned bedding were kept close.

"Tell me what you haven't told me, what I believe you have feared to tell me for some time," Honora said when it was only she, Addie, and Zia in the room.

Zia hesitated and attempted to reassure her.

Honora held up her hand before she could begin. "It's time for the truth."

"Please," Addie said. "Something has been on your mind about the babe. Honora and I have both seen it."

A pain suddenly struck Honora and she yelled out, grabbing Addie's arm.

Zia placed her hand to Honora's stomach and probed for further evidence of what she suspected.

"What is it?" Honora begged once the pain had passed.

"I think you carry more than one babe."

"Twins?" Honora asked with excitement.

Zia nodded. "Twins who may not be in the right position for delivery."

"Will you be able to do anything to help them?" Addie asked.

"I can't say for sure. Only time will tell."

"Don't say anything to Cavan," Honora said. "He is worried enough. Wait until you know something for certain."

"I will discuss it with you, and the decision will be yours," Zia said. "In the meantime, let's be prepared for anything." She turned to Addie. "The bread I asked left to mold, could you please get it?"

Addie nodded and left.

Hours passed, the pains remaining too far apart for the birth to be anytime soon. Still Zia wouldn't leave Honora's side, especially since she had calmed considerably since the first agonizing scream.

With the birth apparently hours away, Honora asked to see Cavan. She didn't want him to worry needlessly, and knew he wouldn't if he saw that she was doing fine.

When Cavan entered the room, Zia left, giving husband and wife some privacy, though both were anxious over her departure. She assured them that she would be in the great hall having breakfast with Artair.

She no sooner sat down beside him than Artair asked, "What did Cavan say to you that upset you?"

She reached for the pitcher of cider, but he brushed her hand away and filled her tankard. She flavored her bowl of porridge with a drizzle of honey before answering. "He didn't upset me. He surprised me."

"Why was that?"

"He told me to use witchcraft if it would help save his wife and child."

Artair was struck silent.

"He spoke out of fear, not reason," she said.

"I never would expect him to say such a thing," Artair admitted.

"Would you use witchcraft if you feared I would die?" she asked, or was he too sensible to believe it even possible?

"I would do whatever was necessary to save you."

"Even believe in witches?" she asked, amazed, for he had made it known that he did not believe in such nonsense.

"I would believe for you," he said, and stole a teasing kiss, not giving her a chance to respond.

She placed her cool hand to his cheek, and the warmth of his flesh sent tingles rushing up her arm. "You really do love me."

"You doubted?" he asked, alarmed.

"No, I'm startled by the depth of your love. It makes it so very real."

"More real than I ever thought possible," he said, and kissed the palm of her hand.

She shivered from the pleasurable tingles that continued to race through her. "You always excite me."

"If only we had time," he whispered.

"I must stay with Honora."

"I know, but know I will be waiting for you," he said, nuzzling her neck.

She giggled. "Believe me, I won't forget."

By mid-afternoon Honora's pains had subsided, and it worried Zia. She feared it would only prove to be a long laborious time for Honora until the babes were finally ready. And of course she worried too that perhaps there might be something wrong with the babes.

Only time would tell, and she had plenty of that . . . or at least she thought she did.

Addie entered the bedchamber, having gone to see how her sons were doing, and returned with a look of concern.

"What is it?" Zia asked, her heart already sensing something was seriously wrong. "Has something happened to Artair?"

"Is Cavan all right?" Honora asked frantically.

Addie looked to Zia. "Bishop Aleatus arrives by nightfall and requests to meet with you immediately."

Chapter 29

Artair and Cavan climbed the stairs to speak with Zia, while Lachlan and several clansmen were sent to escort the bishop's caravan the remainder of the way to the keep.

"We need the cleric's signature and official seal for this to work," Cavan said, shaking his head. "And he's still about two days away."

"One and a half if he didn't stop to rest," Artair said, hoping the man just might think the same, after all the message sent to him spoke of the immediacy of the situation.

"We'll have to find a way—" Cavan stopped, almost bumping into his mother as he turned a curve on the stair.

"Oh dear," Addie said, and laid a hand on his shoulder.

"What's—"

The agonizing scream reverberated down the stairs, causing everyone to say a silent prayer for Honora.

Cavan rushed past his mother, though she remained close on his heels yelling, "Wait! Wait!"

Artair came up behind them and, entering the bedchamber, almost collided with Cavan, who had stopped abruptly. Zia and Honora were laughing.

"What goes on here?" Cavan demanded, going straight to his wife.

"I've come up with the solution to the problem," Honora said proudly. "I intend to scream loud enough for the bishop to realize my dire circumstances, and to force him to see the wisdom in delaying his talk with Zia."

"I was just about to go down another level to see if her scream was loud enough when I bumped into you," Addie said to her son, then turned to Honora. "It was perfect."

"I'd say so, since it scared the hell out of me," Cavan complained, though he smiled at Honora. "Good idea, wife."

"Is it feasible?" Artair asked Zia.

"Women can sometimes take days to birth a babe, often due to complications, which I'm certain any woman asked will confirm," she said.

"But Honora is all right? She'll deliver the babe sooner than a few days, right?" Cavan asked cautiously.

Honora took his hand. "The babes."

"Babes?" Cavan and Artair said in unison.

"Oh my, I didn't mean to tell you just yet," Honora said, though she grinned happily. "I will give you two children."

Cavan looked utterly confused. "But you are so tiny, how could you—" He turned directly to Zia. "She will be all right?"

"So far so good," Zia said with a firm nod.

Cavan seemed satisfied with her answer, but Artair knew better. He knew Zia well enough to realize that she would never make a promise she might not be able to keep. And she was informing him that everything looked fine now, but beyond that, she could not say.

He wanted to talk with Zia alone, not only about Honora's condition, but about the bishop and what she might face. He walked over to her and took her hand.

"I'm going to steal my wife for a while," he said, easing Zia away from the bed. "We'll be right outside in the hall."

"It's good that you stay close, and it's good that you refer to her as your wife," Cavan said with a curt nod that appeared more like a command.

"Nonsense," Honora scolded. "Zia will be locked away in here these next couple of days. Take her to the battlements, Artair, so she can get some fresh air."

Zia smiled and Artair thanked Honora, while Cavan scowled but said nothing. Artair grabbed his brother's cloak from the peg near the door and hurried Zia up the stairs to the battlements.

"It's gorgeous," Zia said and snuggled in Artair's arms after he wrapped the heavy wool cloak around them.

"The stark barrenness of the moors can either shiver the soul or still the heart," he said looking out over the familiar scene that never failed to still his heart. "I'm glad to finally share it with you and glad you feel the same."

"How could I not? It's stunning, and now . . . " She smiled and kissed his lips softly. " . . . it's my home."

Artair returned the kiss with a more passionate one wrapping his arms more tightly around her until her body was firm against his and he could feel the entire length of her.

As he ended the kiss, he whispered, "A home where you will always be safe."

She shook her head slowly. "No, it is in your arms where I will always be safe."

His heart soared along with his love for her, and he spoke from his heart. "I never expected to love the woman whom I would make my wife as much as I love you. I never realized what it meant to love until you showed me."

"You were an apt pupil," she teased.

"And I will continue to be."

She shook her head. "No, we now teach each other."

They kissed again, and Artair realized that if they continued kissing it would certainly lead to them making love, and they needed to talk.

"I wish there were time—"

Zia stopped him. "As do I, but we have urgent matters at hand."

"Tell me the truth about Honora and the babes," he said, and smiled. "Two. How wonderful for my brother and her. That is, if all goes well."

"I have no reason to believe it won't, but the babes can't seem to decide if they're ready to be born or not, and that worries me. But there is nothing I can do at the moment. Only time will tell, and to be honest, it is better I remain with her and not have to concern myself with speaking to the bishop. But what of the marriage documents? He'll want to see them right away, won't he?"

"I can easily delay, explaining that the papers were left at your village and someone is on the way here with them. But we need the cleric here as fast as possible, for he will settle the problem by marrying us and providing the proper documents."

"You haven't said it, yet you know."

"I've told you that I love you," Artair said, confused.

"Not that."

He shrugged. "I don't know what you mean."

"You haven't flaunted the fact that you were right and I was wrong about us getting married right away."

He looked over her lovely face, lingering on her delectable lips, plump from their kisses, her green eyes so vibrant with passion, and her dark red hair fired with blond streaks. They gave the illusion of flames, which matched her fiery nature. He slowly shook his head.

"You weren't wrong."

"What?" Zia asked, startled.

"It would have been wise of us to wed, but it was much wiser that we fell in love and *chose* to wed."

She gasped, then smiled. "You're right. My wish has come true. I wed for love."

"And my practical nature wisely gave way to—"

"Passion!" Zia cried out with joy.

Artair laughed and hugged her tightly. "I love your zest for life."

"What will you do if we have a daughter with such zest?"

Artair shook his head. "I will need to—" He stopped and stared at her wide-eyed. "Are you with child?"

She grinned. "I'm not sure yet, but there is a strong possibility."

He scooped her up and swung her around. "I didn't think I could be any happier than I was, but this is beyond happiness. This is sheer bliss."

After he put her down, she said, "We mustn't tell anyone yet. I'm not certain, and besides, it would not be good for the bishop to hear."

"Agreed, but you will let me know—"

"As soon as I know for sure," she said.

"We will have a good life together, Zia. I promise," he said, knowing he would do anything to keep her safe.

"Zia!"

They turned to see Cavan approach.

"The pains have started again."

Zia nodded, gave Artair's cheek a quick kiss and hurried off.

"I would die to see her safe," Artair said, his glance fixed on where Zia had disappeared through the open door.

"I understand," Cavan said. "I would do the same for Honora."

"Then perhaps we should leave this situation to Lachlan's discretion," Artair joked.

"If only the bishop were a woman."

Both men laughed, but stopped when they heard the horn that heralded the bishop's approach.

"Are you ready?" Cavan asked with a firm hand on his brother's shoulder.

"I will always be ready to defend my wife," Artair said, and both brothers went to greet the man who would decide Zia's fate.

A warrior was waiting in the great hall when Artair and Cavan entered.

"A group from the village Black follows a few hours behind the bishop's caravan," he informed the brothers.

"This could present a problem," Cavan said after sending the warrior to the kitchen for food and drink. "Supposedly, you were married in the village Black. It would be odd if those from the village knew nothing about it."

"Zia had sent word to her grandmother about our ruse. Bethane is an intelligent woman. I would have to believe that she made it known to the village," Artair said. "But I can send Patrick to intercept them and make certain of it, since he knew of the ruse."

Cavan shook his head. "How so many knew and yet kept the secret."

"Bethane is widely respected, especially by those she harbors."

"Do you think she comes as well?"

"I believe so. She would know when Zia needed her," Artair said, somehow knowing himself that Bethane was close.

"Then perhaps she will provide us with more information about Ronan."

Artair smiled. "Bethane is a wise woman. She will learn more about you than you will of her."

"You admire this woman," Cavan said.

"You will too, but first we must deal with the bishop."

Addie entered the hall from the kitchen, directing servants with platters of food and pitchers of drink.

"All will be ready for the bishop's arrival," she said to Cavan.

"Honora?" he asked.

"Is in good hands. Do not worry. Besides, Zia said her grandmother is close and will be here to help with the birth."

The brothers looked at each other, and Artair's grin said *I told you so.*

Addie hurried off to finish with the servants.

"I just realized," Artair said. "We planned on telling the bishop that we sent for the marriage documents left behind, where the ceremony took place."

Cavan shook his head. "The village Black, and with Bethane's arrival—"

"The story is no longer viable. Unless . . . " Artair nodded slowly. "Unless Bethane forgot the papers and realized shortly after beginning their journey and sent someone back for them, which means he should arrive within a day or two, giving us just enough time."

"I suggest as soon as we greet the bishop, you ride out and accompany Bethane's entourage to the keep. As far as we know, the marriage papers are on the way, though we will not discuss them unless asked."

"Agreed," Artair said.

A messenger entered the hall and informed the brothers that the bishop's coach had entered the village.

Cavan and Artair went outside to greet the man who could bring disfavor down on the clan by claiming Zia a witch.

Bishop Edmond Aleatus wore a dour expression as he alighted from the coach, and his sharp green eyes appeared to miss nothing. His regal attire bespoke his station, his handsomely stitched green and gold garments crafted perfectly for his tall slim frame.

Artair watched his brother greet the bishop with the dignity expected, but Cavan also greeted him with the confidence of a mighty warrior. His brother would not bow down to this man, though he would show respect for his position.

"Please let me offer you food and drink and then a place to rest," Cavan said.

"Where is the woman Zia?" the bishop asked, following Cavan into the keep.

"She is detained looking after my wife, who is presently in the middle of a very difficult birth."

The bishop halted in the great hall with a scowl. "I will not be kept from my duty by excuses. You will command this woman to—"

A bloodcurdling scream ripped through the keep, sending icy shivers through Artair. He could only imagine what his brother must be feeling, for it sounded much too authentic not to be real.

The bishop crossed himself and mumbled a prayer. "I shall pray for your wife, and in the meantime enjoy your generous hospitality."

"Go see to your wife, Cavan," Artair said, knowing his brother worried.

"If you will excuse me a moment, Bishop Aleatus," Cavan said. "My brother Artair, Zia's husband, will see to you until I return."

"Yes. That is fine," the bishop said with a dismissive wave to Cavan.

Artair sat with the bishop at the table before the hearth where his family always gathered, and it was here where he would protect his family. Zia was no witch, and he would make certain the bishop understood that.

He thought the man might wait to question him, hungry and thirsty from his travels, but the bishop questioned in between enjoying the abundant offering of foods and drink.

"I was told by those at Lorne that you paid handsomely for Zia's release."

Artair knew an accusation when he heard one, and knew this was one time Zia would be pleased with his sensible nature.

"I had need of her," he replied.

"You gave no thought that she may have bewitched you to secure her release?"

Artair gave caution to his responses, knowing that any answer could be misconstrued, which could do more harm than good.

"If she had such powers, wouldn't she have convinced those in Lorne to release her?"

"The men at Lorne tell me that she tried but they fought against her powers."

Artair wanted to shake his head, but knew better. He had to convince the bishop that Zia was no witch.

"I found her to have no such powers. She is a woman who generously uses her skills to heal the ill."

"Miraculous healings, I hear," the bishop said, sounding once again as if he accused.

"They are no miracles, just hard work by a healer who cares for those she treats."

"We shall see," the bishop said sharply. "I will talk to those in your village she has treated."

Artair simply nodded, staring at the bishop. Something about him appeared familiar, but he couldn't say what. And oddly enough, he sensed that the bishop could be a fair man. He had no idea why. It was something he sensed and it gave him a shred of hope.

"Where were you and Zia wed?"

"The village Black."

The bishop tried to cover his startled look, but he failed. He remained unnerved.

"You know of it?" Artair asked, though the man obviously knew something.

"Some believe a place of healing, while others—" He glared at Artair. "—believe it a place of pagans."

Chapter 30

Artair hurried along the road to intercept Bethane and her people, worried over their safety. If the bishop thought the village Black a place of pagans, how would he treat them when they arrived?

He hadn't wasted a minute once Cavan returned to the hall. Cavan had appeared relieved, so Artair assumed all was well with Honora. He had signaled his brother that this wasn't the case with the bishop and that he should approach with caution.

Cavan had fabricated a mission that required Artair's immediate attention and served as a ruse for his necessary departure from the keep. The bishop hadn't been at all suspicious, though he made it known that he would speak with Cavan there and then.

Artair caught up with the approaching group from the village Black only a few hours from the keep.

Bethane greeted him with a hug and a smile. "It is good to see you again."

Artair could not get over her beauty. Though her lines and wrinkles attested to advanced years, Bethane still seemed young. She walked alongside a cart with firm and steady steps. Her long white braid lay over her shoulder, on her chest, and shined silky soft, and her skin glowed as if the sun kissed it pink.

"You have grown more beautiful than when I last saw you," Artair said, walking alongside her and searching the surrounding area for Nessie.

"Tall tales will not set you in my good graces, for you are already there, *dear son*."

Artair felt a thump to his chest when she referred to him as son. It pleased him to know that she thought of him that way. "I speak only the truth."

Bethane patted his arm. "I know, which is why it soothes my heart to know that you would lie to protect my granddaughter."

"I fear I need to ask the same of you and your people, and advise that you may be placing yourselves in danger by your visit."

"Tell me," Bethane said softly.

Artair detailed the entire situation.

"And this bishop's name?" Bethane asked when he was through explaining.

"Bishop Edmond Aleatus."

She nodded and raised her hand signaling the group to stop for a rest. She took Artair's arm and walked with him to sit beneath a tree, the fallen autumn leaves providing them with a cushion.

"I believe once the bishop meets with Zia, he will see that she is no more than a good woman and good healer."

"I have hope," Artair admitted with a sigh.

"Keep hope strong. It is the best you can do for Zia. Besides, your plan is sound and I am sure it will work." She smiled. "I am glad I will be here when you exchange vows with my granddaughter."

"Zia will be too. She misses you."

"And I her, but you two will visit me often, as I will you. After all, I will want to see my great-granddaughter and all the grandchildren to follow."

Artair stared at her dumbstruck. "Zia is not sure she is—"

"She is," Bethane said, nodding. "And Zia will give you a daughter first. All women born of our line have daughters first."

"Every one of them?"

"It is so as far back as our lineage goes," Bethane confirmed.

The thought struck Artair like a blot of lightning. "She will—" He stopped and grinned. "My daughter will be a healer like her mother and all those before her."

Bethane nodded, her smile growing.

"I will keep them both safe," he said adamantly.

"As they will you. As for this bishop," she said, "I think it would be best for me and the others from our village to keep our distance from him, for a while at least."

"It might be best until we see how things go, or perhaps until after Zia and I wed."

Bethane nodded, agreeing, and then the nod slowly turned to a shake. "Zia tends a troubled birth?"

Artair might have thought the woman a witch if he believed in witches. But he understood that Bethane had a special connection with Zia, and sensed when her granddaughter needed help, needed her.

Artair explained about Honora.

"Twins, how wonderful," Bethane said joyously. "But Zia will need help." She sprang to her feet far more easily than one would expect, and laughed when Artair stood and his knee cracked loudly. "I have something that will help that aging knee."

They both laughed.

"Where is Nessie?" Artair finally asked, not having caught sight of her.

"She refused to the leave the village."

"I believe she has chosen a new home and if it makes her happy then that's where she should stay," Artair said.

"It is a wise man who gives a woman what she wants," Bethane replied with a grin.

Dusk covered the land by the time they reached the keep. Bethane went with Mave to see how James was doing and help settle the young woman in his cottage, while Artair saw to it that the rest of the group had places to stay. Once he finished, he went to James's cottage to escort Bethane to the keep.

"She's already gone to the keep," Mave said. "She knew Zia needed her."

Artair didn't linger. He immediately set out, hoping Bethane had been able to avoid the bishop. He was relieved to discover that the bishop had retired to his room with a request not to be disturbed for the remainder of the evening.

Artair hurried to see Zia and cringed when he heard the moans drifting down the hall on his approach to the room.

He knocked and Addie let him in.

"Don't be long," his mother warned. "We have our hands full."

Artair almost ran to Zia and scooped her up into his arms. She looked utterly exhausted though alert. Her sleeves were rolled up and a white bib apron covered the front of her. Her hands were sparkling clean but then he had noticed that she washed them often when treating the ill.

If he thought Zia looked exhausted, he turned pale when he saw Honora.

"Now you know why Cavan can no longer enter this room," Zia said, standing alongside him.

A forceful tug at his arm had him turning away and looking at Zia. "She is—"

"Doing her best and needs no audience." Zia escorted him out of the room and into the hall. "I have only a few minutes."

"Is there anything I can do?"

"Keep Cavan away, though let him know that all is

well, and don't tell me anything of the bishop until the delivery is over."

"The babes are being stubborn, not wanting to be born yet?" he asked hopefully.

Zia shook her head. "One is turned the wrong way, which is what I suspected, and it prevents both from being born."

"What will you do?" he asked anxiously.

"What I've been taught. What I know. Now go and see to Cavan. I will send word now and again with your mother."

She turned and hurried back into the room before Artair could even give her a kiss. This was going to be a long night, for he knew that Cavan, Lachlan, and he would not sleep until the ordeal was over.

Artair stretched the aches from his shoulders as he raised his head and worked the kinks out of his back. He had fallen asleep along with his brothers at the long table in the great hall hours ago. Cavan had sworn he wouldn't sleep, but as the night wore on and pitchers of ale were drunk, the three of them dropped one by one into a sound slumber, Artair being the last, and now the first to wake.

When he saw his mother enter the hall, he shook his brothers awake.

Cavan jumped up wavering, the deep sleep not yet gone from him.

Addie smiled and took Cavan's hand. "Come meet your sons."

"Honora?" Cavan choked.

"Is tired but well."

Artair and Lachlan slapped their brother on the back and teasingly praised his prowess for having not one but two sons.

Addie looked at the two of them before she walked off with Cavan. "Well, do you want to see your nephews?" she called over her shoulder as they moved away.

The two men stumbled over each other, eager to meet the new babes, but Artair more eager to see how his wife was.

Damn, but he could think of her no other way. To him Zia was his wife and always would be. The vows they exchanged would see them properly bound, but he was bound to her far deeper than any documents could make them.

Love had seen to that, and love would continue to bind them.

He was the last to enter the room, Lachlan teasingly pushing past him, but he didn't mind. His eyes were set to find his wife before anything else. He didn't have to search for her, she came right to him, slipped her arms around his waist and rested her head on his shoulder.

It was her special place there nestled against him. She came there when she needed comforting, when she was tired, when she wanted to be near him. It was familiar to her and to him and he did what he always did, wrapped his arms around her and hugged her to him.

Soft mewling cries caught everyone's attention, and all eyes went to the twins yawning in their mother's arms.

"They're so small," Cavan said, looking on his sons with pride.

"So were all of you," Addie said with a laugh. "And glad I was of it."

The women laughed.

Cavan knelt beside the bed and reached out to tenderly touch his wife's face. "I can't believe—"

"Neither can I." Honora laughed, then winced.

"You are in pain?" Cavan asked anxiously, and turned to Zia.

"It is normal and will pass," she said, to Cavan's relief.

Soon everyone was taking turns hovering over the twins, taking hold of their tiny hands.

It was Lachlan who asked, "Have you thought of names?"

Cavan looked to his wife and she smiled. "The first-born . . . "

Honora nodded to her right to let everyone know who that twin was.

" . . . will be named Tavish, for Father."

Addie wiped a tear from her eye.

"The second," Cavan said, pointing to the little lad in Honora's left arm, "will be named—" He stopped and looked to his mother. "—Ronan."

Addie couldn't contain her tears, and it was Bethane who went to her and slipped an arm around her. "What an honor that will be for him when he returns."

Artair felt a sting to his heart. Did Bethane know something they didn't? But then, that seemed to be her way. He caught the same questioning look in Cavan's eyes that had to be in his own, and sensed that his brother would speak with Bethane about Ronan.

"I think there are some who need rest," Bethane said, glancing around the room. She nodded to Addie, and the two women each took a babe from Honora. "Cavan, you may visit for a while with your wife and sons, though they will sleep. And Zia . . . " She turned to her granddaughter. "You need to rest."

Artair was pleased that Zia didn't argue. She simply nodded, and along with Lachlan, they were shooed out of the room.

"I'll see to the bishop," Lachlan said, and gave Zia a hug. "Thank you for helping Honora and the babes. This is surely a joyful day."

"I am pleased to help and will do the same for you and your wife."

Lachlan walked off laughing.

Artair walked with Zia to their bedchamber, yawns attacking Zia the whole way.

"I am bone-tired," she said when they entered the room.

"I'll see you settled in bed and then I must go see to the bishop. With Cavan occupied, I can't have the bishop roaming around on his own, especially with those from your village here."

Zia sighed as if she didn't want to ask but felt it a necessity. "Tell me of the bishop."

Artair told her as he helped her disrobe and slip into a soft wool nightdress. Her beauty wasn't lost on him, but he contained his passion. She was tired and he had to see to the bishop.

"He is a man sharp of mind and clear of sight. I do not believe he is a man easily fooled, though I do believe he is a fair man."

"Why?" she asked, standing still as he tied the ribbon at her chest.

"I can't say why. There's something about his eyes that tells me as much." He shook his head. "It doesn't make sense. It's as if I know him, and yet I don't."

"I trust your opinion," she said on a yawn.

"And you trust me to keep you safe?" he asked spreading his arms around her to draw her up close against him.

"You needn't keep asking me that," she said, and with another yawn rested her head on his shoulder. "I know without doubt that you will protect me."

He scooped her up into his arms, fighting the notion to drop down in bed with her and make love to her. "Good. Then you can sleep without worry."

She slipped her arms around his neck, nuzzling the crevices with her lips before whispering, "If I weren't so tired we would—"

"Don't say it!" he snapped. "I'm already fighting the overwhelming urge to make love to you."

"Good, then it isn't only my passion I feel."

He laid her carefully down on the bed and pulled the wool blanket over her.

She grabbed his arm and tucked him down close to her. "It is you, not I, who cast a spell, for I cannot be near you without my passion soaring."

"You tempt me too much, woman," he said with a growl, fighting the lust that had grabbed firm hold of his loins.

"We could be quick," she teased with a gentle nip at his lips.

"Damn," he mumbled, and continued mumbling as he threw the blanket back to touch her intimately, only to find her wet and ready. That was it, he was finished, he had to have her and he entered her with a sharp quickness that had her crying out in pleasure.

It was a fast mating, but a thoroughly satisfying one that had both of them sighing with the beauty of it.

"Tonight, I will take my time with you," he said, bending over the bed to kiss her before he left.

"Promises, promises," she chortled, and waved him off.

He playfully grabbed her chin. "I will make you squirm with the want of me."

"You always make me squirm with the want of you."

"Then I will make you beg."

She laughed, though a yawn interrupted. "You've done that too."

He caressed her cheek gently. "Then tell me what it is you want."

She sighed, her eyes already closing. "Simply love me."

Chapter 31

Artair went in search of Cavan an hour later. He found him just coming out of the bedchamber after visiting with his wife and newborn twins.

"They all sleep," Cavan said softly. "Now what of the bishop?"

"He is exploring the village and talking with the people," Artair said.

Cavan said nothing until after they walked down the stairs and entered the solar, closing the door behind them. "He will also come upon those from the village Black."

"They have been made aware of the situation."

"Zia knows to remain out of sight?" Cavan asked.

Artair nodded. "No doubt it will be hours before she wakes, and when she does she will immediately want to check on Honora and the babes, and then there is her grandmother to visit with."

Cavan nodded. "Bethane. A most gracious and wise woman, so I've learned. And I believe one who knows more than she says."

"You intend to speak to her about Ronan."

"I do, and she knows it, for she told me privately that she would talk with me about my brother when I was ready."

"Ready?" Artair asked.

"I wondered what she meant, the same as you. Then I thought perhaps I should be ready to hear dire news."

Artair shook his head. "I don't believe so. Besides, Bethane could have meant that with so much going on—the birth of the babes, the bishop's arrival—you had no time to talk about Ronan just now."

"And she would have been right. We must settle this matter and see that Zia is freed of these senseless, vicious, and dangerous charges. I will feel better when you two finally exchange vows, for then she legally has the Sinclare name to protect her."

"My thoughts as well," Artair said.

Cavan rubbed the back of his neck. "I suppose the bishop knows of the birth of my sons?"

"He does, though I let it be known that mother and sons still required Zia's attention. He asked that you, Lachlan, and me, and also Mother if she is not needed to help with the babes, to join him for the noon meal. It was more of a command than a request, I must say."

"It is best we comply. We don't want to give him any reason to believe us uncooperative."

"Agreed."

"In the meantime keep a close watch on him."

"I have Patrick trailing him."

A knock interrupted any further conversation, and a warrior who had been sent to see that the cleric made it to the keep as soon as possible entered.

Artair felt his stomach plummet. From the warrior's dire expression, he could sense that something was wrong.

"The cleric has been taken ill at a village and isn't fit to travel," the man said. "It might be a day or more before he is able to resume his journey."

Artair refused to allow this setback to defeat him. If he did, he could very well lose Zia. "We must keep the bishop busy with his investigation until the cleric can get here," he said to Cavan when the warrior left.

His brother was about to agree when another knock sounded at the door.

Another warrior entered. "One of the sentinels has reported a lone rider approaching from the east."

"How long before he arrives?" Cavan asked.

"Thirty minutes or more."

"Intercept him and find out what he wants on Sinclare land," Cavan ordered.

The two brothers looked at each other, both sensing something was not right. It wasn't long before their fears were confirmed. The rider was from the village Lorne. He was sent to bear witness to marriage documents and to talk on behalf of his village with the bishop. Cavan couldn't prevent his arrival. If he did, his actions would only make Zia appear guilty.

The man was greeted as any other visitor would be, and when the bishop found out who he was, requested his presence at the noon day meal.

The great hall was empty except for the Sinclares, the bishop, and the messenger, Neil. The tension was thick in the air. Even Champion felt it, the dog standing stiffly to the side of the hearth as if on alert and ready to protect.

The servants were quiet and solemn whenever they entered the hall, and didn't remain long. The mood remained dour as the meal began and the silence hung heavy. At Champion's bark, everyone jumped, but then had to smile at the way he ran to greet a smiling Addie.

"Bishop Aleatus, it is an honor to have you in our home and at such an auspicious time," she said with a respectful bow to the man. "I would be honored if you were to bestow blessings on my grandsons."

"A gracious request to which I would be only too pleased to consent," the bishop answered with a smile, the only smile since his arrival. "Please sit by me."

Addie eagerly joined him, her smile still brimming.

Talk turned general, and seeing that his mother's smiling presence had changed the charged atmosphere, Artair was grateful to her. She talked of the beautiful service a cleric had conducted for her husband's funeral and the strength she derived from her daily devotionals.

The bishop conversed mainly with her, which Artair noticed made the messenger Neil, all the more uncomfortable. Finally, the wiry little fellow snapped.

"The witch has bewitched her," he blurted.

"Why say you that?" the bishop asked.

He stammered for a moment before regaining control of his tongue. "The witch told us to pray for our loved ones."

"She did?" the bishop asked curiously.

He nodded. "She claimed she'd pray too, but it was the devil she prayed to."

"But your people got better, didn't they?" Artair asked, knowing full well they had.

"Every one of them," Neil said, his hands trembling. "And that isn't right. Not a one of the ill died. Even the ones everyone thought for sure wouldn't make it survived."

"Zia is a good healer," Artair confirmed, and his brothers agreed with a nod, as did Addie.

"No, no," Neil insisted. "She let the devil steal their souls, and when they die they'll burn forever in the fires of Hell."

"That's pure nonsense—"

Before Artair could finish, the bishop held up his hand for silence. "I will decide what is nonsense and what is not."

"Speak to the witch," Neil insisted. "Speak with her soon or she will bewitch you too, just as she did to everyone in our village. If it were not for the strength of our leader, Harold, to fight her powers, we would have all been doomed."

"The man you speak of is the one who sold her to me?" Artair asked.

The bishop raised a brow as he regarded the messenger from Lorne. "This is true, is it not?"

Neil pointed an accusing finger at Artair. "She bewitched him into trading coins for her release."

"Did she then bewitch the man to take the coins?" Artair asked with a sneer, growing annoyed with such nonsensical talk, and meanwhile concerned that the bishop just might agree with the ridiculous man.

"Aye, she did," Neil said firmly. "She even commanded it to rain so that we couldn't light the wood to burn her."

Artair wanted to reach out and strangle the idiotic man, but that wouldn't help his cause. Calm rationality would.

"Bishop Aleatus," he said calmly, "my wife is not a witch. She is a remarkable healer schooled in the art by—"

"Other witches," Neil interrupted with a trembling voice. "They all live in a village together. A village no one can get to for they have cast a spell around it to keep it invisible."

Lachlan laughed.

"You find this humorous?" the bishop chastised.

Lachlan was wise enough to assert otherwise. "No sir, it is just that I have watched my sister-in-law heal many, and she uses no such witchcraft to do it."

"What of James?" the bishop asked.

"What of him?" Artair said.

"He survived a severe wound. He claims Zia worked a miracle to save him."

Artair knew James meant only to help but his choice of words had done the opposite. "Hard work by my wife is what saved James's arm."

"I have found no one who speaks harshly of your wife," the bishop noted, nodding.

"She is loved and respected by all," Artair said with pride.

"It seems odd that not even one person—"

Neil interrupted the bishop. "She's done it again, bewitched the whole village."

Artair almost lunged at the man, ready to beat him unmercifully. It took great willpower not to do so. Instead, while inwardly fuming, he retained a calm exterior composure.

"She has not," he asserted.

"That will be for me to decide," the bishop said curtly, and looked directly at Artair. "Tomorrow I will speak with your wife so that this matter can be settled. And you have two days more to produce a wedding document. If you fail to do so, I will assume she is not your wife and take matters from there."

Artair stood. "Conduct your investigation, Bishop Aleatus, but know this. Zia is *my wife*. She is not a witch and I will not see her condemned and punished because of ignorance and lies."

He stomped off, his hands fisted, itching to punch someone. He swore beneath his breath until he realized he was swearing aloud. One last oath and he clamped his mouth shut, taking the stone stairs two at a time.

He was furious and couldn't calm himself down. Because of some ignorant, foolish, selfish men he could very well lose Zia. And he would be damned if he'd let that happen.

He burst into Cavan's bedchamber without knocking, and his temper cooled in a flash when Zia jumped up off the chair where she sat with a firm finger pressed to her lips.

He saw that Honora and the babes were asleep, and from where Zia had sat, it looked as if she and Bethane had been talking. She walked over to him and took his arm, turned her head to give Bethane a nod, then headed out the door with him.

"You look as if you've lost your temper, but knowing you, that would make no sense."

He caught her smirk and shook his head, realizing the stupidity of his actions.

She placed a gentle hand on his arm. "Who was the unfortunate recipient of your seldom exposed temper?"

He wasn't only reluctant to tell her, he was reluctant to admit it. "The bishop."

"Really?" Zia asked, stunned.

His nod turned quickly to a shake. "I may have just made the situation worse."

"But you did it anyway."

"Stupidly."

"No," she admonished softly, and smiled. "Passion-ately."

Artair took hold of her face; her lovely green eyes glistened as if ready to tear. "You sound proud of my foolishness."

She laughed softly while a single tear drifted down her cheek. "You weren't practical."

"That I wasn't, and still you sound proud of me." A smile crept over him and he gently wiped the single tear away, and at that moment realized he loved her even more. "I can't believe that you're proud of my foolishness."

Another tear slipped down her cheek. "Love pro-duced your foolishness. Love for me." She giggled. "I love a fool, how wonderful!" She threw her arms around him.

He hugged her tight and laughed. "You forever make me smile, and over the most senseless things."

They were about to kiss when they heard footsteps on the stairs. Artair hurried her into the bedchamber. Closing the door on her smile, he said, "We will talk later. I love you."

Lachlan appeared in the hall, his anxious foot-falls slowed when he spotted Artair, and he looked as if he approached with a cautious grin. "Are you my brother?"

Artair clipped him on the shoulder when he got close enough. "Have I made a mess of things?"

"Cavan handled it."

"He soothed the bishop?"

"Not exactly," Lachlan said. "Cavan told the bishop that you take your vows seriously and your duties to your wife even more seriously. And part of your vows is protecting your wife and you will do that no matter what the circumstances."

"My brother defends me."

"You doubted he would?" Lachlan asked, surprised.

Artair hesitated.

Lachlan laughed. "You gave thought to nothing but defending your wife, and I don't blame you. Everyone can see how madly in love you two are."

"Even so, that doesn't help the situation."

"True enough, which is why Cavan wants to see you in his solar," Lachlan said. "Once we can't produce the marriage document . . ." He shook his head. "Zia is no longer considered under our protection and the bishop—"

"Can take Zia from us."

Chapter 32

Zia rejoined her grandmother, easing into the empty chair beside her only a short distance from the bed where Honora slept peacefully. She sighed softly, stretching out her legs in front of her.

"Content, are you?" Bethane asked.

"Ever so much," Zia said, giving herself a huge hug.

"Artair makes you happy?"

"I never imagined such happiness or that he would fall foolishly in love with me."

"He is good for you," Bethane confirmed with a strong nod.

"So you told me from the beginning."

"You needed to find out for yourself," Bethane said, glancing at one of the babes, who stirred restlessly in his cradle then settled once again.

Zia sat forward in the chair and took her grandmother's hand. "All will turn out well, will it not?"

"A problem with the bishop?"

"I'm not sure."

The door creaked opened and Addie slipped in, closing it quietly behind her. Zia got up and plopped down cross-legged on the floor, leaving the chair vacant for Addie. She shook her head at Addie when the woman tried to protest, and Addie relented with an appreciative smile and sat in the chair.

"There is some trouble," she whispered.

Bethane and Zia leaned in closer, not wanting to wake Honora or the babes.

Addie continued. "The bishop insists on seeing the marriage documents by tomorrow."

"Shouldn't the cleric be here sometime today?" Zia asked.

Addie shook her head. "He's been detained due to ill health."

Zia almost laughed for here she was a healer and out of reach of healing the man who could possibly solve all her problems. "What happens now?"

Addie shrugged. "I don't know. Cavan will meet with Artair to talk over possibilities."

"Can the bishop's mind be changed?" Bethane asked.

"I don't know how," Addie said again. "The bishop seemed adamant in his edict."

"What is the bishop doing now, at this moment?" Bethane asked.

"He strolls the village again, visiting, or so he says, but it seems he investigates and interrogates without anyone realizing it. And while many offer praise, they unknowingly provide fodder for doubt."

Bethane nodded knowingly. "Many do not realize

that generous praise can be misconstrued to make an innocent healer appear a witch who works magic."

"What am I ever to do?" Zia asked, wishing she possessed a magical potion that would chase away ignorant notions.

"Leave it to my sons," Addie said. "They will find a way."

"Addie is right," Bethane said, and reached her hand down to Zia. "What say we talk?"

Zia looked to Addie. "Would you mind watching Honora and the babes for a short time? We'll be close, in my bedchamber."

"What a silly request to ask of a new grandmother," Addie said, grinning proudly as she got to her feet and shooed them toward the door. "You have had no time alone to talk. Go, I will send for you if necessary."

Zia thanked her with an exuberant hug and a kiss on the cheek. "I won't be long."

"Take as long as you want," Addie assured her.

Zia eagerly ushered her grandmother into her bedchamber and fixed cups of their favorite brew, a mixture of herbs that soothed and relaxed. They settled in chairs she arranged in front of the hearth, the heat of the flames toasting their feet stretched out in front of them.

"I have missed you so much, Grandmother," Zia said.

"And I you, my child, but there is an important reason I wished for us to talk . . . there is a tale I wish to tell you."

Zia settled comfortably in her chair, tucking her warmed feet beneath her, ready to listen as she had when she was young. Her grandmother's tales never ceased to fascinate her. "I am listening."

"Many years ago in our village there was a young beautiful girl schooled in the Old Ways of the healers. She was an exceptional healer, always had a kind word for everyone and always generous with her time to those who required her talent. She traveled when necessary to different villages, just as you do. During her travels, she met and fell in love with a young man, and he with her, but there was a problem. The young man came from a noble lineage that expected obedience from their son, which included an arranged marriage. The couple dreamed of a life together, marriage and family, and when the young man's father denied him his dreams, he and the young woman wed in an old ceremony forgotten by many and acknowledged by few.

"Unfortunately, the young man's family refused to recognize the ceremony as valid and forcibly took him from his bride. They sent him away, and try as she might, his young wife could not find him. She was brokenhearted and missed him more each day. She soon realized that she was with child, but her heart refused to heal, and hope died slowly with each passing day, so that when she delivered a daughter, she smiled and took her last breath."

Zia had tears in her eyes. "You speak of my mother."

Bethane nodded.

"Why didn't you tell me sooner that my father was forced to leave my mother?" Zia asked, sniffing back her tears. "I would have looked for him."

"That was exactly why I didn't tell you. You would have insisted on searching for him, and that would not have been good for you or for him."

"If he loved my mother, surely my father would have been overjoyed to learn that she had given him a child," Zia said, fighting back the tears that refused to remain locked away.

"I have no doubt he would have, for he loved your mother very much."

"She certainly must have loved him, to die of a broken heart." A tear slipped free and ran down her cheek.

Bethane reached out and took her hand. "Don't think for one moment that your mother didn't want or love you. She knew she carried a daughter and spoke of you often to me. It was just that she lost her passion for life when she lost your father."

Zia nodded, slowly wiping away her tears. "I never truly would have understood that if I had not fallen so deeply in love with Artair. I don't shed tears for myself, but rather for my mother and the love that was stolen from her—not only my father's love, but mine."

"You are much like your mother, and she would have been proud of you."

"That means a lot to me," Zia said, her eyes drying. "I'm curious, though. What has changed that led you to tell me all this now?"

Bethane gripped both her hands tightly. "The Bishop Aleatus, the man sent to judge and condemn you, is your father."

Zia shook her head slowly. "The bishop? My father?"

Bethane nodded.

"I cannot believe . . ." Zia continued shaking her head, astonished by what she had heard. The man who would decide her fate was the man who had given her life.

"I know this is hard for you to believe."

"Are you sure?" Zia asked, thinking it must be a mistake.

"Yes, I am certain. I learned several years ago that he had become a bishop."

"And you didn't tell me?" she asked, not angry with her grandmother, but rather, disappointed.

"What good would it have done? Even now you must be very careful what you do with this knowledge, for it can be more dangerous than claims of you being a witch."

"Do you think if he knew who I was, he would want to do me harm?"

Bethane pressed a gentle hand to her granddaughter's face. "I believe he would love you immediately, for you look exactly like your mother."

Zia gasped with the realization and jumped out of the chair. "Then I surely must stay out of bishop's way until . . . " She shook her head. "Eventually, the bishop will insist on speaking with me. What then?"

"You will know what to do," Bethane assured her.

Zia collapsed back into the chair. "This news stuns me, but what could happen because of it startles me even more. The only thing I know for sure is that I will not see my husband—" She shook her head, correcting herself. "I will not see Artair suffer because of me."

"To you, Artair is your husband. You need no document to prove that to yourself. Follow your heart," Bethane advised. "You can't go wrong when you follow your heart."

Zia looked after Honora and the babes, and later that day realized she wasn't needed. Both Honora and Addie had the situation well in hand, and Cavan too. He visited with his wife and sons as often as he could.

She wished she could leave the keep for at least a short while, just to breathe the cold autumn air, feel it fresh against her cheeks. She recalled her visit to the battlements, and grabbing a wool cloak from her room, hurried up the stairs, rushing to taste the joy of a moment's freedom.

The cold air stung her cheeks and whipped through her hair and she stuck her chin up enjoying the invigorating assault. She hugged the cloak around her and couldn't help but think of her father.

Was he still the man who once loved her mother, or had he become cynical and indifferent to others because of what had been done to him? And did she dare take a chance and find out?

It wouldn't be only her life she placed in danger, and

she couldn't live with the possibility of being the cause of the Sinclares suffering because of her. What choice did she have then?

"You frightened the hell out of me!"

Startled, Zia swung around to see Artair descend on her. He looked in a rage, and grabbed hold of her and gave her a shake.

"Don't ever frighten me like that again," he ordered sharply.

"What have I done?" she asked, perplexed and concerned, for she had never seen him so upset. His dark eyes glared and he actually looked pale.

He shook his head and then rested his forehead to hers. "I couldn't find you, and feared the bishop had sped off with you when I wasn't watching."

You mean my father. She almost said it aloud, but the words were so foreign to her that they never reached her lips.

"I would fight like a wild animal if anyone tried to take me from you," she said with a soft kiss to his flushed cheek.

"I would kill anyone who tried."

She thought she heard him snarl, and shivered at the thought of the animal inside him that could materialize when necessary.

"You're cold," he said, and scooped her up in his arms.

She wanted the crisp air to sting her cheeks and shiver her flesh, but she could get the same from her husband, and much preferred to do so.

"Make love to me," she whispered in his ear.

He laughed. "You read my mind."

"That is because we are one and will always be."

He stopped abruptly before going through the arched doorway. "Promise me that. Promise me we will always be one no matter what."

"I promise," she murmured against his lips and then let him have his way with the kiss and he took it. Instead of quenching her lust it ignited it and shivered every inch of her flesh.

"You are cold," he said, hurrying to take the stairs down to their bedchamber.

"I am hot," she teased with a nip to his ear.

"I intend to make you hotter."

"Then hurry, for I am already near boiling."

He laughed. "This will be a night you long remember."

How appropriate that the day remained consistent, for it surely was a day she would never forget.

Zia stretched her naked body along the bed, arching her back to welcome Artair deeper inside her. They had wasted no time in divesting themselves of their clothes and falling on the bed together. And she had wasted not a moment of getting him inside her.

She needed him and the satisfaction he would bring her, though he would take none himself, not yet. He would wait and bring her to pleasure over and over, making her body squirm with his intimate touches and breath-stealing kisses.

It was a dance of sorts, and one she never tired of. And how could she when he would sweep her off her feet with a new step or two and in no time have her groaning, whimpering, pleading, and crying out in pleasure?

"You are the witch," she breathed heavily as his mouth tormented her nipples with the most delicious swirl of his tongue. "You bind me with a wicked—" She gasped as he plunged into her suddenly and steadily.

They both were soon lost in a maze of lovemaking, twisting, turning, grasping, gasping, as they made their way through the tormenting maze that took them ever deeper into the center, the apex of it all. When they could no longer contain themselves, they burst like a torch ignited and allowed the fire to consume them and the maze.

After her sanity returned, Zia bounced up, crawling over Artair to slip off the bed.

"I'm starving," she said, and went straight to the table where hours ago platters of food and pitchers of wine had been left for them. Once there, she munched on a hunk of cheese and reached for a slice of black bread.

"You should eat while naked more often," he said sitting up to rest against several pillows he piled behind his back. " I enjoy watching you."

With a start, while still munching, Zia hurried into a soft green silk robe Addie had given to her recently.

"I am so hungry that I forget myself," she said with a grin.

"Forget yourself all you want. I love seeing you naked. You are beautiful."

"For that," she said raising a finger, "I will bring you food."

"I feared you would let me starve."

"Never," she said hurrying over to him with one of the smaller platters of cheese, to which she'd added cold mutton and bread.

"Mother tells me that you had time to speak with your grandmother today," Artair said while digging into the plate of food.

Zia knew it appeared a casual question, but it was far from one. And she would give him his answer if . . . "Ask me directly what you wish to know and I will tell you."

But would she? She had given thought to her grandmother's warning, and knew that Bethane was right. The information could prove more harmful than helpful to far too many people. With that in mind, Zia had decided that for now her father's identity would continue to remain a secret.

"Did you discuss Ronan?" Artair asked anxiously.

Zia shook her head. "But then, that wasn't really your question. You think my grandmother and I keep something from you about your brother."

"Do you?"

"I have confided everything to you except one thing. I gave my word to someone and I cannot go back on it."

Artair rubbed his chin and nodded.

Zia knew he would remain calm and think over

her response. He was and would no doubt always be a sensible man, except when it came to her. She almost sighed at the beauty of it.

"Does this promise interfere with me locating my brother?"

"No, it would no way impede your search for Ronan."

He nodded again. "What of Bethane? Does she know more than she tells me?"

Zia sighed and dusted her hands over the plate. "I truly don't know. I was surprised when we returned to my village and found Ronan gone."

"What you tell me is that it would have been difficult for him to leave your village without someone knowing of his departure. You said so yourself when you told me and my men about the posted sentinels."

"You're right. Someone would have seen him," Zia confirmed.

"Or helped him?"

Zia nodded.

"And you know who that is?"

"As do you," she said.

"Bethane."

Again Zia nodded. "She had to have given her word if she has not confided this to you."

"Which means—"

"She will not tell you why your brother left or where he goes."

Chapter 33

"**Y**ou know I will need to tell Cavan of this," Artair said with a sense of betrayal that disturbed him. Either way, he felt as if he betrayed someone with his decision. If he didn't confide in Cavan, he would betray his brother, and if he told Cavan, then he felt as if he betrayed Zia. He did not like the position he was in and would not tolerate it.

"I assumed you would, but then I believed you and Cavan already had plans to speak with my grandmother," Zia said, gathering up morsels of the food that fell on the blanket, to place them on the empty plate before bouncing off the bed to take it to the table.

"I would have spoken to you first."

Zia turned, slipping her robe off and walking toward him. "I know that."

Artair's loins tightened rock hard and his mind began to muddle with each lazy step she took toward him. "I—I—"

"Want me," she said, her voice dripping with a sultry passion.

Or was it simply what he wanted to hear? Artair shook his head.

"You don't want me?" she asked, pouting as she stopped by the bed.

Artair had lost all sound reasoning, and while somewhere his mind reminded that he should pursue questioning her about Ronan, another part urged him to assuage his aching loins.

Zia settled it by throwing the covers off him and crawling over him with a sexy grin that promised paradise on earth. Then he surrendered to her with each tantalizing touch and intimate kiss.

Artair paced in Cavan's solar.

"Everyone tried to help," Cavan said.

"And made it worse," Artair spat. "The village makes Zia appear a saint, which only fuels the bishop's perception of her as a witch. And that fool Neil gloats over what he assumes is a victory . . . the witch will burn."

"We both know that will not happen."

"How do we stop it?" Artair asked desperately, looking to his brother as the powerful laird who could do the impossible.

"I don't know, but we will stop it," Cavan said with a firm grasp of his brother's shoulder.

Artair calmed and nodded. He and Zia weren't alone in this. His family was on his side and would do all they could to keep Zia from being taken away.

A knock interrupted their concerns and forced a different set of worries on them.

"You will be kind to her?" Artair asked of his brother, knowing Bethane waited beyond the closed door.

"I want my brother home," Cavan said sharply, and called out for her to enter.

Bethane entered with a flourish, her cheeks dashed pink, her green eyes aglow and her smile generous.

"What an honor to be invited to your solar, Cavan," she said, and extended her hand to his.

He took it, and she held firm to it with both hands for a moment, then smiled wider and released his hand.

Bethane nodded. "You will serve your people well."

"I am more concerned at the moment with finding Ronan," Cavan said, and directed her to one of the chairs in front of the large hearth where he stood.

She stretched her hands out to the warm flames. "Winter will be upon us soon."

"And I would like my brother home for the solstice."

"Your brother is a strong one. I have no doubt he will find his way home," Bethane said.

Artair stepped forward and sat in the chair beside Bethane. "Why did Ronan leave your village?"

"Someone followed him," she answered.

"Why didn't you tell me this when I first asked?" Cavan asked, bewildered.

"I had given my word."

"To who?" Cavan demanded.

"Your brother," Bethane said softly.

Both brothers shook their heads.

"Yet you tell us now?" Artair asked, as confused as Cavan.

"Enough time has passed to ensure Ronan's safety, which was what he had asked of me."

"But we're his brothers," Cavan said.

"Yes, you are."

Cavan and Artair stared at each other, shaking their heads until Artair looked at Bethane and glared at her.

"Ronan was protecting us!"

She nodded, smiling.

"From what?" Cavan demanded.

"That I'm not at liberty to say," Bethane said regretfully.

Cavan began pacing in front of the hearth. "This makes no sense."

"Did Ronan know of our victory against the barbarians?" Artair asked Bethane.

"Yes, he did," she confirmed.

"Then why not simply come home?" Cavan asked with annoyance.

"It isn't that simple for your brother," she said. "And I would suggest that you let him be, for his own safety."

"Ronan's in trouble?" both brothers asked at once.

"He will tell you all of it when he sees you," she said.

"That's not good enough," Cavan said curtly.

"I'm afraid it is all I can offer you."

"Do you tell me you refuse to answer any more questions?" Cavan demanded.

"Of course not, but I doubt my answers will satisfy you," Bethane said firmly.

"You speak in constant riddles, while I want facts," Cavan said.

Bethane stood. "Riddles lead to facts. Think about it and you may learn something. Now I must go see how my people fair."

She had dismissed Cavan rather than him dismissing her.

"I should be furious with her," Cavan said after she left. "I should lock her up in the dungeon until she decides to tell us what we want to know . . . and yet I can't, for I feel I have something to learn from her words."

"Besides, we don't have a dungeon," Artair said, grinning.

"Shut up," Cavan warned, and dropped into the chair beside his brother. "Don't tell me this doesn't disturb you. It sounds as if our brother is in more trouble than we first thought. But with whom and how, and how the hell do we help him?"

"According to Zia, we can't. It would appear that our interference would only make it worse."

"We can't just leave him," Cavan said, exasperated. "We must do something."

"Then let us find out what is going on before we rush into anything," Artair suggested. "Once we know what we're dealing with, we'll be better able to formulate a plan of action."

"Good idea," Cavan said. "But where do we start?"

Artair smiled. "I will talk with Bethane and find out."

Lachlan burst into the room. "You better hurry. That fool Neil is causing more problems."

Artair entered the great hall behind his brothers to hear Neil complaining to the bishop that the witch was working her magic on them and they would soon be under her spell like all the others there.

"Zia helps my wife and sons," Cavan said.

"We do not know that!" Neil shouted. "She could be hiding away mixing her potions, casting her spells . . . " He lowered his voice. " . . . bringing evil down upon us."

"I'm going to kill him," Artair whispered to his brothers.

"I'll help," Lachlan offered.

What angered Artair even more was the way the bishop let the man rant on. In any other village or keep, Neil would have had others believing him by now, and if he were allowed to keep it up, he might just get a few in Caithness to start doubting, and that would be all they would need.

The bishop finally raised his hand for silence, then turned his attention to Cavan. "When night falls, I will have the wedding documents in my hands and speak with Zia, or I will inform the council of your reluctance to cooperate and have a troop dispatched here to take Zia into custody until further notice. And then the Sinclares would be investigated for harboring a witch. "

Fury rushed through Artair like a raging fire, and he barely managed to contain himself. No options were left to him. How did he protect his wife?

"See it done," the bishop ordered Cavan before retiring to his bedchamber for afternoon prayer.

Artair took a menacing step toward a retreating Neil, but Lachlan blocked his path. "There are more important things to worry about. Save him for last."

Bethane entered the hall then, and Artair stared at her, as did his brothers, as if she might provide them with a solution.

She walked over and patted Artair's arm. "Speak to Zia."

"What good will that—"

She shooed him away. "Speak with her."

He didn't argue, and as he walked away he heard her order Cavan, though in a pleasant tone, to visit his wife and sons, and Lachlan to take his mother for a much needed walk.

Artair shook his head. He wondered how it seemed that Bethane always sensed how people needed healing even if they appeared well. She always knew the right thing to say or the right advice to offer or how to listen. He truly admired her.

He found Zia alone in the sewing room working on a tiny robe.

She laughed, patting the seat of the chair next to her. "Honora just realized that she would need to double the clothes she had made, so I'm helping her."

"She and the babes do well?"

"They are wonderful, and ready to leave the confines of her bedchamber," Zia said, placing the garment aside and reaching for Artair's hand. "But you didn't come looking for me to ask me about Honora. What has happened?"

He covered their clasped hands with his other hand, hoping in some strange way that they would be bound together so no man or force could separate them.

"Speak up," she ordered, "for your silence frightens me."

He kissed her softly, brushing his lips across hers, then recounted in fine detail what had just happened in the great hall.

Zia sat silently for a moment and then spoke. "For your family's safety, it is better I leave here."

Artair stood and yanked her out of her seat. "Don't you dare let me ever hear you say that again."

"But—"

"Never!" he warned adamantly.

Zia pressed her hand to his chest. "You tremble—"

"With anger that you could even think to leave me."

Zia gasped. "I do not choose to leave you. I choose to keep you safe."

"*I,*" he said empathically, "keep you safe."

"*I,*" she emphasized equally, "keep you safe."

He lowered his lips to hers. "Then we do it together, but never, ever, do we part. Promise me."

She did, and he captured her promise with a kiss.

They hugged each other tightly.

"What are we to do?" Zia asked.

"I don't know, but your grandmother suggested I speak with you, and I'm glad she did. Just holding you in my arms make me feel better."

Zia nestled closer against him. It wasn't until a few minutes had passed that he realized she was crying softly.

"What's wrong?" he asked, upset, trying to pry her burrowed face away from his chest. He finally managed to grab her chin and force her to look at him, and her tear-filled eyes broke his heart. "Everything will be fine, don't worry."

She sniffled and shook her head, freeing her chin from his grasp. "It isn't that. It is when I see your passion flair that I know and feel down into my soul how very much you love me, and I know how lucky I am to have found you."

"We're both lucky, and I intend for us to stay that way. As for how it happened?" He shook his head. "I don't know, but I believe the magic of love will find a way to help us now."

"That isn't practical," she teased.

"We—our love—were never practical from the start. Why should it be any different now?"

They both laughed, and after a brief kiss Zia said, "There's something I must tell you."

He sat in the chair, pulling her into his lap. "Tell me, I'm listening."

"I want to tell you the story I just heard, about my mother and father."

Artair nodded. "I'd like to hear it."

Zia recited the story her grandmother had told, growing teary-eyed once again.

He kissed her and hugged her close. "How sad for them and for you. I would have never believed someone could die from a broken heart, but now I know it is possible."

"I felt the same as you when my grandmother told me, but there is more."

"More that causes you hurt?" he asked with concern.

She nodded.

He held her tight. "I am here for you and always will be."

She smiled and rested her hand to his cheek. "That is good to know, for my father is in your home at this very moment."

Artair scrunched his brow and shook his head. "I don't under—" He grew pale. "Oh my God! Bishop Aleatus is your father."

"Yes, he is. My grandmother warned me that the information could prove more dangerous than helpful and told me to be careful what I did with it. That is why I waited to tell you."

"It is a secret no one would have blamed you for keeping," he said, "but I'm glad you entrusted me with it."

"But what do we do with it? Will it help us or harm us? That is what I have been trying to decide."

Artair thought a moment. "Your grandmother claims

that your father loved your mother beyond all reason. I cannot see a man who loves a woman so deeply do any harm to the child born of their loving union."

"You think I should tell him who I am? Though my grandmother says he will know, for I look just like my mother."

"Then how can the bishop not love you, his daughter?" Artair encouraged.

"We don't know that for sure. Perhaps the years have not been kind to him and he is now bitter."

"A few moments ago I told you I believed the magic of love would help us find a way out of this mess." He smiled. "I believe it just has. You need to believe the same."

Chapter 34

Zia held firmly to Artair's hand as they approached the solar. She was grateful to him for speaking with Cavan and assuring that their meeting would be a private one with the bishop. She was also grateful that Artair chose not to divulge her secret to his brother. He left that choice to her.

Zia fussed with her short hair, though it had grown longer since it had first been cut, she wished it was at a more proper length.

Artair grabbed hold of her hand. "You are beautiful. It makes no difference about your hair or anything else. Your father will only see his daughter, and see the woman he loves in you."

She released a sigh. "I am so glad you are here with me."

"I'll be right beside you the whole time. You can depend on it."

Artair opened the solar door, and she kept hold of his hand as she entered the room.

The bishop sat in a chair facing the burning hearth.

She couldn't see him, or he her. The only part of him she did see was his hand draped over the arm of the chair. His fingers were lean and long, like hers, and showed little signs of age, and he wore a sizable emerald ring on his middle finger.

"Come stand in front of me, woman," he ordered. "I wish to see this supposed witch with my own eyes. And don't think you can bewitch me, for I am a man of God."

Zia looked to Artair, and he kissed her cheek quick and gave her a little shove to get her moving.

"Do not keep me waiting," the bishop said curtly.

He loved your mother beyond reason. I could see it in his eyes the day his family tore him from her arms.

Her grandmother's words rang strong and clear in her head, and she lifted her chin with pride and walked forward to meet her father.

The bishop lifted his head when she came to stand in front of him.

"I have been—" His ringed hand flew to his chest and he gasped. "Oh my God! It can't be." He shook his head. "Is that you, Blythe?"

Tears instantly filled Zia's eyes and spilled down her cheeks upon hearing her mother's name. "No, Father, it is your daughter Zia."

The bishop struggled to get out of his chair as tears raged from his eyes, and Zia reached down to help him. He immediately grabbed hold of her.

"My daughter? My beloved Blythe gave me a daughter?"

Choked with tears, Zia could only nod.

The bishop's slim hand touched her face tentatively, as if trying to prove to himself that she was real. "You look exactly like your mother."

"I didn't know if you would remember her."

He shook his head and kept hold of her arm. "I could never forget the woman I love. It broke my heart when I was forced to leave her, and my heart broke again when I heard that she had died. I wanted to die too, but it seemed life had different plans for me." He smiled through his tears. "And now I know why."

"You're not angry?"

His smile turned sad. "I could see why you might think that, but I'm relieved that you had the courage to face me anyway."

"I wanted to meet you," Zia said. "I wanted you to know I was your daughter and that I prayed every day to the Heavens, since I was young, to bring my father home to me."

"If I had known, I would have left the Church and come for you. Nothing would have stopped me." He shook his head. "I should have been stronger and fought harder for your mother. I should have clawed my way out of the cell my parents locked me in."

"They locked you away?" Zia said incredulously.

"Until I agreed to study and commit my life to the Church," he said sadly. "And once I learned of your mother's demise, I knew there was nothing left for me. I would never love another woman as I did your mother, and there isn't a day that goes by that I don't think about her."

"You and Mother suffered a cruel fate."

"But look what our love produced," he said, his whole face lighting with a smile. "Sit . . . Sit and tell me all about yourself."

Artair nodded to Zia and slowly backed out of the room, leaving father and daughter to discover each other.

Artair sat in the great hall at the table before the hearth, enjoying a tankard of ale for the first time in days. He took his time, didn't have to rush, didn't have to worry. Zia would be his wife, and she would be protected not only by him, but by her powerful father. And though he had no confirmation of this from the bishop, he knew it to be so. One only had to see the look of love in the bishop's eyes to know that he would see no harm come to his daughter.

The magic of love had worked magic.

"You look mighty content for a man whose wife may be burnt at the stake," Lachlan said, joining him at the table.

Artair filled a tankard for him. "I believe all is going to work out well."

Lachlan leaned across the table and whispered, "Learned how to cast a spell, did you?"

"Learned how to perform magic," Artair said with a gleeful grin.

Lachlan looked aghast. "Are you sure you're my brother? He's too sensible to believe in magic."

"The magic of love proved me wrong."

"Good Lord, another brother lost to love," Lachlan said, laughing. "Where is the love of your life?"

"Talking with Bishop Aleatus."

"What?" Lachlan near choked on his ale. "I thought that meeting wasn't until later, and what are you doing sitting here so calmly?"

"To answer both questions, Cavan arranged for a change of time, and I know something you don't," Artair said smugly.

"And you're not going to tell me, are you? You . . . " Lachlan muttered a string of oaths only his brother could hear.

Artair just laughed feeling free to really enjoy.

Cavan entered the hall from outside, swinging his cloak off his shoulders and dropping it on the table next to where his brothers sat. "By the happy look on your face, Artair, I would assume the meeting with the bishop and Zia went well."

"It's still going well," Artair said.

"You didn't stay with her?" Cavan asked, surprised.

It was Bethane who answered, entering the hall. "It wasn't necessary for him to stay. All goes well and will continue to do so. Isn't that right, Artair?"

Artair saluted her with his tankard. "That's right, Bethane, but then you knew this day would come, didn't you?"

"It was inevitable," she admitted. "Now I will go tell Addie and Honora we have a couple getting married tonight in a private ceremony."

Cavan scratched his head. "Who will perform the ceremony?"

"The bishop," Artair said with a smile and a nod to Bethane.

The older woman turned to leave, then stopped and looked once again to Artair. "You have a question to ask me. I will do my best to answer it for you." She turned then and disappeared up the stairs.

"How does she do that?" Cavan asked. "Know things before people even say anything?"

Artair shrugged. "She's a wise woman."

"Or maybe it's magic," Lachlan said, and nodded at Artair. "Our brother here believes in magic now."

Artair draped his arm around Cavan's shoulder. "So does this brother, and we don't want to be the only ones who were struck by the magic of love."

Cavan caught on and nodded. "That's right. So let's cast a spell of love on Lachlan."

Lachlan laughed.

"Get away from them," Neil shouted, having emerged from the shadows.

The three brothers looked at him.

"They've been bewitched and now they try to bewitch you. Run before it's too late and you find yourself saddled with a witch of a wife," he shouted, and ran from the hall like a madman, his arms waving up over his head as he continued shouting.

"You know, that's the first smart thing that man has said since his arrival," Lachlan said, laughing.

* * *

Zia stood in the sewing room while her grandmother altered the dark green velvet dress that Addie had gifted her with for her wedding ceremony. A few tucks and a sizable hem and it was perfect for her. The velvet fell in swirls from beneath her breasts, and her long sleeves ended in points over the back of her hands. Velvet slippers completed the outfit.

While the dress was more beautiful than any garment she had ever owned, it was her father who dominated her thoughts.

"He knew me at first sight," she said, standing still while her grandmother worked on the hem.

"Of course he would. You are the picture of your mother."

"So he remarked, though I saw bits of him in me as well," Zia said proudly. "And he spoke with such pride of Mother and her healing skills, and knew I possessed the same. He told me how Mother told him their first child would be a daughter and that she would be a healer."

Zia placed her hand over her stomach.

"You know the same. Have you told Artair?"

Zia smiled and shook her head. "Not yet, but soon enough."

"Your father will be pleased. He will have the family long denied him."

Zia's smile faded. "But he will never be able to openly acknowledge me as his."

Bethane comforted Zia with a hug. "He protects you by not letting anyone know you're his daughter."

"I know," Zia said sadly. "It's just that he has suffered so much, and merely because he loved my mother."

"But think how much joy this night will bring him. He will unite in marriage his daughter, whom he never knew existed, to the man she loves. While it may seem a small consolation to you, I believe he thinks otherwise. Besides, he also saved you from being condemned a witch, and now with his blessings no one will ever dare try to accuse you of witchcraft again."

Zia wiped a lone tear from her eye. "I don't want him to leave. I want him to stay so I can learn more about him and tell him more about me, and hear stories of him and my mother . . . And I want him to hold my newborn daughter in his arms and know that it all started with the love he had for my mother, and how that love will live on forever."

"I think he realized that when he laid eyes on you. Besides, he won't rush off now that he knows who you are. He will delay his departure, claiming an illness perhaps, that the healer advises would best heal with rest, not travel."

Zia brightened. "I forget how wise you are."

"Do not worry. I will remind you."

Zia laughed along with her grandmother.

A soft knock sounded at the door and Honora entered. She looked beautiful wearing a purple gown her long hair tucked up with combs.

"I made this for you while the babes slept." Honora handed her a crown made of heather.

Zia blinked back tears, placed the lovely gift on her head, then hugged Honora. "Thank you so very much. You must be well, for you look beautiful."

"I feel wonderful, thanks to you," Honora said. "But this night is not about me. It is about you, and everything is ready, and everyone waits in the solar."

Bethane rushed through the last of the hem, and the two women escorted the bride downstairs.

As Zia approached the door, she grabbed hold of her grandmother's arm. "Behind that door—"

"Your past and future unite," Bethane whispered softly.

Zia smiled and took a step toward her future.

Chapter 35

The ceremony was short, and a light fare had been prepared and arranged in the solar, with plenty of wine and ale to help celebrate the special occasion. It was very late so that no one would be the wiser of what took place there that night.

Some of the servants speculated, but were happy that at least whatever did take place was a celebration, which meant that all was well.

Artair watched his wife . . . Finally, he could truly call Zia *his wife*. He watched her speak with her father and Bethane.

He and Zia had decided it would be best if no one else knew that Bishop Edmond Aleatus was her father. It wasn't that he and Zia didn't trust his family to keep the secret. It was just that he had learned from experience that the more people who knew a secret, the more people found out about it. And besides, he felt it was safer for his family not to know the truth, and Zia had agreed with him about that.

He couldn't get over how utterly beautiful she looked

and how utterly happy she was. He wished he could say that it was all because she had married him, but that most of her happiness was the result of learning about her father, and he couldn't blame her for that.

He had to laugh quietly, for the bishop hadn't smiled much when he first arrived, and since finding out about Zia, he hadn't stopped smiling. Those in his entourage who saw him wondered if the witch had cast a spell over him, and in a strange way, it could be said that she had, though it was a daughter's love that freed him from a spell. Once it was learned that the bishop had declared Zia free of all witchcraft charges, his people sighed a breath of relief and went about their tasks contentedly.

Bethane drifted over to him. "Happy?"

"More than I ever expected," Artair admitted, then smiled. "But you knew that. What else do you know?"

"What is it you want to know?" she asked.

Artair looked around the room, taking in each person. "Cavan and Honora are happy, and even more so with the birth of their sons, this *I know*. What of Lachlan?"

Bethane smiled. "He finds love where he least expects it, and if he fights fate, he will lose her."

"I will remember that," Artair said with a nod. "What of my mother?"

Bethane sighed. "She will love again."

"Never," Artair said adamantly. "She loved Father far too much to ever love another man."

"This man will be persuasive—"

"My brothers and I will get rid of him fast enough."

"Be careful, for your mother's heart will go with him," Bethane warned. "Odd that you ask of everyone before—"

"Ronan," Artair finished with a firm nod. "I saved him for last. Tell me how to find him."

"He travels a road you cannot follow."

"No riddles, Bethane, just tell me where to start. I want my brother home where he belongs."

"Then let him be, and he will find his way home," she said.

Artair shook his head. "I cannot do that, and neither can my brothers. Just point me in the right direction and leave the rest to me."

"As you wish," Bethane said. "Find the barbarian leader's daughter and you will find Ronan."

"Thank you," Artair said, certain now that he and his brothers would find their brother and bring him home.

"Do not be so fast to thank me," Bethane warned, and walked away as Zia approached.

"You look confused," Zia said, taking hold of Artair's arm.

"Your grandmother has a way of doing that to people." He gave her a quick kiss, whispering afterward, "I have been a patient husband. Can we take our leave now so that I can make love to *my wife* for the first time."

Zia smiled. "I thought the same myself, *husband*."

"You've been patient too?" he asked teasingly.

She pressed close against him and whispered in his ear, "Far too long."

Her warm breath sent shivers racing through his body, and he felt her shiver along with him. "We need to leave now."

"We'll slip out. No one will notice," she whispered.

He agreed with a nod, but it took longer to take their leave than they hoped, and by the time they reached their bedchamber, they both breathed a sigh of relief and fell on the bed together.

"I thought they would never let us go," Zia confessed.

"It is I who will never let you go," Artair said with a kiss, soft, gentle, and tempting.

They took their time undressing each other, kissing as they went. Each lingered along favorite spots, so it took a long lazy time to undress completely, and when they finally did, they settled naked into each other's arms.

They kissed as if for the first time and lingered in the exquisite beauty of its sweet innocence. And laughed like new lovers eager to continue exploring. Then they began to touch, discovering each other for the first time as husband and wife and cherishing the joy of it.

They didn't rush, not once. Not even as their passion consumed them. It was as if they intended to treasure each and every moment and remember it always. When they finally joined, it was with an exquisite slowness that drove them both wildly mad until neither could prevent the other from exploding in a blinding climax that left them completely spent.

Later, tucked beneath the blanket and wrapped around each other, with sleep not far off, Artair whispered in her ear, "You have bewitched me from the start."

She laughed softly and snuggled against him. "Maybe so, Highlander, but it is you who have kept me under your spell."